ADVANCE PRAISE FOR JUSTICE HILL

"Macleod's brisk tale of a brutal murder and flawed investigation, replete with intriguing clues, surprising twists, detestable villains, compromised heroes, and enduring friendships—all wrapped up in questions of morality and justice—is a great read."

Chuck Rosenberg, former U.S. Attorney, senior FBI official, and DEA administrator

"A delightfully atypical murder mystery, *Justice Hill* takes the investigation of a crime deep into a captivating tale of lifelong friendships entwined together in love, jealousy, deception, trust, family, and faithfulness. Macleod's wealth of experience shines exceptionally in his lyrical prose. Quite simply, mesmerizing."

Christopher Rosow, bestselling author of *False Assurances* and *Threat Bias*

"*Justice Hill* is an exceptional legal thriller, deftly written and full of gritty, fascinating details about the work of lawyers and crime investigators. The bizarre nature of the murder leads to startling revelations and a wholly unexpected conclusion. The protagonists, Jessie and Sam, are strong, complex women who face devastating choices. Highly recommended."

Marcia Trahan, author of *Mercy: A Memoir of Medical Trauma and True Crime Obsession*

JUSTICE HILL

JUSTICE HILL

A SAVAGE MURDER, A LOVE STORY

John Macleod

JUSTICE HILL

ISBN No: 978-1-7355213-0-5

Library of Congress Control Number: 2020917266

This is a work of fiction. Some place names are real, as are references to certain
historic events, but the characters and the story are entirely made up.

*To my former colleagues at Crowell & Moring
and also, and always, to Ann*

Good people do all the things bad people do, Lazlo.
It's just that when they do them, they call it justice.

Laini Taylor, *Strange the Dreamer*

AUTHOR'S NOTE

This story is about lawyers and the hard choices they face: How do I navigate the annoyingly grey ethical zones in discharging my duty to represent my client zealously? Is it proper for me to defend someone I believe is guilty? In resolving conflicts of interest, do I side with the big new client or the smaller one I have represented for years? Most lawyers I know, and certainly the lawyers at the firm that was and is my home, act with principle, integrity, and sensitivity in sorting out issues such as these. But getting it right is not always easy, particularly when there is tension between professional duty and personal relationships.

People tend to admire or despise lawyers, with good reason either way. Some even favor killing lawyers, as Shakespeare's Dick the Butcher famously did in *Henry VI*. Dick's urgings have not come to pass, fortunately, but we still read from time to time about a lawyer or judge who has been killed in an act of revenge.

None that I know of, however, has been killed with a chain saw. Until now.

The story also touches upon the fascinating world of coal mining, which was forever changed by a massive explosion that occurred at an underground mine near Farmington, West Virginia, in 1968. Of the ninety-nine miners who were underground, only twenty-one made it out. Seventy-eight were killed, and the bodies of nineteen were never recovered.

The Farmington disaster was the catalyst for a comprehensive federal mine safety and health law that was passed in 1969. That law represented a huge step forward in reducing accidents, injuries, and fatalities in the nation's coal mines. In 1968, 311 coal miners lost their lives in work-related accidents. That figure has since been reduced to the low double digits. Still too many, but a remarkable advancement.

In my early years as a lawyer, I was privileged to visit many coal mines and work with many coal mining companies as the 1969 law was implemented. The coal miners I worked with were good people—down-to-earth, generous, honest, and fun. The coal companies were professional and took their safety responsibilities seriously. As the federal Mine Safety and Health Administration has acknowledged, the dramatic improvement in coal mine safety is due not only to more stringent laws but also to the impressive efforts of most coal mining companies to assure the protection of their employees.

And yet every barrel has a bad apple or two. I didn't know the one in this story, but he's out there.

PROLOGUE

June 8, 2017

The Honorable Jessie Macaulay
Charlottesville Circuit Court
315 East High Street
Charlottesville, VA 22902

Dear Jess,

I was in your courtroom today when Kate Strange was convicted of murder. Your facial expression, the one I know so well, told me you were pleased. Why?

I followed this trial because I knew Jason Worthy. I hated the man. But that young woman didn't kill him. There was a ton of reasonable doubt. You know it and I know it. But you let her go down. Why?

We've known each other our whole lives. Except maybe for Jimmy, no one knows you better. Or so I thought. Maybe I don't know you at all.

What the hell happened to you?

Sam

June 12, 2017

Samantha Picken, Esq.
Picken & Lloyd, LLP
127 Court St.
Woodstock, VA 22664

Sam, oh Sam—

You really are a good friend. No one, not even Jimmy, knows me like you do.
What can I say? I did what I had to.

Let's get together soon.

Love, Jess

CHAPTER ONE

The murder scene was gruesome. Emma Mancini, the medical examiner for Bath County, Virginia, estimated that Jason Worthy had been dead three days when his body was found. Blood was all over the living room at Justice Hill, the magnificent retreat near Hot Springs that Jason had lovingly called his "log cabin" in the wooded hills of western Virginia.

The blood was all Jason's. Some was from his forehead where an X had been carved by the box cutter found next to his body. Some was from similar X marks carved across his mouth and on his penis. Most was from his femoral artery, which had been severed when his right leg was cut off by a chain saw. It was easy to see what had happened because the leg and the chain saw were also next to the body. Jason's shirt was on, but his pants had been pulled off, probably to allow access to his leg and penis. A diamond ring was on the floor near the body.

"Someone sure must have hated that guy," said Emma.

Deputy Sheriff Scott O'Hanlon agreed. He had investigated several homicides in his twenty-five years in law enforcement. "Out here, killing's usually done with a gun. This took a lot of trouble. It also took some strength, or maybe some misdirection by someone he knew and trusted. There aren't the signs of struggle you'd expect with a killing like this."

"Wonder who the victim is. Do you know?"

"Yeah, he's some kind of a big-shot lawyer in Washington, D.C. Should say he was a big-shot lawyer. He doesn't look like anything special right now."

"What was he doing out here?" Emma wondered.

"I didn't really know him, but I met him once. He bought this place, Justice Hill he called it, eight or nine years ago. Spent a fortune fixing it up. He'd come out here several times a year, usually in the spring or autumn. Always brought that old hound dog Slouch with him."

"Slouch? What kind of name is that for a dog?"

"A last name, I'd guess. First name was probably something like 'I'm No,' or 'Don't,' or maybe . . .'"

"Never mind."

"I don't know. I just heard he called the dog Slouch."

Scott and Emma were joined by an earnest young man who looked like he wanted to be anywhere else. Scott welcomed him with a hearty "Hey, hotshot. How they hangin?" Emma smiled and quietly said, "Hi, Angelo. Murder scenes are always tough, but they get easier after the first."

Angelo Jones (his grandfather had traded Giovanetti for Jones at Ellis Island) had joined the Bath County Sheriff's Office four months earlier. A handsome young man who had gotten an MBA at the University of Virginia, he had unaccountably passed up a promising Wall Street career to take a job that paid peanuts in one of the least populated parts of Virginia.

"Are you nuts?" Scott had asked him.

"Probably," Angelo had said, "but I don't like crowds, and I don't care about money. Living here and being a part of this community feels right to me."

Now, staying as far from what was left of Jason Worthy as he thought he could get away with, Angelo whispered to Scott, "Did you see all those X cuts . . . and the leg? That's really ghastly."

"Yeah, I did. And what're you whispering for? He can't hear you."

"I guess not. I just thought it was, you know, respectful. There are easier and cleaner ways to kill a guy than this. What do you think it means?"

"The killer was sending a message," said Scott. "We're going to find out what it was. When we know that, it shouldn't be hard to find the perp. All I can say for now is there's an awful lot of hate involved. Or an awful lot of love."

CHAPTER TWO

O'Hanlon took a long look at the body. "I'll nose around a bit, walk the grid, and get this place dusted for prints. My guess is we aren't going to find much that isn't in the open. Doesn't look like the killer made much of an effort to cover his tracks."

"*His* tracks?" asked Angelo. "How do you know it was a man?"

"I don't," said Scott. "That was just loose talk. But if I had to make a guess right now, I'd say it was a man. This crime scene doesn't look like a woman's work."

He paused, thinking out loud as he worked out a preliminary investigation strategy. "You know, figuring out who his friends and enemies were is a good place to start. Angelo, you take that on. And see if you can find the dog."

"On it," said Angelo, starting to walk away.

"One more thing," Scott called. "I heard there was a young woman who used to come out here with him. Never met her and don't know her name. Be sure she's on your list. I guess that would be the friends' list because people don't usually vacation with their enemies. And don't say I never did anything for you."

Angelo got into his car and began to drive back to town. A half mile down the road, he saw a small, well-kept house near the entrance to Justice Hill. *Never too early to begin the investigation,* he thought, and turned into a driveway flanked by two beautifully carved eagles.

His knock on the door was answered almost immediately by an older woman who, Angelo judged, must have been a beauty in her day. Her name was Eliza Dawkins. She had lived in this house for forty-two years, alone for the last four since her husband died. That must have been difficult for someone her age; the area was sparsely populated, and the only road in, the gravel road that went past her house and ended at Justice Hill, resembled a bucking snake. The rocky terrain accounted for the curves. *Probably a good thing,* Angelo thought. *You could go much too fast if the curves weren't there.*

"Sorry to bother you, ma'am. I'm with the sheriff's department, and we're doing an investigation over at Justice Hill. I'd like to ask you some questions, if I may."

"Yes, of course. What kind of an investigation?"

"I'm afraid it's a homicide investigation. The owner of the place, Jason Worthy, was killed."

"Oh, my goodness. I'm so sorry," said Eliza. "I was afraid something was wrong up there. The dog was howling frantically a few nights ago. That isn't like Slouch. It was around 4:30 in the morning. I managed to get back to sleep, and when I woke up at 6:15, the howling had stopped. I figured he must have been frightened by a bear or something."

"Did you know Mr. Worthy?"

"No. Well, I mean yes, I guess I knew him a little. We're the only two houses this far up the road, and out here, it's a good idea to know your neighbors. My husband and I went over to say hello when Mr. Worthy bought the place. He was gracious but never made any effort to reciprocate. He was a lawyer in Washington, and when he was out here, he pretty much stuck to himself."

"If you didn't see much of him, how do you know the dog's name was Slouch?"

"I saw it on his name tag when he came down here to sniff around, shortly after Mr. Worthy moved in. He was a bloodhound, I think, or maybe a coonhound. Very friendly. The first time he came, I gave him a treat. After that, he was a regular visitor when they were here. He knew there would always be a treat waiting for him." Eliza paused, then asked, "How did you know to come out here to investigate? How did you know something was wrong?"

"Our office had a call from one of Worthy's law partners. He said Worthy wasn't in the office this morning but should have been because he had a court date. That wasn't like him; he would never miss a court date. We said we'd go to his place and have a look around. That's when we found the body."

"I see," Eliza replied. "It's a good thing someone called. Otherwise, it could have been days or even weeks before the body was discovered. No one ever comes out this way. Just Mr. Worthy, or sometimes a contractor if he's having work done at the place. And me, of course."

"You seem to have a good view of the road from your living room. Do you notice people as they come and go?"

"Yes. It's very quiet here. You can usually hear a car go by, and you see the dust from the road unless it's been raining. I saw Mr. Worthy when he and Slouch drove in last Friday. I don't think anyone else has been here since then, unless it was after 9:30 at night. That's when I go to bed."

"By the way, do you know where the dog is?"

"Oh. Oh yes, and your question reminds me that there was one other visitor. There was a girl, well, actually a young woman, but they're all girls to me. She used to come out with Mr. Worthy, pretty regularly for quite a while. She was his girlfriend, I guess, but something must have gone wrong because I hadn't seen her for several months until last Saturday. It was early in the morning. I saw her driving away, and Slouch was with her."

"Did you notice what time it was?"

"It was 6:30. I was having my first cup of coffee."

"Do you happen to know her name?" Angelo asked.

"I believe it was Kate."

CHAPTER THREE

Sam's friendship with Jessie Macaulay—well, Jessie Spaulding then—went back as far as she could remember. They lived in West Virginia coal country. Their daddies, Big Joe Spaulding and Bill Picken, worked underground at the Merriman No. 3 Mine. They were best friends. Their mommas got along well too. Maybe they had to because their husbands and little girls were so close.

Life was good in Owl Hollow, where Sam and Jessie grew up. It had been a coal town for as long as the mine had been there, going on fifty years. It was along the Big Coal River in Boone County. Just about everyone there worked for the mine one way or another. No one would choose to live in Owl Hollow without a reason, and the mine was the only reason.

There are people who talk about living in Appalachia like it's a sin or a sorrow. They say the word *Appalachia* like it's dirty and they can't wait to get on to happier subjects. And they show pictures of Appalachia that are always sad and depressing—kids with no shoes, stores with broken windows, grim women with broken spirits, oppressed men with no options other than the mine.

Sam thought those people didn't understand coal mining. Coal miners are proud and being underground is in their blood. Sam's granddaddy was a coal miner, and that's all her daddy ever wanted to be. The same was true in Jessie's family. Big Joe Spaulding was born to the mines. He was a powerful man who thought he was John Henry.

The miners Sam knew in Owl Hollow liked being in the mine. It might have been different if they had to work low coal, but the coal seam at Merriman No. 3 was high enough that they could stand and move around easily. There was a freedom in the mine, a pride, and the pay was good for guys who didn't go to college. Everyone knew everyone in Owl Hollow. The land was peaceful, with streams and mountains and trees and none of the sirens and screeches of cities. The hunting was great too; there weren't many miners at work on the opening day of hunting season.

Sam knew the places in those pictures of Appalachia must exist because the pictures showed them, but that wasn't what she remembered. Her family had a nice house. It wasn't big, but it had three bedrooms and two bathrooms, and her momma always kept it clean, which wasn't easy with all the coal dust around. And Sam had shoes and three or four sets of clothes to wear, one fancy and the others for everyday. Her family was a little better off than most because Bill Picken was a section foreman. Being in management meant a little more money. It also meant a lot more responsibility.

Big Joe could have been a foreman too, but he preferred to be in the thick of things, running coal. He liked just being one of the guys. Big Joe gave Bill a little crap about being in management now and then, but it didn't affect their friendship. They were both good workers, safe workers. They knew the mine was dangerous, and they didn't cut corners. They trusted each other and looked after each other.

Jessie and Sam were classmates at the small public school in Owl Hollow. They played baseball and basketball and skipped stones on the river with the guys and always held their own. In grammar school, it didn't feel like boys and girls were all that different. Everyone had plenty of chores to do and went to the same church and shopped at the same Dollar store. Most of the guys and some of the girls thought they'd go to work in the mine after high school.

Jessie was born in 1975 and named after her momma, Jessie Farrell Spaulding. She had a younger brother, Kevin, but he caught pneumonia and died when he was seven. Sam was a few months younger than Jessie and an only child. Her daddy had wanted a son and took some of the edge off his disappointment by calling his little girl Sam. Actually, her name was Samantha, her momma insisted on that, but she was always just Sam.

Sam thought Jessie was prettier than she was, even though it was later before they noticed those things. Jessie had blond hair, but sometimes it looked almost red. There was no mistaking the blue of her eyes, though; they were pure crystal and had a depth to them, particularly when she looked at you intently, as she often did. Sam had brown hair and some freckles and wasn't bad looking, at least when she wasn't next to Jess. Sam also thought Jessie was smarter than she was, even though their report cards said otherwise. Jessie was plenty smart anyway, and Sam was a little jealous of her because boys almost always choose a pretty girl over a smart one.

It was a happy growing-up time in Owl Hollow. Then, when Jess and Sam were in high school, a section of roof fell in at the mine. Big Joe Spaulding was under it.

CHAPTER FOUR

Big Joe was lucky, at least he said he was. Several miners led by Bill Picken worked desperately to free him. His leg had been crushed, and he underwent three operations to fix his broken back. He left the hospital in a chair. He was partially paralyzed, but his mind and spirit were intact.

"I'm so sorry," Bill said. "I should have been there for you."

"There was nothing you could have done. It was just a freak deal. You know, the old man of the mountain taking a little revenge for us poking and clawing at him all these years. Hell, if it wasn't for you, Bill, I'd be a dead man. Big Joe can live with being Wheelchair Joe. My right leg's gone, but my right arm's as good as ever, and I can still hoist a few with the guys. And I've got my two Jessies. I feel blessed."

Bill Picken was not so lucky. His body was intact, but he was broken inside. After weeks of stewing, he gave his notice at Merriman No. 3 and he and his family moved to Blacksburg, Virginia. "I can't stay there," he told his wife and daughter. "Every time I look at Joe, I see my failure. My job was to keep the men safe. I didn't even keep my best friend safe." He took a job as a campus cop at Virginia Tech.

Bill was done with responsibility. He was done with religion, too, because "How can you believe in a God who would let something like this happen?" For all practical purposes, he was done with living. He just sat. And stared. And drank.

The accident drove a wedge between Bill and Big Joe, and of course their wives. Ironically, it brought their daughters even closer. They no longer saw each other at school every day, but they visited often, particularly in the summer months. They usually got together at the Spauldings' home in Owl Hollow so Jessie's presence wouldn't remind Bill of the accident.

Jess and Sam talked about school, which came naturally to both of them. They talked about boys. Jessie had gone out with several, one of them seriously, she said, but Sam could tell it hadn't been all that serious. Sam had sort of been seeing Chris Lloyd, a boy she met in Blacksburg and liked pretty well.

"Have you done it?" Jessie asked Sam once.

"No!" Sam said, feeling embarrassed. "How about you?"

Jessie just got a funny little smile on her face but didn't answer. Sam thought she probably had. Jessie was always ahead of her.

They talked about the accident and how it changed their families. "I love your parents," Sam told Jess. "They've had so much to deal with, and they're still so positive about everything."

"I know. It's weird, but I actually think it's made our lives better. For one thing, I know I want to get out of Owl Hollow. I want to go to college, and my folks agree. But tell me, how are your folks? How is your daddy? I wish he wouldn't take it so hard, because it wasn't his fault."

"I know, and Momma and I keep telling him that. Big Joe has certainly never blamed him. But Daddy just can't see it that way. He's so sad—they're both so sad. He's given up. Momma is trying to be there for him, but she really doesn't know what to do. The funny thing is, their despair is why I'm at the same place you are. I want to go to college."

Jessie graduated with honors at Owl Hollow, and Sam was valedictorian of her high school class in Blacksburg. They both got scholarships to Stanford.

CHAPTER FIVE

Sam ended up not going to Stanford. Her dad wasn't getting any better and was more than her mom could handle. She stayed in Blacksburg and went to Virginia Tech.

She felt some jealousy as Jessie left for Palo Alto. If the shoe had been on the other foot, Sam didn't think she would have gone to Stanford and left Jessie behind. She didn't begrudge Jess—she just wished things had played out differently and they could have gone together. *Our school mascots say it all,* Sam thought. *Jessie's a beautiful red Cardinal and I'm a Hokie.* She smiled as she remembered having to google Hokie and finding out it was a turkey.

Things worked out well despite Sam's regrets. Virginia Tech is a fine school, and she was close to home, which meant a lot to her mom. She was also close to Chris Lloyd, who had gone to nearby Radford University. They were still seeing each other in an on-and-off relationship that was definitely tilting toward on.

Sam really admired Chris. His family didn't have much money, and he had held odd jobs all through high school and college. He was the most honest person she knew. He lived in a black-and-white world in which shades of gray didn't exist. He simply wouldn't cheat, in school or in life. He was incapable of it.

Chris was a better-than-average student but not by a landslide. He studied hard for his B grades, but he earned them on his own. He had a logical mind and a good helping of common sense. In his senior year of high school, he was voted "most dependable" by his classmates. Sam thought he was certainly that, and also very cute.

Life had dealt Chris a challenging hand, and he made the most of it. He had strong values and was unfailingly optimistic. There was so much to admire about him, and Sam did, absolutely. It's easy to confuse admiration with love when you don't have much experience to fall back on. Sam came to realize that later, after she and Chris were married, and she had a period of doubting her choice and thinking she could have done better. But they hung in there, and many years later, Sam came to learn that admiration and dependability can alchemize into real love.

Because of her family background and absent a passion for anything else, Sam chose to study mining engineering. She found it fascinating to learn what's involved in siting and developing a mine. The technical elements didn't turn her on, but the economic factors were captivating. She took two extra courses on the financial aspects of operating a coal mine. It was quickly apparent there's a lot of money to be made. It's no surprise that the owners of coal mines are often referred to as coal barons.

The money is in the land. It's in the coal seam within the land. Profits are influenced by the quality of the coal and the extent to which it can be easily and efficiently mined. They're dependent on the value of the long-term contracts negotiated with utility customers and the price of coal on the spot market. They're also influenced, very heavily, by the operator's ability to keep costs down. There's big money in closely managing personnel costs, equipment costs, and maintenance costs.

Life is what it is when you're a kid, and Sam didn't think about these things then. Now she found herself wondering why the living conditions weren't better in Owl Hollow. They were OK, and she and her family were happy, but things could have been a lot better.

George Rafferty, the president of Black Bear Mining Company, lived very well. Black Bear operated seven mines in the area, including Merriman No. 3. George had a huge estate in the next county. The grounds, maintained by a full-time crew of eleven, were beautiful. George even had a private hunting reserve on the estate. *If he had so much,* Sam now thought, *why couldn't he have paid the miners at Merriman No. 3 a little more? Why couldn't he have taken five percent of all the money he made and pay it to the miners? That wouldn't have made any difference in his life, but it would have made a world of difference in theirs.* The answer, Sam knew, was that he didn't have to. The people in Owl Hollow either worked at the mine, or they didn't work. George could get away with paying whatever he wanted.

There was a separate set of issues: *Did George cut corners on maintenance? Did he cut corners on safety? When the roof fell in at Merriman No. 3 and took Big Joe's leg and Dad's will to live, was the roof control system everything it should have been? Or was George cutting a corner, maybe skipping a roof bolt here or there, so he could make a little more money?*

Sam became fixated on the increasingly probable injustice of Big Joe's loss, her family's loss, and her loss, frustrated by the knowledge there was nothing to be done about it. Even if legal claims were not time-barred by the statute of limitations, even if they had not been waived by taking the workers' compensation money needed for medical expenses, it was folly to imagine the miners would testify against George Rafferty. They would want to, of course, to support Big Joe Spaulding and Bill Picken. They would want to because they knew the conditions at the mine, they knew Black Bear's practices, and they knew the accident might have been avoided. But they also knew better than to take on George Rafferty.

Sam couldn't fix this one. But maybe there were others she could fix. She decided to go to law school after graduating from Tech.

CHAPTER SIX

College was the most time Jessie and Sam had ever been apart, but they stayed in touch as regularly as they could. They talked by phone every week or two and spent time together at the Spauldings' place in Owl Hollow when Jessie was home for the summer.

They kept up to date on each other's lives. Jessie had a dual major in Brit lit and poly-sci, had made the softball team, and had pledged the Alpha Phi sorority. Sam's extracurriculars revolved around Chris Lloyd and helping out at home. Jessie regularly asked Sam how her folks were doing. The words varied in Sam's responses, but the message was always the same.

"It's awful. Dad's in total despair. I try to ease his guilt by telling him the accident was on Black Bear and George Rafferty and not on him, but he simply shrugs and says in that case he'll see them in hell. That accident ended his life. And Mom's. She's the one I really feel sorry for. She didn't do anything to deserve the life she's living."

Jessie called Sam in October of their junior year with sad news. "Mom's and Dad's spirits are good," she said, "but some complications have set in for Dad. He's having circulatory problems that trace back to the loss of his leg. He's gotten pretty frail and spends too much time with doctors, tests, and medical crap. Mom is worried sick. And it's costing them a bundle, even with insurance."

Sam was saddened by the news. Big Joe was a rock to everyone in Owl Hollow. "Jeez, Jess, that breaks my heart. Are you going to have to go home?"

"I don't think so. The scholarship money covers most of my costs, and whenever I raise the subject, Mom tells me to put it out of my head. She says how proud she and Dad are to have a daughter at Stanford, that I'm all he talks about when he gets together for beers with the guys. They want me to finish up here, and I guess I will. It's only a year and a half to go."

When Sam asked Jessie about her social life, as she did every call, Jess inevitably said she was dating around, but there was no one special, nothing serious. That changed toward the end of their junior year. There was this guy named Jimmy.

Jimmy Macaulay was from Walla Walla, a quiet town in southeastern Washington. His parents produced small-volume cabs and cab blends at their winery in nearby Horse Heaven Hills. They were fans of the great James Taylor, and when they had a son in 1976, they called him Sweet Baby James. Everyone else called him Jimmy.

Jimmy had his Grandpa Jock's strong Scottish jaw and gray-green eyes, and his mother's thick black hair. He was exceptionally gifted but used his gifts selectively. On the athletic fields, he pushed himself relentlessly. He lettered in three sports and led his high school football team to the state championship his junior and senior years. He was less inclined to push himself academically. He didn't need to. With remarkably little effort, his grades consistently put him in the top 10 percent of his class.

Jimmy went to Stanford on a football scholarship. Jessie met him one night at an Alpha Phi party. There was an instant attraction.

"Tell me all about him," Sam said. "Is this going anywhere?"

"He's handsome, charming, smart, and fun. He's also taken. He has a high school sweetheart at Yale, and he's annoyingly committed to her. We've gone out a number of times, but only as friends. I like him a lot and want to give this a chance to play out, but so far, I'm not making much headway. I'm giving it my best shot, but I can't say I think it's going anywhere."

Sam heard the sadness in her friend's voice. *She's nuts about the guy*, Sam thought. *Jimmy may have a girlfriend at Yale, but that's three thousand miles away, and Jessie's right there. I'm not betting against her.*

A month later, Jessie stopped seeing Jimmy. Her feelings had grown beyond friendship and weren't being reciprocated. She had too much pride to stay in that kind of relationship.

Jessie told Sam all about it. *I'm still not betting against Jess,* Sam thought.

CHAPTER SEVEN

S cott O'Hanlon called a meeting of the Justice Hill team. It was 2:00 p.m. on Wednesday, April 13, 2016. The body had been discovered on Monday morning, and Scott wanted to know where things stood. Not all the results would be in, not by a long shot, but there should be at least some progress by now.

He had invited Emma Mancini to the meeting, and he started with her. "Thanks for coming, Doc. I know you've got other things to do, but this is important. What have you got?"

"I'm placing the time of death between 7:00 p.m. on Friday, April 8 and 5:00 a.m. on Saturday, April 9. I know that's a bigger window than you want, but it's the best I can do right now."

"I'm actually surprised you can narrow it down that much," Scott said. "What do you base it on?"

"Mostly lividity and the absence of rigor mortis."

"Why don't you take a minute to explain what you mean by that, Doc? Angelo's new here, and this is as good a time as any for him to start learning this stuff."

"Sure, happy to. When the heart stops pumping, gravity takes over, and the blood pools in those parts of the body closest to the ground. That's called lividity. It's a pretty fast process, usually no more than twelve hours, but it varies from person to person. Worthy was on his back, and there were reddish-bluish concentrations, blood pools, where his back and legs touched the carpet.

"Also, the blood was completely dried, even the large pool next to Worthy where his leg had been cut off. Blood dries at the edges of a pool first, then moves toward the center. Here it was all dry, confirming he'd been dead for well over a day when we found him. The problem is, we don't know how much more than a day. Rigor mortis, or I should say the absence of it, helps us figure that out."

Angelo looked confused. "I thought rigor mortis set in after you died, and fairly quickly. How could there be an absence of it?"

"It does set in quickly, and the stiffness of the body lasts for a period of time, usually a couple of days, and then the body becomes flaccid again. The fact that Worthy's body had gone through rigor mortis and was back in a re-laxed state indicates it had been at least two days and more probably two and a half days since his death."

Scott smiled inwardly, marveling once again at Emma's teaching skills. She was an eight-year veteran when he came aboard, and she had helped him more times than he could count. "Thanks, Doc," Scott said. "Good report. Not perfect, but at least it gives us a frame of reference. One thing that keeps nagging at me is there were no signs of a struggle. Was Worthy incapacitated in some way? Was he tied up? If someone comes at you with a box cutter and a chain saw, you don't just sit there and take it."

"That is troubling," said Emma. "We'll know a lot more once we get the body on the table and take a closer look. There were no abrasions on his extremities or mouth, so it doesn't appear he was bound or duct-taped or otherwise physically incapacitated. But there are a couple of things that may be pertinent. First, there was alcohol in his system, a lot of alcohol. His blood-alcohol level was more than twice the legal limit. Second, he had a needle mark in his left arm, and there are no indications he was a user."

"What kind of alcohol? What was injected into him?"

"You'll be the first to know after I open him up."

"And when the hell will that be?"

"Hopefully tomorrow. No later than Friday. Don't worry, Scott—the body won't give up its secrets before then."

"Well, the picture begins to fill in," said Scott. "Tom, what can you tell us about the forensic findings so far?"

Tom Mahaffey had been doing crime lab work for a long time. There was little he hadn't seen. "Not much help with the prints, I'm afraid. Worthy's prints are all over the place, of course, but he didn't do this to himself. We couldn't find any prints on the chain saw, which suggests the killer was wearing gloves. We found smeared prints on the box cutter. They may have been older prints that were largely rubbed away by the killer's gloves. There is one partial print we might be able to work with."

"OK. Any hair or fiber samples?"

"We did take a couple of hair samples from the carpet near the body. We need to analyze them, but we already know they didn't come from Worthy. They look like a woman's hair. Blond. No fiber samples and no footprints. One thing we'll want to run down is the chain saw. It's an old one, one of the early Hammersmith models. It looks commercial grade and has a partial serial number on it. Maybe we can track down where it was bought and by whom."

"What about the diamond ring?"

"There are fingerprints on it. We'll analyze them."

"Thanks, Tom. Good work. Anything else?"

"Just thinking about what T. S. Eliot wrote in *The Waste Land*." Tom loved poetry and usually managed to work in a poetic reference when reporting on his findings. "He wrote that 'April is the cruelest month.' That was certainly true for Worthy."

Delighted, Angelo jumped in. "Yes, but Robert Browning had a contrary view. In one of his sonnets from abroad, he wrote, "Oh, to be in England, now that April's there.""

"Well, isn't this just great, a goddamn poetry reading," Scott barked. "For the record, I think Eliot's right on this one. Besides, we're not in England. We're in Bath County, Virginia, where we're supposed to be doing the people's work. Let's get back to business, shall we?" His eyes were fixed on Angelo. "Your turn, hotshot. What've you got?"

"I know what happened to the dog. He was taken from Justice Hill by a woman named Kate."

"Who the hell is Kate, and how do you know that?"

"She's the one who used to come up here with Worthy sometimes, the one you told me about." Angelo filled the team in on his conversation with Eliza

Dawkins. "I should know a lot more after tomorrow, and with luck, I'll get a fix on this Kate person. I have a meeting in Washington with Terry Gomez. She was Worthy's secretary at the law firm for the last nine years. Secretaries usually know stuff about their bosses. I'm thinking Terry will be a good source of information. Then I'll follow up on the leads I get from her."

"OK," Scott muttered, reminding himself that Angelo was still new at the job and trying to hide his annoyance that he wasn't farther along. "Keep on it. What else have you been doing?"

"Finding out all I could about Jason Worthy from old newspaper stories and public record searches."

"And?"

"And he's not the Goody Two-shoes everyone thinks he is."

CHAPTER EIGHT

Jess was surprised to receive a call from Jimmy in late November 1997. She was preparing a quick dinner at her Logan Circle apartment in Washington, D.C. before heading back to the library at Georgetown Law for a night of study. It had been more than a year since they had talked.

"Hey, Jess," he said. There was a long silence as she caught her breath. "I'm up at Wharton. I've been thinking about you, and I'd love to see you. Would you be up for dinner sometime soon?"

"Sure, sounds like fun. When can you come down?"

A light snow was falling in Washington when Jimmy knocked on Jessie's door eight days later. "Hi," he said, giving her a hug. "Hi, yourself," said Jess. "It's good to see you. Let's have a glass of wine and go get something to eat. There's a lot to catch up on. For openers, what happened to Miss Yale?"

"The short, evasive answer is that it didn't work out. The longer, more interesting answer is that she eloped with one of her professors."

They enjoyed a leisurely seafood dinner at the Maine Avenue waterfront and traded stories about what they had been doing. They were comfortable with each other, just as they had been at Stanford.

"I didn't know you wanted to go to law school," said Jimmy.

"I didn't either," replied Jessie. "But as graduation neared, I realized there wasn't much I could do, at least not much I wanted to do, with a liberal arts degree. I had read a book about a trial lawyer, Earl Rogers, and it inspired me to go to law school. I chose Georgetown because it's really good and also close to the world of politics, which I love."

"How are you finding it, now that you're a semester in?"

"It's been wonderful so far. I know it's weird to say that since law school gets such a bad rap, but it's very logical and involves real people with real problems. It engages me as nothing I've done ever has. But how about you? Why an MBA? Are you after the big bucks?"

"It seems that way, doesn't it? The truth is, I didn't know what I wanted to do. I don't think I would have made it in pro football, and besides, I didn't want to get my head beaten in. I've always liked business, and Dad used to say he wished he'd known more about it when he started his winery. I decided to give it a try. Wharton was willing to take me, so there I am."

On the long walk back to Logan Circle, Jimmy asked what Sam was doing.

"She's finishing her first semester of law school at Washington and Lee. It's a good school, ranked in or near the top twenty-five, and it's not that far from her folks. Her boyfriend, Chris Lloyd, is there too, so it works out well all the way around."

"So, you're both studying law," Jimmy laughed. "Why am I not surprised? Is the thing with Chris serious?"

"We haven't had that exact conversation," Jessie said. "But I think it is."

When they got to her apartment, they kissed gently, and Jimmy asked if he could come in. "No, I don't think so, Jimmy. I've been very fond of you as a friend, but things are different now. I need some time to process. I hope you can understand that."

"Actually, I do. My dad's a winemaker, and he always used to say great wines take time and so do great loves. I'm OK with any pace that works for you. Thanks for a nice evening, Jess. I'll call you soon."

After he left, Jessie grabbed her phone and called Sam. "When can you come up? We have to talk!"

"Well, exams are around the corner," Sam replied, "but not for a couple of weeks. There won't be much traffic this late at night. I'll jump in the car and see you in four hours."

Jessie shared her news with Sam. It was warm, exciting, and enveloping. So was their lovemaking.

That was the first time.

CHAPTER NINE

It came to them naturally, like falling asleep. They were drinking wine, and Jessie was telling Sam about Jimmy, and Sam hugged Jess to share in her joy, and then they were kissing, and then it was a runaway train. There wasn't shock, surprise, or regret. It was like they both knew it was coming, like it was their destiny, and now that it was here, they welcomed it. They were willing and active participants. It was spontaneous and lovely.

They lay together quietly when it was over, each trying to sort out what had just happened. "What the fuck was that?" Sam asked, trying to interject a light note.

"Beats me, but I loved it," Jess said, propping herself up on one elbow. "I was excited about Jimmy, but I was even more excited to share the news with you."

"I know. We've done everything together our whole lives, and now this. But I don't think it changes anything."

"No," murmured Jess. "It doesn't. Our lives go on. You have Chris, and Jimmy and I will find our way to each other. And you and I will always have this moment."

Sam's thoughts returned to her law school reality as she made the long drive back to Lexington. Final exams are a big deal; they cause extreme stress because at most law schools, there are no other tests, and your grade on the final is your grade for the course. They are particularly stressful in the first semester of your first year because it's all new, and you have no context for evaluating the process or your place in it. All you know is based on the interactions in your classes, where most of the other students seem smarter than you.

On top of that, the grading is subjective. At the beginning of the period allotted for the exam, you are given a narrative that states a problem. Your job is to analyze the problem and spot the issues. You may be given the role of a counselor advising the client who has the problem, in which case you are to tell her what the issues are, analyze the strengths and weaknesses of each according to the facts and the law, and advise her as to the course she should follow. Or you may be given the role of plaintiff's counsel or defense counsel and asked to prepare an outline of a brief arguing one side of the matter or the other. It's actually quite intriguing, and if it weren't for the stress would be a lot of fun.

Sam had final exams that semester in five courses: Contracts, Torts, Real Property, Constitutional Law, and Civil Procedure. She thought she passed them but beyond that had no idea what to expect. When the grades were posted, she was surprised and pleased to see that she had finished seventh in the first-year class. Throughout it all, she had been thinking about Jessie, who was going through a parallel experience at Georgetown. Jess, too, did well, finishing in the top 15 percent of her class. Sam wasn't worried about Chris—he was a survivor who would steadily plod his way to a good result. He did, comfortably finishing near the top third of his class. All three held serve throughout the remainder of law school.

CHAPTER TEN

Jess and Jimmy did find their way to each other, and it took less time than Jess had expected. Jimmy was an "all in" kind of a guy, and his attraction to Jessie intensified now that she could be more than a friend. They saw each other every couple of weeks, generally alternating between Washington and Philadelphia. Jess wanted to keep it cool, and Jimmy respected her boundaries, so whoever was visiting stayed with friends or at a hotel. If it was meant to be, it *would* be, they told themselves, and both believed it would be. Neither could deny the growing comfort of the relationship as intellectual compatibility, a common affinity for wry humor, and sensual attraction settled in.

In June 1999, after finishing her second year at Georgetown Law, Jessie Spaulding became Jessie Macaulay. It was a small wedding for family and close friends. Big Joe couldn't travel, and it was unthinkable to Jessie that her parents wouldn't be a part of it, so she asked Jimmy if he and his parents would mind coming to Owl Hollow for a firsthand look at coal country and, by the way, a wedding. They understood the situation and readily agreed.

Despite Jessie's dedication to keeping expectations low, it was a lovely occasion. The families bonded with genuine warmth, due in part to their common Scottish roots. Jessie didn't have to worry about her maid of honor's expectations. Sam was thrilled to be with her best friend on the biggest day of her life.

Two weeks and an abbreviated honeymoon later, Jimmy and Jess moved into a small but charming apartment in Brooklyn. Jimmy had just graduated from Wharton, finishing near the top of his class. He was fascinated by business and for the first time in his life found a desire to push himself academically. The effort rewarded him. Barclays offered him an investment banking job, working with foreign exchange products. Jessie took a job as a summer associate with the prestigious Cravath law firm.

The next year flashed by. Jimmy worked long hours and loved it, enjoying short business trips to London, Frankfurt, and Paris. Jessie and her partner, Veronica Lynch, had won the second-year moot court competition the year before, with Jessie getting the best speaker award. She was articulate and had a quick and active mind, and moot court played to her strengths. She loved it and devoted substantial time in her third year to managing the moot court program and serving as a judge whenever she could. She skipped graduation to rejoin Jimmy in New York and study for the bar exam. Once that was behind her, she would start her new job as a law clerk for Ed Belson, a highly regarded trial judge in the Southern District of New York.

CHAPTER ELEVEN

Sam's life was far less glamorous. She worked hard and had some wins, but her family's needs and her more limited ambitions gave her a smaller stage. Sam saw Jessie as an eagle who soared, while she flapped her wings at a much lower altitude and was satisfied to get from branch to branch.

Chris and Sam started living together during their second year of law school. It just seemed like the natural thing to do. They had been going out pretty steadily for several years. They were in law school together and saw each other every day and most nights. Living together wasn't much different and saved rent money.

When she looked back on it later, Sam wondered why she had settled on Chris so early. *Maybe I should have looked around to see what else was out there. It wasn't like guys were beating down my door trying to date me, but there were opportunities.* Somehow, it just hadn't taken with the other guys she went out with. It always seemed like too much work and usually ended up being a disappointment in one way or another.

Chris was different. He was just a good guy. Maybe it was because she had known him for so long and there weren't any surprises. He was an old shoe. But he was an honest and sturdy old shoe. He was who he was, and he wouldn't back down or change just to please someone. She admired him and felt comfortable with him. He also knew her folks and why her dad was the way he was, and so she didn't have to go through all that and try to explain it. It wasn't that exciting with Chris, but it was steady. She knew what she was getting, and it worked for her.

After Jessie's wedding, Sam went to Charleston and spent the summer clerking at Jackson Kelly, one of the premier law firms in West Virginia. Chris had wanted to be with his family and went back home to work with a small firm in Blacksburg. Sam chose Charleston because it was the capital and largest city in a coal mining state, and her desire to use the law to help coal miners and their families was still strong. It was a good summer, and she did interesting work with fine lawyers who were also nice people. She did learn, though, that it's not easy to do the kind of work she wanted to do at a big firm in West Virginia. The big firms typically have a stable of coal company clients, and they can't sue those clients because it would be a conflict of interest. Besides, it's just bad business for big law firms to sue coal companies in West Virginia.

When Chris and Sam hooked up again in Lexington to start their third year, Sam realized she had missed the little shit more than she thought she would, and he had apparently missed her too. They talked about it as they lay in bed one night. "Why don't we just get married then?" Chris asked suddenly. Sam had no good answer.

At 10:00 the next morning, they went to the Rockbridge Circuit Court, got a marriage license, and found a judge who was willing to marry them. There was no planning and no ceremony. There were no parents and no Jessie. It was just Chris and Sam doing what they always did, falling toward each other without making a big deal of it. Sam never wanted a big wedding anyway, and Chris sure as hell didn't, so this seemed about right. They celebrated by going to the Dive Bomber, one of their favorite bars, for burgers and fries and a few beers.

Their third year of law school was actually a lot of fun. Sam spent thirty or forty hours a week helping her friend Blue run the law review. Blue had narrowly beaten her out for editor in chief, but she was OK with that because they liked and admired each other. Blue made Sam executive editor, and they ran the review as a partnership.

Chris didn't make the law review, but he wouldn't have wanted to do that kind of work anyway. He liked corporate law (why, Sam didn't know), and he liked counseling. He found avenues to pursue both interests. He was a research assistant for his corporate law professor, and he also got real-world counseling experience working in the school's pro bono clinic.

When you're on law review at a good school, opportunities open up for you. Sam went through the recruiting process to see what was out there and got offers from several first-rate firms up and down the East Coast. She thought about them, but none seemed right, even though she had to admit the money was appealing. She also had an attractive clerkship opportunity for a respected judge on the Fourth Circuit.

"What do you think I should do?" Sam asked Chris one night.

"There's a lot of money and a lot of prestige tied up in all these offers," he replied. "And whichever one you took, you'd crush it. But I think the important question is this: What does your gut tell you?"

It felt good to have to confront what she really felt. "I don't want to be a junior associate at a big law firm, and I don't want to waste a year or two of my life clerking. I don't care about the money, not all that much anyway, and I'm trying hard not to care about the prestige. When you ask me straight out what I want, I come back to what I've always wanted: to help my people. I want to make it a better and fairer life for coal miners and their families. Wherever I live, I want to help the people in the community who have a hard time helping themselves. I guess that makes me a Pollyanna, but it's what I want."

"Good by me," Chris said.

"Well that was easy," Sam said with relief. "And how about you? What do you want to do? Where do you think we should live?"

"I'd like to do corporate work for small businesses. I want to help the have-nots too, though not through litigation. That's your thing. I don't really care where we live. I'll go wherever you want as long as it's not too far away. I can be happy wherever you're happy."

"Then let's go to Charleston," Sam said, with a conviction she hadn't known was in her. Chris looked at her and smiled. "Done," he said.

CHAPTER TWELVE

There are two federal judicial districts in West Virginia. Sam took a job as an Assistant United States Attorney for the Southern District, headquartered in Charleston. Her job would be to prosecute violations of federal laws occurring in the counties for which the Charleston office had jurisdiction. Boone County, where she grew up, was one of them.

Almost every judicial district in the country has a steady flow of drug cases. It was no surprise when Pete Gage, the United States Attorney, welcomed Sam by telling her, "The Assistants here cut their teeth on drug cases. There will also be some gun cases—you know, young men buying guns under false pretenses like lying about their age, prior convictions, that sort of thing. Maybe a fraud case now and then; consumer fraud and bank fraud both come up. And probably some public corruption cases because the people who run the government in this state can't seem to turn away when there's an easy buck to be made."

"That works for me," Sam said. "How about environmental cases, or cases against coal companies for safety violations?"

"They don't come along too often, but when they do, they're usually big. The coal industry largely runs this state. It has a big say in who gets elected and ready access once they are elected. It isn't tenable, politically, to hassle the coal companies over minor stuff. Most of that gets handled in Washington anyway, by Labor Department lawyers and administrative law judges. But when there's significant graft or a mine explosion or environmental disaster, we jump in. Remember the mine explosion near Farmington that killed seventy-eight miners and led to the first serious federal mine safety law? Remember when the dam broke at Buffalo Creek and wiped out the downstream communities? That stuff is our meat."

"Please sign me up if cases like that show up," Sam said. "I come from a coal mining family. I've always wanted to help miners and their families not get hurt or killed or screwed unnecessarily."

"I'll do that," Pete promised. "My people are also from coal country. I know where you're coming from."

Sam knew he meant it. Pete Gage was a hard charger. He had earned his spurs taking on the powerful who trampled over the less powerful, even when it was politically dangerous or downright stupid to do so. He had put away a handful of prominent business leaders and government officials in West Virginia, and he had made some enemies. But his enemies' list didn't include any of the Assistants in the Southern District. They thought he was a god.

One of the great joys (at least in hindsight) and benefits of working as a prosecutor is the trial experience. Federal prosecutors don't get the fire hose treatment that state prosecutors do, but they have more than enough work to consume their days. Fortunately, many of the cases, particularly the drug cases, are uncomplicated, and basically, all you have to do is put the arresting officer on the stand to testify. Even with those relative breathers, there is constant pressure, and you're screwed if you can't think on your feet. You quickly get over your fear of being in a courtroom.

Four months into the job, Sam was taking a break and checking messages with a happy heart after convicting a bad guy. He was real scum, and it had taken the jury less an hour to find him guilty of selling crystal meth to high school kids. Sadly, one of the kids had gotten totally wired and killed himself by driving into a concrete abutment at high speed. That wasn't relevant to the crime Sam was prosecuting, but everyone knew about it, and everyone was pissed. This creep would be off the streets for a long time. She felt great.

Then one of the messages brought her up short. It was from Jessie. Big Joe was dying.

CHAPTER THIRTEEN

Jessie had booked a flight to Charleston. She asked if Sam could pick her up and drive her home. Sam cleared it with Pete, who said he'd cover for her. Then she called Chris to let him know and headed to the airport.

There is unbearable sadness when a long illness is nearing its end. The signs of suffering are everywhere. They show themselves in the body, where folds of loose skin recount how eating has progressed from joy to duty to unwanted agony, where a wrenching welter of bruises screams that there have been too many needles and not enough blood flow, where the mouth that has smiled a million times is an angry grimace, where the eyes look down or away or simply close in search of respite from the long and losing struggle. They show themselves in the spirit. The resignation and defeat are unmistakable. Sam looked at Big Joe, and she hated George Rafferty.

The room was quiet, as death rooms always are. The man in the bed, once a fun-loving second father to Sam, lay still. He had come back home from Boone Memorial Hospital in Madison two days ago. He had told the doctor he was done with medicines and treatments. He knew he had lost the battle. He just wanted to go back home. He wanted to die in the place he loved. He wanted to die with the people he loved, his two Jessies.

From a corner of the room, Sam watched this man she knew so well but now could barely recognize. Once so vibrant, so full of piss and vinegar as her daddy used to say, he lay motionless, and colorless almost to the point of translucence. Sam watched the hospice nurse, quiet in her own corner of the room, step forward to wipe down his face and smooth the sheets. She watched Jessie's momma, seated in the chair by the bed, dry-eyed and seemingly bewildered, as if she were trying to understand what was happening, trying to accept that her life would never be the same. Her hand was on the bed next to his shoulder, not quite touching it but providing a steady presence he knew was there, would always be there. Sam could only wonder at her thoughts, her memories, her clarity, and her confusion.

Is this what is meant to be? You could never have imagined it so long ago. You meet a guy. He seems nice and laughs a lot. He works hard and plays hard. You go out a few times and realize he's better than nice. He's lovely. Then suddenly, you're married and raising a family. Disaster strikes, but you deal with it; together you have the strength to deal with it. You have the sorrows and the joys and the challenges of every life. A young son gets sick and dies. A daughter grows up and makes you proud. You cry together, you laugh together, you can deal with anything as long as you're together. And then one day, this. Is it what always happens? Is it what has to happen? Is this God's will?

Sam watched Jessie, her best friend, and her heart ached. Jessie sat on the side of the bed, where she and her father and mother formed a close triangle. She wept quietly as she held her father's once-giant hand. It was now thin and crooked and weak, so very weak. She looked at it in wonder, finding it incomprehensible that this small and withered hand once shoveled coal, hoisted beers, fired up a chain saw, carried a daughter, and fished and threw a baseball and skipped stones on the river with her. Jessie loved her mother, but she was her daddy's girl.

As if by their special osmosis, Sam felt Jessie's feelings as she sat there, at one with her dad but moving away. She felt her love and gratitude. Big Joe hadn't been perfect, but he had done his best, and it had been pretty damn good. Jess needed him to know that clearly and fully, and she willed the oneness of their joined hands to be a vehicle for her feelings to flow into him, to appear on a screen that he could see so he would know, unmistakably, how much she loved him. She wanted him to live, but she willed him to die so he would find peace.

Sam watched for a very long time. The picture didn't change. The people didn't move. Then Big Joe closed his eyes for the last time.

A few hours later, a lifetime later, after all the necessary little things that must be done when a loved one dies, after bracing against the tides of grief and sadness that roll in like an angry ocean, after the many unwanted calls and visits from well-wishers, after a quiet dinner of so much to say and nothing to say, Jessie's momma hugged her daughter and went to bed.

Then Jessie and Sam puttered around in deafening silence, not knowing what to say, knowing nothing needed to be said. This was the hardest part. "Jess," Sam started, but no more words came. There were only tears. Then they were in each other's arms, crying uncontrollably and holding each other desperately.

That was the second time. It was frantic and passionate and impossibly precious. It was like the strong, cold wind of the mistral roaring through the south of France on its violent path to the Mediterranean, clearing and cleansing the land as it went. It came out of their deep, deep need to share everything with each other, to be everything to each other. And it got them through that awful night of Big Joe's death.

CHAPTER FOURTEEN

Jessie went back to Cravath when her clerkship with Judge Belson ended. The money, prestige, and high-profile clients were attractive, and she jumped into the work eagerly. She didn't mind the grueling hours that are the life of junior associates at large law firms, but she soon began to feel like a small cog in a giant machine. She spent her days doing document review and found it stultifying. It would be years before she saw the inside of a courtroom. Being a partner at Cravath was a big deal, but she wasn't sure it was worth the price. A simpler life in a less frenetic city was alluring. So was the greater responsibility she would get at a smaller firm.

After stewing and fretting for weeks, Jess raised her concerns with Jimmy. He was sympathetic and supportive but saw this as her call. He was a rising star at Barclays. He liked New York, but he loved Jessie. If they were to move, it would be to Washington, where Jess had lived and been happy, and Jimmy knew he could do his job in Washington. There would be more travel, but that wasn't a problem. He would do whatever Jessie wanted.

Jimmy grabbed a meal when he could with Patrick O'Leary and Ray Delfino, two of his Wharton classmates who had remained good friends. They met for an early breakfast at Windows on the World on September 11, 2001. They had a great time catching up and telling lies, but it ended all too quickly. Jimmy left a little before 8:00 to make an important meeting at Barclays.

"Next time, we're doing this up *my* way," he said as he was leaving. "You guys don't get the easy commute every time."

"We're going to have another coffee, and we'll still be at work before you," Ray laughed.

As analysts at Cantor Fitzgerald, a leading financial services firm, Patrick and Ray only had a short elevator ride down to their offices on the 102nd floor. They had another cup of coffee and were at work by 8:25. Twenty-one minutes later, their building, the World Trade Center's North Tower, was struck by American Airlines Flight 11. They were among the 658 employees of Cantor Fitzgerald who died that morning.

Jimmy was devastated. He felt the grief, shock, outrage, and profound sadness that all Americans and particularly New Yorkers felt, but the loss of Ray and Patrick made it personal. The North Tower collapsed 102 minutes after it was struck. *What did they do in those 102 minutes?* Jimmy wondered. *The impact was between the 93rd and 99th floors, so any hope of escape down through the building was gone. Patrick and Ray were smart guys—they had to know the building would collapse, particularly after another plane struck the South Tower and it was clear this was no freak accident.*

Was the electricity out on their floor? It must have been. Had the fire on the floors below, where the impact had occurred, reached their floor? Were they running from the flames? Or were they simply waiting to die, knowing there was no way out? They had surely called or texted or emailed their loved ones or tried to anyway. Did they think about jumping to avoid the agony of the countdown? Did they jump? How terrified they must have been—did they pray? They weren't religious guys, but they must have prayed. What would I have done in those long, fleeting, last minutes of life? That could have been me. But for God's grace, that was me.

The terrorist attack got Jess and Jimmy off the dime. They decided to move to Washington, not out of fear of living in New York, because Washington is a terrorist target in its own right. But they were on the edge of making the decision anyway, and the sadness and the aftermath and the memories and all that came with 9/11 were a tipping point. It would be good to make a fresh start.

In the spring of 2002, they bought a brownstone on Q Street, near DuPont Circle. It was a four-story affair, counting the basement. The house had twelve-foot ceilings, reflective of the style when it was built. The top floor featured a large and wonderful light-filled room at the front. Half a block to the east was the venerable Trio, where they could go for good pizza; the secret recipe, it was said, was the grease. Two blocks to the west, on Connecticut Avenue, was Kramerbooks, where they could grab coffee and a bagel and get their book-browsing fix. They had everything they needed.

Jessie took a job with Watson Worthy, a litigation boutique of forty-seven lawyers that was the hot new firm in Washington. She thought it would be perfect.

CHAPTER FIFTEEN

Watson Worthy was formed in 2000 when Nick "Pudge" Watson and Jason Worthy left megafirm Skadden Arps and took a small army with them. Good friends who enjoyed practicing together, Pudge and Jason were effectively driven out when a conflict of interest developed between Jason's largest client and an even larger firm client. Conflicts are a common problem as firms grow, and the almost inevitable outcome is that the firm will keep the bigger client and jettison the smaller one. This case was no exception. Jason had to give up his client or leave the firm.

It wasn't an overly difficult choice. Jason didn't want to give up his client, an up-and-coming private equity firm called Sand Ridge Partners, but other factors were also at work. The unquestionable upsides of practicing at a giant firm were accompanied by unquestionable downsides, and Jason and Pudge had been talking for months, with increasing excitement, about going off to do their own thing. They were hard chargers in their early forties, and they were good guys. When they decided to pull the trigger, they had their pick among the young partners and associates who wanted to join their new venture.

Jessie interviewed with Watson Worthy and was instantly won over. She saw a firm of big-time lawyers with big-time experience who had escaped the bonds and burdens of what the trade refers to as Big Law. The energy in the firm was palpable. The associates were working on important cases, the kind Jessie wanted to do, and they were handling depositions and arguing minor motions in court as early as their third year. She spent an hour with Pudge and Jason, who delighted in telling her about a small antitrust case they had just tried to a successful verdict. They were the senior partners at the firm, but they seemed way too young and cool to be senior partners—hell, there wasn't a gray hair between them. Pudge, a very fit and handsome guy whose nickname was a hangover from an overweight childhood, came across as open and easygoing. Jason was more serious, slightly guarded even, but he too was engaging and impressive. They made her an offer on the spot, and she accepted.

Chris and Sam went to Washington for a long weekend in the fall of 2002. It had been almost two years since Sam had seen Jessie. There was a lot to celebrate and talk about—the move to Washington, the new house, Jessie's job—and it was way, way past time for a catch-up. As she and Jess had talked about getting together, Sam knew she and Chris would have to do the heavy lifting if it was going to happen. Among other things, that meant going to Washington. There was undeniably more to do there, and besides, the small two-bedroom apartment in Charleston would have been uncomfortably crowded with four. Sam also preferred to ooh and ahh over Jessie's brownstone rather than put her own humble apartment on display, though it shamed her to think of being competitive with her best friend.

Sam and Chris talked about that as they drove up I-81. "Why do you give a shit?" he asked. "Our apartment works for us, and we're happy there. They made different choices that happen to pay more. So what?"

"I know, and you're absolutely right. I know Jessie respects our choices as much as her own and would never knowingly make comparisons between us. She's too good a friend for that. But we've always been even, ever since we were kids. I don't want to trot out the disparity of our homes because I don't want us to be uneven. Can you understand that?"

"No, not really. They're doing what they want, and we're doing what we want. It doesn't mean they're smarter or stronger or faster. We just chose a different course, and choices have consequences. That doesn't make one better than the other. She's your friend. She'll understand and respect that."

"Yes, she will," Sam said. "But you can respect someone's choice and still wish their circumstances were better. I don't want Jessie feeling she needs to give me strokes so we can continue to be even."

After a long moment, Chris took Sam's hand and said, "Jess is great, but you're something special. You don't take shit, and you don't take a back seat to anybody. You're living the life you want to live. I'm proud of you for that."

Sturdy old shoe that he was, Chris got right to the central point and never left it. He always had Sam's back, and she loved him for it.

The weekend together was a poem. Jessie's home was beautiful. It was a work in progress, but extremely comfortable. And so were they, all four of them. That was a particular relief to Sam because Chris and Jimmy didn't know each other well, and if they didn't hit it off, it would put pressure on her friendship with Jessie. She needn't have worried. In less than an hour, Chris and Jimmy discovered a shared fondness for Whistle Pig, neat if you please, and from that point forward, everything took care of itself.

The four friends relaxed, talked, ate, and drank all weekend. They took a long walk on Saturday, enjoying the fresh autumn air and loving the sights and sounds and smells of the beautiful city of Washington. They passed the pickup games of chess that people from all walks of life play nonstop at DuPont Circle, headed northwest on Mass Avenue to sample Embassy Row, then cut down to P Street, where they crossed over Rock Creek Park and made the delightful stroll through Georgetown. The leaves were falling, Jimmy and Chris were becoming fast friends, and Jessie and Sam were just so damn happy to be together again.

When they got back to the house, Jimmy and Chris broke out the Whistle Pig to ease their exhaustion from the trek. Jessie was an aspiring mixologist and dazzled Sam with a few concoctions that Sam found very tasty. And they talked, Jessie and Sam, and Chris and Jimmy, and the four of them together, until they knew everything there was to know about each other and had solved at least half of the world's problems.

Sam had been a prosecutor for a couple of years and had tried almost twenty cases. Jessie was amazed and impressed, as she had yet to take her first deposition. Sam told her not to be, that these were pretty much run-of-the-mill cases, and what Jessie was working on was far more complicated. "But you've been in court," Jess said. "Talking to judges. And juries. And making legal arguments. And putting some bad people in jail." Yes, Sam had to admit, she had been.

In truth, she loved being a prosecutor. The days were long, often frantic, and usually exhausting, but most of them brought contentment and pride.

Jessie was several months into her job at Watson Worthy. She was working on four matters, second-chairing a small contracts dispute and playing more junior roles on the other, larger matters. She itched to get into court, but she knew that would come. In the meantime, she felt she was getting good experience, her work was more interesting and varied than it had been in New York, and she really liked the people she was working with. She knew she had made the right choice.

Chris had landed perfectly. As the junior lawyer at a firm of six kindred spirits in Charleston, he did corporate work for small businesses. His clients had ideas they believed in, and they usually had the energy to see them through. They were generally unsophisticated about business, and Chris enjoyed being their business adviser as well as their lawyer. Cash is always an issue for small companies, and his clients were unable to pay his fees from time to time, but Chris always gave them slack as long as they were honest and did what they could. He genuinely liked his clients; he liked being part of their business families and sharing in their successes.

Chris had also joined the US Army Reserve. His family had a long history of military service. He was proud of that and wanted to uphold the tradition. He didn't enlist in the regular army because he wasn't looking for a military career, and he also had a job and a wife he didn't want to leave. The army reserve gave him the opportunity to have it both ways. He could serve his country without giving up his job, his wife, or his life in Charleston. He only had to report for duty one weekend a month and do two weeks of active training a year. That wasn't much of a sacrifice. Besides, he enjoyed it, and the extra paycheck was a godsend. He was proud to serve, and Sam was proud of him for wanting to.

Jimmy was all over the place—New York a couple of days a week, the financial capitals of Europe several times a year, and China, Japan, South Korea, and Singapore less often but with increasing frequency. Barclays was running him ragged, and he was meeting every challenge. In a quiet moment with Jessie, Sam shared a worry that his travel schedule might impact their relationship. "He loves the energy and the importance," Jessie said. "It certainly wouldn't help if I were to try to take that from him. And I wouldn't want to.

We cherish our time together, but our independence is also important, to both of us. We're good." Sam felt reassured but wondered if there was a message between the lines.

Chris lived in a world of moderation and understatement. His exuberance on the drive back to Charleston was uncharacteristic. He usually entered friendships slowly and carefully, but with Jimmy and Jess, he jumped right in. Sam smiled at his enthusiasm and hoped his judgment was justified.

CHAPTER SIXTEEN

Terry Gomez was a gold mine of information. Deputy Angelo Jones met her for coffee at an out-of-the-way place where the bagels were fresh, and the tables were far apart. She had been loyal to Jason in their nine years together, and she respected him as a lawyer. She was quick to say he had treated her well and always made sure she was more than fairly compensated. She just didn't like his values.

"I feel uncomfortable talking about him," she said at the outset and reiterated two or three times. "He was my boss. I've always felt you shouldn't talk about your boss, and I never have, except for venting to my husband now and then. I guess it doesn't matter now that he's dead, particularly if what I know helps you find out who killed him."

"Thank you, Terry," replied Angelo. "I'll keep this between us as much as I can. Tell me about your husband."

"Eddie is a good man. We were both born in El Salvador and came to America when we were small children. We went to school here, and we fell in love—maybe because we had so much in common in terms of our backgrounds and our hopes and fears. We married young and have three daughters. Eddie is an electrician, and he works hard. He's a good husband, and he loves his children."

"How did you come to work for Jason Worthy?"

"I trained to be a legal secretary. My first job was at one of the big firms. I worked for four associates. It wasn't very interesting. The associates are under so much pressure. My friend Estella worked for Mr. Worthy. She was older, and when she decided to retire, she asked if I wanted to interview for her job. I said sure, and she set it up. Jason and I hit it off, and I was hired."

"Jason?"

"Sure. Watson Worthy isn't a formal place, and when you work with someone ten hours a day, fairly intensely, you quickly get to first names."

"What are your impressions of Watson Worthy?"

"It's a great place to work," Terry said. "The lawyers are smart, and they work hard. Most of the staff are committed and fun to be around. There's a willingness to cooperate with each other most of the time. It isn't that way everywhere. A lot of that's because of Pudge. He must spend an hour a day walking around and talking to people. He sets the tone."

"And Jason?"

"He was good too, but he wasn't as friendly as Pudge. He was more about staying in his office and setting an example by hard work. Don't get me wrong, he wasn't unkind. He was just more private, almost to the point of being secretive, and tended to form one-on-one relationships."

"Was he married?"

"He was, but he and Jennifer got divorced three or four years after I got here. It's too bad. I really liked her."

"Did they have children?"

"No. I think it was a choice, but maybe they couldn't. I never asked."

"Why were they divorced?"

"They were both screwing around. They were too much like each other. They'd get attracted to the next beautiful person who came along, and they had to learn more, experience more. It never lasted long. It's funny, they both thought they were being discreet, but everyone knew. Everyone always knows. They were both highly successful. She was an ophthalmologist. But they were both cheaters. They had everything, both of them—looks, smarts, success. I guess if things come too easily to you, if you don't have to fight for them, you never really value what you have. That's the way it seemed with them."

"If Jason didn't value his marriage, what did he value"

"He valued himself. He valued his reputation, and he worked hard to build and protect it. He valued his partners, and he valued this law firm."

"Did he ever cheat as far as the law firm was concerned?"

"No, he wouldn't do that," Terry said thoughtfully. "I guess you could have a philosophical discussion about whether dating women at the firm was cheating, and some would say it was. Jason did have relationships, or maybe flings is a more accurate word, with at least one partner, two associates, and one staff member that I knew of, but they were all consensual. I thought it was a bad idea, but I wouldn't call it cheating."

"Did he ever hit on you?"

"No, never."

"How were his client relationships? Did he ever take advantage of those?"

"He was very loyal to his clients. He gave them good advice, worked hard for them, and delivered results. They loved him. He had a heavy hand billing his time now and then, particularly if he thought the outcome justified it, but many lawyers do that, and based on my experience, Jason was within the bounds of normalcy. There were certainly never any client complaints. As I say, they loved him."

"I'm struggling with something here, Terry. You've suggested that Jason had issues with his values, but you're painting a picture of a guy who was a pretty straight shooter, at least as far as his partners and clients were concerned."

"I think that's true of Jason Worthy. He was all in for the firm and its clients. Now let's talk about John Wiggins."

"Who is John Wiggins?"

"Jason was a slumlord, though no one here knew it. I don't think even Pudge knew it. He formed a company called Rose Hill, which he used to acquire and manage four apartment buildings in depressed areas in inner cities. And he created an alter ego, John Wiggins, to run Rose Hill."

Angelo was fascinated. His prior research into Jason Worthy had produced an article in a small local newspaper about a case that had been settled three years earlier, involving a tenant group at a Baltimore complex called The Yellow Rose. The facts were vague, but the suit against the building owner, Rose Hill, detailed numerous instances of plumbing defects, heating defects, and rat infestation that persisted despite numerous complaints. The plaintiffs sought damages under a theory of constructive eviction. Rose Hill was represented by Jason Worthy. The article had caught Angelo's attention because he couldn't envision a lawyer of Worthy's quality and reputation representing a slumlord; it hadn't occurred to him that the lawyer was actually representing himself.

"Tell me more," Angelo urged Terry.

"It's pretty simple, really. The four buildings were all out of town so they wouldn't attract attention in D.C. They were in bad shape, and he bought them cheap. Jason, or I should say John, made promises to fix them up, but he never did. Each complex was named after a rose, and John rented the units fairly inexpensively and quite successfully by assuring prospective tenants that 'everything would come up roses' if they lived there. John maximized Jason's income by ignoring the tenant complaints. Although Jason wasn't troubled by being a slumlord, he knew the firm could be badly hurt if word got out. Hence Rose Hill and John Wiggins. Jason set up a scheme to keep his disgusting operation in the shadows. He didn't want his fingerprints on it."

"If he was worried about it, why did he do it in the first place? He was a name partner at a quality law firm and had to make pretty good money."

"He did make good money, I'm sure, but he had some fairly heavy debt from redoing his weekend place, Justice Hill, a few years ago. He needed more money to pay that off. This was easy pickings. Knowing Jason, I suspect he also did it to see if he could get away with it. He was a guy who thrived on excitement."

"And how do you know all this if he was keeping it a secret?"

"Jason kept the Rose Hill stuff on a private computer that wasn't tied into the firm's network. He also kept the evaluations he wrote on the associates and staff on that computer. Like many lawyers, he wasn't good at technology and didn't like it, so he trusted too much and wasn't as careful as he should have been about his passwords. We were talking once about how hard it is to remember your passwords, and he told me his approach was to use street names near Justice Hill. That made it pretty easy to figure out his password—there aren't many streets in that area. I logged on to his computer one day when he was in court because I wanted to see what he had written about me. I shouldn't have, and I'm not proud of it, but I was curious. That's when I stumbled onto the Rose Hill and John Wiggins thing."

"Wow. Did you ever tell him?"

"No. How could I admit I had snuck onto his private computer? I've never told anybody, until now. But I found it harder to work for him after that. It was a couple of years ago. Finding out people's secrets doesn't tend to make you think better of them. Jason was an OK guy, but John Wiggins wasn't. And John was Jason."

Angelo looked at his watch and said, "This has been very helpful, Terry. I know you have to get back to work, and maybe we can have another session in a few more days. But I have just a couple of additional questions before you go, if you have the time."

"Sure," said Terry, "if we can make it quick."

"You mentioned that Jason had some kind of romantic or sexual relationship with at least four women at the firm, a partner, two associates, and a staff member. Were all of these just 'flings,' to use your word? Are these women still at the firm?"

"The staff member was definitely a fling, and she's no longer here. There was a rumor at the time that Jason might have encouraged her departure with a small payment, but I can't say whether that's true. The partner and one of the associates were also flings, you know, people getting together in the heat of battle, or out of curiosity, or boredom, or whatever. They're both still at the firm."

"And the other associate?"

"That one was real. She was an impressive young woman, smart, classy, and substantive. She got to Jason. They'd go away for long weekends and all that. They were together about three years. Then it ended, I don't know why. She left the firm after that. Too bad—everyone said she was our best associate."

"What was her name?"

"Kate. Kate Strange."

CHAPTER SEVENTEEN

Kate Strange grew up in Ketchum, Idaho, the only child of Tim and Debbie Strange. Tim had a Chevy dealership that made good money for a few years. He was an avid outdoorsman and a serious drunk. That proved a bad combination. One night, when Kate was seven, he came home late from a marathon session at Billy's Bar & Grill, decided it was the perfect time to clean his Ruger M77 Hawkeye hunting rifle, and shot himself. Some thought it was a suicide because the dealership was deep in debt, but the coroner ruled it was an accident because Tim was so drunk that if he had been trying to shoot himself, he would have missed.

That left Debbie, a sales representative at the nearby Sun Valley Lodge, to raise Kate. She did a good job of it. Kate was hardworking in addition to being naturally smart and athletic. She breezed through the local high school with high honors and five varsity letters, and then went away to college at Oregon State. Corvallis was further from Ketchum than she would have liked, but Kate wanted to study forestry, and Oregon State had one of the best programs in the country.

Kate hadn't known her father long, but she inherited his love of the outdoors. Hiking in the Sawtooth National Forest, right in her own backyard, was one of her favorite activities. She loved the majesty, the solitude, the wildlife, and the peace. In her junior year of high school, she and a friend spent spring break camping in the Olympic National Forest. She was utterly captivated by the old-growth trees in that spectacular rain forest. She wanted to preserve these incomparable places, this humbling and enriching environment. She believed studying forestry was an important step toward achieving that goal.

After graduating from Oregon State, Kate applied to the Forest Service to become a forest ranger. She spent the next five years living that solitary but satisfying life. She did tours on the Deschutes National Forest in Oregon, the Gifford Pinchot in Washington, and the Idaho Panhandle National Forest back home. She preserved trees, cleared trails, and protected wildlife. She became a smoke jumper and hurled herself out of airplanes fourteen times to fight forest fires. She hiked and thought and dreamed, read books and wrote poetry, and loved every minute of the experience. Her constant companion was Pete, a ninety-pound, sedge-colored hound she had found wandering around lost and confused after a fire had claimed his owners' cabin.

It was an idyllic life, but Kate had increasing misgivings about whether her tree-focused approach was the most effective way to save forests. It was great fun, but there was a larger purpose that was better achieved by passing laws to protect wildlife and set aside national forests, national parks, and wilderness areas, so that these fragile and limited resources would less easily fall victim to poachers, trophy hunters, and thoughtless tourists. Reluctantly, she put her forestry career behind her in order to get a law degree.

Kate chose to study law at UCLA. It was a fine school with a top environmental law program, but Kate's reason for going there was more specific. She wanted to study under Professor Noah Kline, a living legend in the world of environmental law. She had heard Professor Kline speak when she was at Oregon State and was deeply moved by his commitment to environmental protection and his passion for environmental justice. His topic that day was the Endangered Species Act, and he had made his points with eloquence in presenting the plight of his favorite bird, the brown pelican. She remembered it clearly, the words, the devotion, the soul.

Kate did well at UCLA. In her second and third years, she worked as Noah Kline's research assistant. It was an arrangement of mutual admiration and became a true friendship. She had thought she'd go back to the Pacific Northwest to practice, but Noah advised against it. "If you really want to make a difference," he said, "you have to go to Washington. It's where the laws are made. It's where you can have the broadest influence."

"I hear you," Kate answered. "But I don't know anything about D.C. or the law firms there. For that matter, should I be looking at law firms? Or should I try to get an environmental job on the Hill?"

Noah thought for a moment as he looked out his window. It was spring, and the birds were nesting. "I do have some thoughts," he finally said. "You should not go to the Hill, not at this point. You'd be too junior to get anything done. You should get some practical legal experience first. Go to the Hill later on, when you'll be better positioned to accomplish real change.

"As it happens," he went on, "a friend of mine, Paul Jenkins, recently left the Senate to join a small firm that enjoys a good reputation in the area of litigation. It's called Watson Worthy. I don't know anyone there, but the firm apparently wants to start a legislative practice and has brought Paul on board to build it. He seems to think quite highly of the partners there."

Noah paused to assess Kate's reaction. She looked interested. "Unless you think it's a bad idea, I'll give Paul a call and put in a good word for you. We've worked together on environmental legislation, and we know each other well. I believe he would take my recommendation seriously."

Kate joined Watson Worthy as an associate in 2011. Jessie had left years earlier.

CHAPTER EIGHTEEN

In her first five years at Watson Worthy, Jessie worked extensively for Sand Ridge Partners. Jason's pride and joy, Sand Ridge was, year in and year out, one of the firm's top three clients. It consistently produced annual fees in the ten-million-dollar range, and Jason wanted to take it to the next level. When Jessie arrived, he saw his opening.

Karen Woodbine, Sand Ridge's general counsel, had been friends with Jason since their law school days at Harvard. She had gone on to practice corporate law at Latham & Watkins. After handling several matters for Sand Ridge, including the acquisition of its largest portfolio company, she was lured away from a promising future at a great law firm to become the chief legal officer at Sand Ridge. The offer included a substantial equity position. It was too good to resist.

When she thought it was politically feasible, Karen transferred a substantial portion of the Sand Ridge legal work to Jason. He rewarded her with sound judgment, impressive responsiveness, innovative thinking, and hard work. The company prospered with his help, and Karen's stature climbed. He rewarded her further by significantly lowering his billing rate when he and Pudge left Skadden and started Watson Worthy. She reciprocated by giving him even more business. It was a symbiotic relationship, but it caused Jason increasing concern; the work was now more than he could manage comfortably, and it didn't leave him time to develop business from other sources. His mentor at Skadden had once told him that "the job of a partner is to shove as much work down as you can, so you have time to go out and get more." He had never forgotten that.

Jessie had impressed Jason mightily during their interview and in her first weeks at the firm. He saw in her a rare combination of talent, presence, and work ethic. He believed he could bring her into the Sand Ridge relationship with the confidence that she would perform well and bond with Karen. Jessie would be an easy sell not only because of her inherent qualities, but also because Karen was a champion for women in the legal profession and supported them in every way possible. She would love Jessie.

Once Jason had settled on this plan, he called Karen and told her he had a fine young associate who would be working with him on Sand Ridge matters. Her name was Jessie Macaulay, and he wanted to bring her over to meet Karen. They arranged a late afternoon session at Sand Ridge headquarters the following week. It went perfectly, and after less than an hour in Karen's office, the three of them decided to continue the conversation over drinks and dinner at a nearby restaurant. Jason had been optimistic that Karen and Jessie would hit it off, but this was turning into a lovefest. Jason was so pleased that he splurged on the wine order with a spectacular 1985 Sassicaia.

Sand Ridge had expertise in the energy sector, and that was the focus of its investing. It held major ownership stakes in a small fracking company, a regional gas pipeline, a business that franchised independent gas stations and convenience stores, a helicopter company that cleared rights-of-way for power lines, and a water supply company. Jessie ended up working for all of them at one time or another. Jason started her off slowly with small matters on which he took the lead, and gradually, as her experience and the company's confidence in her grew, moved her into larger roles and more significant matters. He was always there, but more as a safety net than a hands-on mentor.

Jessie's relationship with Karen was strong from the outset, but she sealed the deal two years in while working for ClearaLine, the Sand Ridge company that used helicopters to keep power lines clear. ClearaLine was Karen's baby. She had handled its acquisition by Sand Ridge when she was still at Latham. Aerial trimming was a relatively new concept then, and it had not yet gained widespread acceptance, primarily because of safety concerns. Karen immediately understood that trimming trees by helicopter was a revolutionary idea with the potential for huge efficiencies, particularly in rural areas. But she saw the safety questions as serious. After immersing herself in the business, studying the accident history, and riding shotgun on some ClearaLine operations, she concluded the work was safe as long as there was a relentless commitment to having the best equipment and the best pilots. Her belief was a powerful factor in winning over a skeptical Sand Ridge board, and the deal went ahead. ClearaLine quickly became a shining success and earned handsome returns for Sand Ridge.

ClearaLine leased seven helicopters and used them to conduct operations in much of the Appalachian region, particularly West Virginia and western North Carolina. The trimming was done by overflying the power line and cutting the encroaching tree limbs on both sides. That was accomplished by ten rotating saw blades, two feet each in diameter, that hung vertically from the helicopter and were remotely controlled by the pilot to turn at very high speed. It was a noisy business, and tree branches flew everywhere as the devastating blades sliced through them. Not pretty, maybe, but decidedly effective and efficient. And not too big a problem, considering the noise and destruction, because the operations were generally in rural areas, largely mountainous, and there weren't many people around to complain.

The neotropical migratory songbirds that lived in the forests were another matter. The aerial trimming operations killed them by the thousands. This was especially true during nesting season, when the birds couldn't, or wouldn't, fly away. Even if they did, there was no getting the nests and their young occupants to safety.

The songbirds were fortunate to have a powerful ally in Jim Crane. A wire-haired guy who wore wire-rimmed glasses, Jim was executive director of Bless Our Birds, a nationwide avian protection society that went by the acronym BOB. Jim had a long history of environmental activism. After participating in the northern spotted owl wars under the Endangered Species Act, he devoted his life to the protection of birds and punctuated his commitment by forming BOB in the early 1990s. He worked tirelessly, and if he had ever had a sense of humor, it had long since disappeared under the brooding weight of his cause.

Still headquartered along the Willamette River in Portland, BOB now had three additional offices. Jim's friend and fellow birder, John James "Audie" Bill, ran the BOB office in Asheville. Audie was no friend of the timber industry. In defense of the nation's birds, he fought logging operations throughout the Appalachian region. He fought them in the courts and in Congress, in any and every way he could. He fought them fair and he fought them dirty, because in his mind, protecting the birds was a noble and critically important end that justified any means.

Audie watched the ascendance of aerial trimming with growing concern. Its purpose was to protect power lines, but he saw it as just another logging operation. He didn't give a damn why they did it, but he cared deeply about its effects on Appalachian songbirds. Aerial trimming was a problem that would have to be eliminated. Audie shared his concerns with Jim, who came east to get a firsthand look at the situation. They toured some aerial trimming operations together, and Jim was outraged by what he saw. He readily approved Audie's recommendation that the best way to stop this new and egregious form of bird slaughter was through the Migratory Bird Treaty Act.

The problem with this strategy was that the MBTA doesn't provide a private right of action, so any enforcement would have to be taken by the responsible federal agency, the Fish and Wildlife Service. That was a complication, but it wasn't insurmountable. Jim was close to Ed Kite, the deputy director of FWS. Confident that Ed would share his outrage, Jim arranged a meeting and stoked Ed's predictable anger by showing him graphic photographs of dead birds and bird parts that Jim and Audie had taken during their tour. Jim knew from Ed's reaction that he had him.

"It's obviously your call how this should be handled," Jim said. "But I would suggest a criminal enforcement case in federal court in Huntington, West Virginia. The judge there, the Honorable Arthur Plover, is an old friend from NRDC days and an avid birder."

"I know Art Plover," Ed replied. "He's a good choice for a case like this. Since you're making suggestions, and good ones at that, who would be the defendant?"

"The largest aerial trimming company in West Virginia, the one that killed the birds in those pictures. A company called ClearaLine."

CHAPTER NINETEEN

Karen was served with the complaint in *United States v. ClearaLine* and imme-diately summoned Jason and Jessie to her office. They were barely seated when Karen erupted. She was in no mood for pleasantries.

"Have you read this crap?" Karen demanded, waving the complaint in the air. "FWS has asked a federal court in West Virginia to impose criminal fines on ClearaLine because our trimming operations are killing birds. If they win, it will effectively shut us down in West Virginia and that's almost sixty percent of ClearaLine's business. And you know this is just the first step. They'll hit us in other states as well. This is a disaster. We can't let it happen. You can't let it happen!"

"Let's just calm down a bit, Karen," Jason said. "We need to step back and try to understand what we're dealing with. The complaint just came in, and we haven't had much time to analyze it."

"Step back?" Karen roared. "They're trying to put our biggest and most successful company out of business, and you want me to step back? I want you to step forward! You can start by telling me what the hell the Migratory Bird Treaty Act is."

Jason looked helplessly at Jessie. "It's a federal statute that's been around a long time," she said. "It's a criminal statute that gives FWS the power to arrest violators and seek criminal fines and even imprisonment. It was passed in 1918, when there was a significant trade in feathers from birds like snowy egrets, and people were shooting the birds to get their feathers. By its terms, it only applies to migratory birds, but FWS has interpreted it broadly and applies it to many birds that aren't migratory in any strict sense of the term. I think there are around a thousand bird species that are protected. Almost every kind of bird you can think of except pigeons and starlings."

"Why should that apply to us?" Karen wanted to know. "We're not trying to kill any birds, and we're certainly not shooting snowy egrets. All we're trying to do is provide American citizens with an uninterrupted power supply."

"I know," said Jessie. "The problem is that society and business have changed dramatically since the law was passed. Nowadays, when birds are killed by business and land-use practices that have nothing to do with hunting or intended killing, many courts have found violations. The MBTA was applied, for example, when thousands of birds were killed in that huge oil spill off Alaska when the tanker, the *Exxon Valdez*, ran aground."

"So, are we just screwed? Is that what you're telling me?"

"No. But I am telling you we're not likely to find a factual defense. There isn't any question that aerial trimming kills birds."

"But we're not killing birds on purpose. What can we do?"

"Let me look into that and get back to you," Jessie said.

Karen's secretary entered the room. "Sorry to interrupt," she said. "But I know you'd want to hear this right away. Judge Plover has scheduled a status conference for a week from today. He wants to fast-track this case."

"We do too. We have to get this resolved as quickly as possible," said Karen. She looked at Jason. "Can we be ready by next week?"

"We'll have to be," Jason said, "and anyway, this is just a status conference. But I'm in trial in Chicago next week, and the trial is expected to run a couple of months. Jessie will have to do this. Are you comfortable with that?"

Jessie swallowed hard, feeling something between elation and terror. She had done depositions by now, but this would be her first time in open court.

Karen glared at Jason, then looked at Jessie for a long moment. "Yes, I am," she said. Looking annoyed, she said to Jason, "I'm actually glad. She's smarter than you are."

The next week was a long one. Jessie tried to put her fears aside and come up with a defense strategy. Her initial instinct had been right: there was no factual defense. The only relevant fact questions were (a) whether birds covered by the law were being killed, and (b) whether they were being killed by ClearaLine's operations. The answer to both questions was indisputably yes. Jessie would need to come up with a legal defense.

The status conference was unremarkable. Jessie stipulated that ClearaLine's aerial trimming operations killed birds, and the government stipulated that those killings were incidental and not the result of intentional actions directed at the birds. That framed the legal issue for the pretrial motion Jessie would have to file, seeking dismissal of the case because it failed to state an offense. Judge Plover gave her two weeks to file her motion. He wanted it quickly, he said, because birds were being killed.

Jessie had her work cut out for her. The pertinent language of the MBTA makes it "unlawful, at any time, by any means or in any manner, to pursue, hunt, take, capture, kill . . . any migratory bird [or] any part, nest, or eggs of any such bird." A professor at Georgetown had once told Jessie that all you really learn in law school is how to read. That thought came back to her as Jessie read this language slowly, carefully, over and over and over. It was the key to the case. What did it mean?

On its face, the language seemed to be talking about intentional actions directed at migratory birds. ClearaLine certainly wasn't pursuing, hunting, or capturing birds. It was killing them, but not intentionally. The death of the birds was incidental to its otherwise lawful conduct. And what did "take" mean? In traditional wildlife law, taking was equivalent to killing or capturing. The straightforward reading of the language would seem to exonerate ClearaLine.

But Jessie had a nagging doubt because the plain language was seemingly broadened by that pesky phrase, "by any means or in any manner." What did that mean? Did it create enough ambiguity to cause a court to construe the pertinent language in light of the statutory purpose? The purpose of the MBTA was to protect birds. That would argue for a broad reading.

The courts that had previously considered the question had gone both ways. The Second and Tenth Circuits had adopted the expansive view, finding that the MBTA prohibits all activities that kill or injure birds, regardless of intent. The Eighth Circuit had more narrowly ruled that the MBTA only bans actions taken directly and intentionally against migratory birds. The Fourth Circuit, which included West Virginia, had not yet faced the issue. The decisions of the other circuits, while influential, would not control this case.

Jessie carefully crafted an argument based on the plain language of the MBTA. She bolstered it with a statutory intent argument: the MBTA was passed in 1918 to stop the killing of migratory birds so their feathers could be sold, and the statute must therefore be interpreted as prohibiting the intentional killing of birds. She also added a new wrinkle. The Endangered Species Act, enacted fifty-five years after the MBTA, broadened the definition of "take" to include activities that "harm" protected wildlife. The FWS regulations applying that language defined "harm" to include deaths incidentally caused by otherwise lawful land-use activities. The contrasting treatment of "take" in the ESA and MBTA and their respective implementing regulations, Jessie's argument went, demonstrated that Congress intended different meanings of "take" in the two statutes. One included incidental deaths, while the other was limited to intentional acts against the birds.

At the oral argument on Jessie's motion, Judge Plover ruled against ClearaLine from the bench. He gave no supporting analysis other than that the MBTA was meant to protect birds, and he was going to by God protect them. His performance illustrated the principle that strong legal arguments are all well and good, but what really matters is who you can get to hear your case. In Judge Plover, Jim Crane and Ed Kite had chosen well.

The expedited appeal to the Fourth Circuit was a different matter. The three judges on the panel were well-prepared and ideologically balanced. They asked probing questions. This was like moot court all over again. Jessie was in her element and on her game.

Jason, back from his trial, sat with Karen in the courtroom. He was filled with pride. "She's pretty damn good, isn't she?" he whispered. Karen wasted no time answering. "She really is smarter than you are."

The Fourth Circuit issued its ruling a month later, reversing Judge Plover and finding in favor of ClearaLine. The Supreme Court denied the government's petition for certiorari. The case was over.

Karen was ecstatic. She took Jessie out to dinner, just the two of them. They celebrated in style. "What does this mean?" Karen wanted to know. "Are we in the clear, or can FWS and those creeps from BOB take another run at us?"

"It means you're good in the Fourth Circuit, which includes ClearaLine's operations in West Virginia and North Carolina. Unless and until the Supreme Court takes up the MBTA question, which it may at some point because of the split in the circuits, this decision is binding law in the Fourth Circuit. The feds and the creeps could go after ClearaLine somewhere else, but they can't do it here, not under the MBTA."

"The vast majority of our operations are in Fourth Circuit states. We don't have enough to matter elsewhere. Jessie, I just can't tell you what this means to me. I can't thank you enough."

Blushing, Jessie said, "Thanks for giving me the opportunity. It was great fun, and I'm so glad we won. I really enjoy working with you."

They were both a little tipsy now. "I'm thrilled that Jason brought you into the Sand Ridge world. I shouldn't say this, but you're a better lawyer than he is. And he's a great lawyer. From now on, you're my go-to at Watson Worthy. I'll help you, and your career, in every way I can."

"Thank you, I don't know what to say," Jessie offered.

"There's just one thing," Karen added, quite serious now. "Don't ever cross me. If you do, your success in this case won't mean a thing. I'll bury you."

What an odd ending to a wonderful evening, Jessie thought. *I would never cross Karen. Where did that come from?*

CHAPTER TWENTY

On October 13, 2006, at 3:53 in the afternoon, the Rebel Yell Mine blew up. Friday the 13th. Unlucky. Unlucky as hell for the five miners killed in the explosion. Unlucky for their families. But lucky, actually, for seven other miners who had been working at or near continuous mining Section D twelve minutes earlier. With shift change approaching, they had grabbed a mantrip at 3:41 and were near the mine entrance when the explosion occurred. Even at that, even though they were almost two miles away, the concussive force rocked them, and they felt the searing heat. One of them said it was like being in a tornado.

The Rebel Yell was in Boone County, West Virginia, just outside the small hamlet of Londonderry. It was twenty-six miles, as the crow flies, from the Merriman No. 3 Mine, where Bill Picken and Big Joe Spaulding had worked. Rebel Yell and Merriman No. 3 were sister mines, both owned by Black Bear Mining Company. They were driving toward each other as part of a plan to meet and form one giant mine within the next two years. There was a lot of overlap between the Rebel Yell and Merriman No. 3 miners and their families. The news of the explosion hit the Owl Hollow community immediately and hard.

Rescue teams from Merriman No. 3 were quickly dispatched to join the Rebel Yell rescue teams in an effort to locate fourteen miners who were still underground. The mine was nine hundred feet deep, and the combination of smoke and heat prevented the rescue teams from making much headway for several hours. They knew from the seven miners who had gotten out, the lucky ones, that the explosion had occurred at or near Section D. The rescue teams headed for two neighboring sections where it appeared miners might still be trapped. They would do their grim work in those more accessible areas while the firefighters battled the blaze in Section D.

There are few scenes sadder than the surface of a mine when a disaster strikes and keeps hostages below. Most of the community is there, few with dry eyes. They wait. They already know if their loved ones have made it out. Those with family members still in the coughing, smoking, belching mine are in unspeakable agony. They pray, and they weep, and they bargain with God. Mostly, they wait. They say to the others whose men have come out that they are happy for them. They mean it, but they would trade places in a heartbeat. The others, the lucky ones, stay with them to hug and console. And wait.

George Rafferty appeared and moved among the huddled families. A man like George knows the importance of television coverage. So, he was there, the caring mine owner, comforting the stricken families. They didn't want him there. They wanted each other, but they didn't want George. They knew he would speak to the cameras, say nothing was more important to him than the miners and their families, say what a terrible tragedy it was but these things happen in dangerous work like coal mining, even when the most stringent safety precautions are taken. He would talk about how the families needed to be strong for each other, how they would all get through this. It would all be bullshit. The miners knew that. They silently pulled back, pulled away, as he neared them in the crowd. They didn't want to see this man or have contact with him. Not in this moment of darkness and despair.

Suddenly, a cheer erupted and spread through the crowd. It was 10:18 p.m., more than six hours since the explosion. Two rescue teams, one from Merriman No. 3 and one from Rebel Yell, were coming out of the mine. They had seven of the missing miners. A couple were on stretchers; most were walking with help. All had suffered smoke inhalation and a terrible ordeal. But they would live. They were safe. These seven had escaped with a small ransom. There was elation in seven families. But seven other families descended to a deeper level of grief and anxiety. Their loved ones were still underground. They prayed even harder.

Just after midnight, with the odds growing long, a rescue team brought out two more miners. They had been separated from the others, working some distance away. The explosion had knocked them to the ground, but they were clear of the flames. They managed to put on their self-rescuers and, together, started the long walk out. Half a mile from the surface, they encountered a roof fall that blocked the entry. They found a fresh air pocket and holed up there to wait for help, pray for help. Two hours later, miraculously, they heard hollering from a search team. They were exhausted and fading into semiconsciousness, but the will to live is strong, and they managed to make themselves heard. They would need a few days in the hospital, but they would be fine.

The fire was extinguished very early in the morning, halfway through what would have been the graveyard shift on any other night. The families were still there. No one had gone home. Five families still prayed for news, beside themselves with grief, hoping for deliverance from this bleakest and blackest hour. The others were with them in solidarity.

Dawn was beginning to break when the exhausted firefighters emerged from the mine. The crowd mustered a small cheer and moved forward to offer heartfelt thanks for their efforts. These men were part of the community, they were friends, and they had done what they could.

Not far behind the firefighters was the final rescue team. The dejection in their body language told the story. Tim Small, the team leader, looked at the five families, now separated from the others, and sadly shook his head. John Sullivan, Mike Kapaczinski, Roy Chambers, Keith Middleton, and Terrible Tommy Waters were still below. Their bodies would be recovered later.

CHAPTER TWENTY-ONE

Scott O'Hanlon was antsy. It was now April 15, 2016, six days since Worthy's death and two days since he had last met with his team. He had heard nothing further. Emma Mancini had said she'd be doing the autopsy no later than today. Why hadn't he heard from her? The investigative work being done by the others would take longer, but he wanted to hear from Emma *now*. He needed to know the cause of death. He wanted to know more about Worthy's alcohol intake. He wanted to find out what he had been injected with. And had she found anything else? If so, what?

In a perfect world, Emma would present her findings at a team meeting because it was important for everyone to hear what she had to say. Her findings would be relevant to the tasks each team member had taken on. But this wasn't a perfect world, far from it, and Scott wanted to know *now*. Today was Friday; he would call a team meeting for Monday, and she could present her findings to everybody then. He would use the weekend to consider changes that should be made to the course of the investigation based on what he learned today.

Emma wasn't in her office. Scott knew her well enough to know she wouldn't have taken Friday afternoon off to play golf. There was only one place she could be. He went to the autopsy room. She was there, with Worthy's body on the table next to her. It was even more cut up than when they had found it.

"I'm just about done, Scott. Sorry I didn't get back to you sooner."

"That's OK. What was the cause of death?"

"He bled out when the femoral artery was cut. The murder weapon was the chain saw."

"That's what I assumed, but I wanted to hear it officially. And the X cuts on his head, mouth, and penis?"

"Those looked bad but were actually quite superficial. They were deep enough to leave pronounced scars, but they weren't life-threatening. Worthy would have been a walking message board. I wonder what the message was meant to be?"

"Were they made before or after the leg was cut off?"

"Before."

"Why would someone carve him up to send a message and then kill him before the message was delivered?"

"Beats the hell out of me, Scott. You're the detective."

"And my job is to find someone who kills with a chain saw. I haven't had this one before."

"We should talk about my other findings. I told you earlier there was a lot of alcohol in his system, and he also had a needle mark in his arm. I know more about both of those things now. They explain, to my satisfaction anyway, why there were no signs of a struggle. As you said, the absence of any apparent resistance is highly unusual when someone's being worked on with a box cutter and a chain saw."

Scott refocused his attention. "Good. What have you got?"

"The alcohol was whiskey. Scotch whiskey. He had more than half a bottle in his system. Along with a sausage, black olive, and green pepper pizza." Emma paused before going on. "Pizza goes with beer. Maybe even wine. But who the hell drinks whiskey with pizza?"

"Beats me. What more can you tell me about the whiskey?"

"It was single malt. Very peaty, like it was from Islay or around there. I'd say it was either Laphroaig or Lagavulin."

"That's impressive. What about the pizza? Was it from one of the chains? If so, we might be able to check delivery records."

"It was homemade. It didn't look very good. Not what you'd want for your last meal."

"Maybe that explains the single malt. He needed something strong enough to kill the taste of the pizza. Tell me about the needle mark."

"He was injected with propofol. It was a generous dose. Not enough to kill him, but certainly enough to put him in a deep sleep for a good forty-five minutes. And on top of the alcohol at that."

"What's propofol?"

"It's been around twenty or twenty-five years. It's a popular form of anesthesia because it puts the patient out in a matter of seconds, but then the patient revives easily and clears up quickly with no memory of what happened. It's a white liquid, and because of its memory-block characteristic, it's sometimes referred to as milk of amnesia."

"What are its primary uses?"

"Surgery, and also to help ICU patients sleep. Not just human surgery, by the way— veterinarians use it too. Obviously, the dosages are different depending on the use. For surgery, you want the patient to be out cold and then wake up. A sleep aid for ICU patients calls for a lighter dose maintained over time. Not to be personal, but if you've had a colonoscopy in the last ten or fifteen years, there's a fair chance they used propofol to put you to sleep."

"I have, and if that's what they used, it did the job. I was out for the count. Does it have a brand name, or is propofol the brand name?"

"No, propofol is the generic name. It's marketed as Diprivan."

"Who has access to it? Is it available on the street?"

"It's a prescription drug. I suppose anything's available on the street, but this isn't a recreational drug and there wouldn't be much of a market for it other than in medical facilities. Maybe that's not entirely right since it was implicated in Michael Jackson's death. But as I recall those accounts, his doctor was prescribing it for him. Generally, you'd have to be a doctor or pharmacist, or you'd have to know one, to get the stuff."

"Just one more question, Emma, at least for now. Worthy had a lot of booze in him. How would that have interacted with the propofol?"

"The combination could have caused a decrease in his breathing, more than the propofol alone would have. There's no question it would have dulled his mental responses and awareness."

"That actually raises one more. I gather there's no doubt all the cutting was done while he was knocked out by the propofol? Let's say within a half hour after it was administered?"

"That seems right to me. Otherwise, there would almost certainly have been some signs of resistance, however clumsy, at the scene."

At the team meeting the following Monday, Tom Mahaffey nailed down one of Emma's loose ends. "It was Laphroaig," he said.

"How do you know that?" Scott demanded.

"Solid detective work," answered Tom. "We found an empty bottle of Laphroaig in the trash can. There was also an open bottle on the bar, a little less than half-full."

"It's certainly beginning to look like Worthy had a visit from someone he knew," Scott said. "They drink more than a bottle of Laphroaig, then maybe Worthy passes out—that would certainly be enough to do it—and then this mystery guest injects him with propofol and carves him up while he's under."

"That's a reasonable hypothesis," Tom said. "But it's not for sure. We don't know whether all the Laphroaig was drunk in one evening. He probably already had the bottle that was in the trash because it's unlikely the mystery guest would have shown up with two bottles. But we don't know how full it was when he started drinking on April 8."

"Good point. Emma said he had more than half a bottle in him and that's the bottom line, regardless of how it was distributed between the two bottles. But it would still be a good idea to find out what his drinking habits were and see if he was a regular Laphroaig drinker." Looking at Angelo with irritation, Scott barked, "Why's your hand up, hotshot? You got a question or an insight that can help us move this thing forward, jump right in."

"OK, thanks," Angelo said meekly. "Dr. Mancini, as I understand it, the effects of the propofol are relatively immediate and profound, but they don't last all that long. Certainly not more than an hour. What are the chances he regained consciousness before he died? Would he have been able to do anything to help himself at that point? Make a call on his cell phone or something?"

"It's not likely he regained consciousness, Angelo, and it's even less likely he would have been able to function in a rational way if he did. Severing a femoral artery is an almost certain death sentence. Depending on the wound, you bleed out very quickly. It can happen in five minutes, and as it's happening, the blood flow to your brain and vital organs is shutting down. On top of that, this guy was drunk as a skunk. I don't think there's much chance he came to, or for that matter had any awareness of what was happening to him."

"Let's try to summarize where we are and what we're looking for," Scott said. "We've got a killer who apparently knew Worthy, who knew the properties of anesthetic drugs and had access to them, who knew how to give an injection into a vein, and who knew how to use a chain saw. That doesn't sound like your common everyday criminal."

"Could be a doctor in a logging camp," Angelo offered. He laughed at his attempted humor, but no one else did.

"I told you to jump in if you had something to offer," Scott said, "not just because you want to demonstrate what a jackass you are."

"OK. Let me offer this," Angelo said, undeterred. "We're talking like this was done by one person, someone who's a cross between a doctor, or maybe a nurse, and a lumberjack. I'm thinking there aren't many of those people around. What if there were two people involved?"

"That's worth considering, but it seems doubtful to me," said Scott. "I suppose it's possible one person cut him up and left, and then another person cut off his leg. But with no sign of struggle, that all would have had to happen in thirty or forty minutes, while the propofol was in effect. I just don't see how the coordination comes together. Besides, a hands-on murder like this is pretty intimate, in a bizarre way, and it doesn't feel like something that would lend itself to sharing. All this in the wee hours of the morning, in the middle of nowhere? Coincidences that big just don't happen."

The room was quiet as everyone tried to piece things together. Finally, Scott said, "What else is the investigation turning up? Tom?"

"We've analyzed the blond hair samples we found at the scene. Definitely a woman's hair. We've done a DNA analysis. Now all we need is a female suspect who's a match. I shouldn't say all we need, because that match would only tell us the woman had been there, not necessarily that she was the killer. But it's a data point."

"Good. Any luck with the fingerprint on the box cutter?"

"Some progress," answered Tom. "But again, it's only a partial print. Not enough for a definitive match. We've run it against the national database with no result. Either the partial is too limited to be meaningful, or it doesn't belong to a known offender whose prints are in the system."

"How about the prints on the ring?"

"Nothing helpful there. They belonged to Worthy."

"And the chain saw? Anything on that?"

"Still working on it. I'm in contact with the people at Hammersmith. They haven't made this model for about thirty years. They're trying to figure out where their sales records for it would be, if they even have them anymore."

"You got anything constructive, hotshot?"

Angelo filled the team in on what he had learned about Jason Worthy from his conversation with Terry Gomez. "He seems to be a first-rate lawyer who's dedicated to his law firm and loved by his clients. A model citizen respected by all. That's the Dr. Jekyll side of him."

Scott rolled his eyes.

"Then there's the Mr. Hyde side," Angelo went on. "The money-grubbing slumlord he doesn't want anyone to know about and works hard to keep hidden. He's also a ladies' man. He's had several office flings, according to Terry. But the woman I mentioned last week, the woman named Kate—Kate Strange, actually—that was a serious relationship. It went on for about three years. And then it suddenly stopped. She left her job at Watson Worthy right after that."

"Where is she now?"

"She's still in Washington, on the Hill. She's deputy chief counsel for the Senate Committee on Energy and Natural Resources. They have jurisdiction over public lands, and Kate is a tree hugger who wants to protect public lands. She's young for the job, but the word is she's very good, and a former senator who's now at Watson Worthy helped her get it. She lives in North Arlington."

"Have you met with her yet?"

"No. I thought about it, but so far she's the only person we can place at the scene, which I would think makes her a suspect. Superficially, at least, she also had a motive—he dumped her, and she wanted to get even. I thought maybe we should try to get more facts from other sources before talking to her."

"That's a reasonable instinct," Scott replied. "I'd agree we have to think of her as a person of interest, but I don't see her as a suspect. Not yet, anyway. I think we need to get to know her better, hear what she has to say. No third-degree stuff, just broad, open-ended questions. Know what I mean?"

"Yes, I do."

"Then why are you still here? Go talk to her."

"On it, boss," Angelo said, moving toward the door. Scott smiled. He liked the kid.

CHAPTER TWENTY-TWO

Jessie worked primarily for Jason, and now she was functionally on her own much of the time, but she had done a couple of small projects for Pudge in her first two years at the firm. They worked well together and had become friends. Now, as Jessie was midway through her fifth year, Pudge asked her to help him on a major new matter. It was a government contracts case involving allegations of defective pricing and false claims. The client, Landry United, was a large defense contractor that manufactured critical aircraft carrier systems in Mobile, Alabama.

Discovery is a large, important, and frequently overused element of any significant litigation. Each party generally has the right to "discover" what the other party's case is all about before trial. This is typically done in two ways: first, by reviewing the other party's relevant documents, and second, by taking depositions of persons (usually the other party's employees) who are believed to have knowledge of the facts. The object of discovery is to avoid surprise and narrow the issues for trial. Importantly, learning about the other party's case and evaluating it against your own also tends to facilitate settlements.

Requests for document production tend to be very broad. That is partly because the requesting party doesn't know exactly what its adversary has and doesn't want to miss anything. It is also because the requesting party usually wants to create a lot of work for its adversary, straining its personnel and financial resources and thus, the theory goes, leveraging settlement talks.

Not unexpectedly, the government's document production request to Landry was of breathtaking scope. In keeping with good practice, Jessie and one of the firm's young associates went to the Landry facility to review the documents pulled together by the company in advance of turning them over to the government. This type of review assures that the potential turnover documents are relevant, not privileged, and appropriate for production. It also assures that the producing party knows what information it's giving the other side. It is a critical step in managing the litigation and it helps a party understand and assess its own case.

On the third day of their review, Jessie found a document that was devastating to Landry's case. It wasn't a smoking gun, but it was close. Jessie went to Don Tapper, the Landry mid-level manager who had been tasked with supervising the document production. Don read the document, then read it again more closely. "Wow. That's bad," he said.

"Do you know the woman who wrote it?"

"No, I don't know her, but I do know who she is. She's an internal auditor who works at another Landry facility. She was evidently asked to review a set of invoices we submitted to the Navy for one of our systems."

"Does her memo say what I think it does?"

"I'm afraid so," Don said. "She wasn't able to substantiate or sign off on our pricing. She tried several times and then went to her boss with her concerns. He told her to just make the numbers work. It seems pretty clear she wrote this memo to cover her ass."

"That raises a lot of questions, don't you think?" Jessie was trying to be gentle and give Don the chance to show them the way out. When he didn't answer, she said, "At a minimum, this seems to be evidence of pricing irregularities. Conceivably, it could even be read to suggest fraud."

Don was clearly uncomfortable. "That memo could cause a swing of several million dollars in the case," he said. "Maybe get some people fired or even sent to jail."

Jessie asked quietly, "How do you think we should handle this, Don?"

"Lose the document," he snapped. "You're our lawyer. Lose the damn thing."

"What do you mean by 'lose it'? The document is clearly relevant, and I don't see any privilege that we could assert. It has to be produced."

"Just lose it!" Don was agitated. "Burn it. Piss on it and flush it down the toilet. I don't care. Just lose it. That's what lawyers do."

"Not this lawyer. And not the firm I work for. We play by the rules."

They were both quiet for several moments while the enormity of their predicament settled in. Then Jessie tried a new tack.

"Don, I don't know you well, but I consider you a friend. You have a wife and two children. The decision you're advocating could put you at risk, possibly even criminal risk. Why would you do that to yourself, or your family? You don't even know the people you're trying to protect."

His body began to shake slightly. He was starting to cry. "I've worked for Landry for twenty-eight years. It hasn't been perfect, but on the whole, they've treated me well. I retire in two more years, and we need the pension money. I have no choice. Don't you see that?"

"I see you're in a tough position, and I feel for you," Jessie said. "But I'm in a tough position too. Ethically, I can't—and won't—destroy that document."

She thought for a moment. "Let's do this," she added. "This is a legal matter with considerable importance to the company. Let me talk to my supervising partner. He's a terrific lawyer and a straight shooter. I'll tell him I brought it to him because it presents substantial financial implications for Landry and, conceivably, criminal exposure for some in the management chain. I'll say I thought he might want to resolve it at the general counsel level. I won't mention the conversation you and I just had."

"That would be amazing. I hate to look like I'm ducking this, but it's way over my pay scale. I really appreciate your keeping me out of it."

Jessie called Pudge and brought him up to speed. He ended up in complete agreement with her approach. As they talked through the pros and cons, Jessie asked whether he was concerned about putting the GC on the spot.

"Yes, I am," he said, "but I think she'll ultimately thank us for giving Landry a chance to cut its losses and control the narrative. That lets the company avoid a potential PR debacle and possibly even debarment from future government contracts."

"It also gives her the ability to keep some Landry people who should have known better out of jail," Jess added. "I wouldn't bet on them keeping their jobs, though."

"I agree, but better to lose your job than your freedom. They'll soon figure that out. Thank you, Jessie. This is the right way to handle it."

The meeting with Landry's general counsel, Mary Orr, took place a week later. Pudge brought Jessie with him, partly to show her how it was done, partly as a reward, and partly because he liked her company. Once introductions were made and the pleasantries concluded, Pudge showed Mary the document and said, gently but firmly, that it would need to be produced if the litigation went forward. She read it with obvious distress. It didn't take long for her to make a decision.

"This will cost Landry a lot of money," she said, "but without our reputation, we have nothing. We can't have people associating Landry with possible fraud. We can't put members of our management team at public risk, even though we absolutely disapprove of what they did and will almost certainly fire them. There's really nothing to decide here. Settle the case for whatever it takes, with no admissions of any kind and the usual confidentiality provisions."

"Will do, Mary," Pudge said. "We'll take care of it. And thanks."

"No, thank you, Pudge. And you, Jessie. You've given me a problem I'll have to manage but saved me from a much bigger problem that I won't have to worry about. You are good lawyers and true friends, and I am in your debt. I really mean it."

It was late afternoon when they left Landry's corporate offices. They felt good about the meeting and its outcome.

"I could take you to dinner at the fancy-ass Bienville Club on the thirty-fourth floor of an office building in downtown Mobile," Pudge said playfully, "or I could take you to a seafood dive on the water. What's your pleasure?"

"Let's do the dive," responded Jessie. "How do you know your way around Mobile so well? You're not from these parts."

"A long time ago, when I was about as far out of law school as you are now, I spent a couple of weeks here doing depositions. I was up against a partner at one of the white-shoe New York firms. He was a real jackass. He thought he was too good to talk to me because he was a partner and I was only an associate.

And he adopted some clever, if unprofessional, approaches to the deposition witnesses. I remember one of our witnesses was an ex-Navy admiral, and the jerk tells him on the record that he knows he's a man of honor since he's an ex-admiral, and asks him, as a matter of honor, not to talk to me so he won't corrupt the record by using coached testimony. It's a load of crap; of course the guy can talk to me because he's there for his employer and so am I, but the poor guy doesn't know what to believe, and since he's a man of honor, he figures he'd better not take a chance and refuses to talk to me about the case. My own witness! He hopes I'll understand, blah, blah, blah. It was the worst two weeks of my professional career. I learned a lot from that jackass, but most of it was about how not to act as a lawyer or a human being."

Pudge was always entertaining. It was easy and fun to be with him.

They soon settled in at Felix's Fish Camp with a nice table at the water's edge. Shrimp and wine were the order of the evening. They talked about some of Pudge's past cases, and about Watson Worthy and what it was like to start a firm, and eventually, they got around to Jason.

"What makes him tick?" Jessie wanted to know. "What's he like?"

"Why are you asking me? You've worked with him as much as anyone at the firm."

"Yes, I know," Jessie said. "But he never really opens up. He's there, but he doesn't let you in. I know he's a fine lawyer. He's given me real opportunities, particularly with Sand Ridge, and I'm grateful for that. I've learned a ton from him. He's perfectly willing to engage about legal issues at length and in depth. But I couldn't say he's a friend. Not like you. I feel I know him as a lawyer but not as a person."

Pudge was thoughtful. "I don't know that I can help you. Our long friendship is an office friendship. We don't hang out together outside of work. I absolutely trust him. Hell, I wouldn't have started a law firm with him if I didn't. But he's a secretive guy. I think he's pretty insecure, or rather, let's say very insecure. I couldn't tell you why. He's not good at personal commitment, that's for sure."

"What's his deal with Karen Woodbine?"

"That's an interesting relationship," Pudge mused. "I think they had some-thing going a long time ago. She may be exhibit A in support of my point that he doesn't do personal commitments well. Or maybe exhibit B, after Jennifer."

"Jennifer?"

"His former wife. You and he really don't talk, do you? Jennifer's a nice person, but they weren't good together. It's a long story, too long to waste this evening on."

"Did Karen give him the Sand Ridge business because of their former thing?"

"That may have been a small part of it. The truth is they really are friends. And the bigger part is that Jason is a sensational lawyer, and Karen knows he'll make her look good. Theirs is an odd brew of mutual friendship and mutual ambition. You may have noticed that Karen is ninety-nine parts about herself. She demands loyalty and knows Jason will always be there for her. Funny, now that I think of it, her insistence on absolute loyalty is part of the reason she transferred so much Sand Ridge work to Jason."

This was getting interesting. Jessie thought back to the weird ending of her dinner with Karen. "Meaning?"

"Meaning the guy who had the business before she gave it to Jason picked a bad time to get married. He was a fine lawyer with an excellent firm, and he and Karen had worked together for years. But an important Sand Ridge trial was scheduled to begin the day of his wedding. Karen asked him to move his wedding date. He wouldn't, and she gave the case, and a ton of other work, to Jason. She saw the guy's fealty to his new bride as a breach of his duty of absolute loyalty to her."

"Good Lord," said Jessie, wondering what she had gotten herself into.

"Don't be too hard on her," Pudge countered. "I hear she's pushing Jason to put you up for partner next year. This isn't really my news to tell—you should hear it from Jason—but here we are."

"Holy shit," Jessie exclaimed. She was beaming. "That's two years ahead of schedule. Do you think it will happen?"

"I do. Jason's very high on you and doesn't need much pushing. It'll take some politicking up front so none of the other partners get their noses out of joint, but I think it will happen."

Jessie couldn't stop smiling. "What an honor. Thanks, Pudge."

"Don't thank me. You've earned it."

They were silent for a long moment. Then Jessie said, "OK, we've talked about me. Now let's talk about you. How does it happen that a wonderful guy like you isn't married?"

"I was married for a brief time twenty-three years ago. We got pregnant in our first year and were over the moon. As the months went by, we learned we would be having a baby boy. We got the room ready, talked about names, all that stuff. But something went wrong. There were complications, and we rushed Becky to the hospital. They tried to do a makeshift delivery of some kind, but she died. They couldn't save the baby either."

"Oh my God, I'm so, so sorry." A tear ran down Jessie's cheek. She took Pudge's hand to console him. "I had no idea—I shouldn't have asked."

"I know you didn't know. It was the low point of my life, and it isn't something I talk about. Anyway, I took a few months off and then plunged back into work with a vengeance. Work was my escape and became my life. When I was working, I wasn't thinking about what I had lost, what might have been. And no one came along to fill the void, or if they did, I couldn't see them through the barricade I had built. It's funny, I've never talked about this to anyone. Why you, why now, why Felix's Fish Camp?"

"I don't know, but I'm pleased and honored that you did."

They looked down at their hands, still joined. But it was no longer in consolation. They were joined in a shared recognition of a new and very personal connection. Instinctively, they leaned toward each other and lightly kissed. It felt warm and good.

"I don't know what to say," Pudge stammered, pulling back and trying to regain his composure. "I shouldn't have done that."

"It's OK. It was nice. But despite my feelings for you, I think we'd better leave it there."

"I'm glad for our friendship, Jessie. I'll always be here for you."

CHAPTER TWENTY-THREE

Jessie had a hard time getting to sleep that night. It had been a productive day and an extraordinary evening. She had learned from Pudge, and she enjoyed being with him.

Partly, there was her excitement about the prediction that she would make partner next year. She hadn't seen that coming. Associates who did well ordinarily made partner after eight years. And she would be making it in six! She couldn't wait to tell Jimmy. She couldn't wait to tell Sam!

Oh yes, Jimmy. He was what caused most of her sleeplessness. Where were they, anyway? She was genuinely confused about her feelings. They seemed to be all over the place. She knew she loved him and wanted to be with him. And she was pretty sure he felt the same way about her. Then what the hell was tonight all about? Jessie couldn't deny her feelings for Pudge. She was comfortable being with him. And that kiss was lovely. She had wanted things to go farther, she knew that. And if she were being honest with herself, she had to admit that if she had had one more glass of wine, she would have gone to bed with him. She had wanted to, man, had she wanted to. And he had too, and it had been genuine. So why did he have to be such a gentleman? Annoying, even though she admired him for it.

Jessie tossed and turned. She couldn't tune out her thoughts. *What was that wine anyway? Damn, it was good. Pudge said it was a Bordeaux. Cos d'Estournel, I think it was. I'll have to remember that and pick some up. It was really good. And we drank two bottles of it. I didn't know I could drink that much wine. I wish I had drunk more. Then I would have gone to bed with him.*

Why didn't I? Why did I stop things when they were just getting started? Because I love Jimmy. We're together, we want to be together. But he travels so much. And sometimes, I wonder if he's sleeping with other women now and then. I shouldn't have those thoughts, but I can't forget the time he introduced me to someone he works with at Barclays, and the two of them seemed just a little too familiar. I thought there were knowing looks passing between them, looks I wasn't supposed to see, and that made me think they might be sleeping together.

If he is sleeping with a work colleague, why wouldn't he sleep with women when he's on the road? He works with a lot of women, just like I work with a lot of men, and he's a great-looking guy, an interesting guy. I'm sure he wouldn't have any trouble finding women to sleep with if he wanted to. Does he want to? If he does, I don't think it's because he doesn't love me. It's just something to do when he's away, a diversion like watching TV or reading a book. It doesn't mean anything.

So why didn't I go to bed with Pudge? He didn't ask me or even hint at it, but it was in the air. It was definitely in the air. If Jimmy's sleeping with other women now and then and it doesn't mean anything, why shouldn't I? Jimmy and I are good together, we love being together, and we're comfortable that way, but we also both value our independence. What would be the harm if he sleeps with someone now and then and I do too? It would make life a little exciting.

I wonder what it would be like to sleep with Pudge. I haven't slept with another man since Jimmy and I started going out. I'm glad I said no tonight.

As Jessie tossed and turned, Jimmy was having breakfast in Frankfurt. He had woken up thinking about her. They had talked by phone, and he knew she and Pudge were in Mobile yesterday for a client meeting. He wondered how it went. He wondered if they had gone to dinner last night. He wondered what their relationship was. He had met Pudge a couple of times and thought he was Jessie's type—well, that is, if she was into other men. He was good-looking, charming, smart, and very curious, so why wouldn't she be attracted to him? She wouldn't do anything about it, though, at least he didn't think so. He knew she loved him, and he sure as hell loved her. But she was a bit of a free spirit.

He thought about his own dinner last night with Monica Fertig, a foreign exchange counterpart of his at Deutsche Bank. They had worked together off and on for two years, and she was a regular stop when he was in Frankfurt. Even if they didn't have business, they always had dinner. They adored good food and great red wines, and they adored each other. She was a Teutonic beauty, tall, with very blond hair cut short and large brown eyes. She was single, he couldn't imagine why, and she was mischievous. They flirted with each other shamelessly and loved it. As their dinner ended last night, he kissed her hand, as he always did. She asked him to come to bed with her, as she always did. He said no, but maybe next time, as he always did.

CHAPTER TWENTY-FOUR

Sam's phone rang. It was Jessie. "We have to get together," she said excitedly. "I've got news."

"So do I. When?" Sam responded. Hearing from Jessie made her day better. The prospect of seeing Jessie made her heart sing.

They quickly agreed to meet the following Saturday. Jimmy would be in Seoul and Sam knew Chris would be just as happy without her, the little shit, having the place to himself and pigging out on football and Route 11 potato chips. They settled on Staunton, Virginia, which is more or less halfway between Washington and Charleston. It has the bonus of being a charming small town, deep in culture and history. It is also, for those who care, the birthplace of Woodrow Wilson.

Sam booked a room for them at the Stonewall Jackson Hotel. She considered getting them separate rooms, now that they were all grown up, but a single room would save some bucks. Besides, they had shared a room many times before.

When Sam got to Staunton and checked into the hotel, she called Chris. She wanted to let him know she had arrived safely. She also wanted to be sure he was OK. They had a matter-of-fact kind of relationship, nothing lovey-dovey, and friends had told her more than once that she was a little tough on him. They had a point. But she was trying to be better since his return from

Iraq a year ago. His army reserve unit had been called up to participate in Iraqi Freedom.

They had assumed he'd be gone a year, but he came home after four months. He hadn't been in the thick of the fighting, but anywhere in Iraq was dangerous. On a routine mission in an area thought to be safe, the jeep he shared with a buddy was blown into the air by an IED. That brought him home early with shrapnel in his hip that couldn't be removed, a Purple Heart, and a permanent limp.

"Hey babe," Sam said. "Just checking in. All good?"

"Oh jeez," he said. "Are you going to call me every five minutes? I've been looking forward to this time alone all week. Please go and play nicely with Jessie and have a good time."

It was their usual sort of banter. They did it so they wouldn't have to get all teary talking about what they really felt. They were so lucky he came back alive, in pretty good shape, really, and they were together again.

Reassured by the call, Sam went down to the lobby to meet Jessie. They spent a couple of hours walking around town, enjoying the various shops and bookstores Staunton has to offer. By 4:15, they had seen what there was to see and they were tired, so they fell into a cute little wine bar.

They had pre-inventoried their respective discussion topics, without revealing their substance, enough to know that Jessie had two agenda items and Sam had one. They had agreed to hold them off until dinner, when they could give them their full attention. But they couldn't stand it any longer and, over a crisp Sancerre at the wine bar, amended the agreement to allow Jessie to reveal one of her items now. That would even things up at dinner.

"I'm going to make partner next year," she blurted out.

"Holy shit," Sam exclaimed. "Are you kidding me? By my count, you aren't due for two more years."

"Yeah, I know. And there are no promises and it's not for sure, but it's looking good. I have a strong relationship with one of our biggest clients, Sand Ridge Partners, and their general counsel is pushing my boss to put me up early. Fortunately, he likes me too, so he's supportive."

"What's in it for him?" Sam asked, suspiciously.

"Sand Ridge is his biggest client. Their willingness to rely on me, usually in a lead role, frees Jason up to do some other things. And Sand Ridge is giving me business directly now. Jason gets the origination credit since it's his client, so it's a win-win for him. Plus, Pudge says Jason wants to lock me in to Watson Worthy because he's afraid if I leave and go to another firm, the Sand Ridge account, or at least some of it, would go with me."

"Jason? Pudge? Who are they?"

"The name partners at the firm. Pudge Watson and Jason Worthy. They're both my bosses. Pudge is also a friend."

"Hmmm. What kind of a friend?" Sam teased.

"Let's save that for dinner."

Sam was tantalized, but she let it rest. "That's such fabulous news, Jess. A real feather in your cap. I'm so proud of you!"

They shared a hug and followed up the Sancerre with a nice rosé from Cassis.

Dinner at Emilio's was lovely, if you like the kind of good Italian pasta Mama used to make, and they did. A small-production Barbaresco from the Piedmont was a perfect pairing for their antipasti. Then they got down to the serious business, gnocchi with a Milanese sauce for Jessie and pappardelle with sausage, peas, and mushrooms for Sam. Not to mention the exquisite bottle of Guado al Tasso.

They also got down to the serious discussion. Sam went first. "So, here's my news. You know, of course, about the recent Rebel Yell Mine explosion."

"Yeah, it made me heartsick. It brought back some sad memories from our days in Owl Hollow. I didn't know anyone at Rebel Yell, but I'm sure our folks did. This must be tearing them up."

"It is, but not entirely in a bad way. I went to see my parents a couple of weeks ago. They're angry. This thing has Dad so pissed off he's slowed down his drinking and come halfway out of his depression. He's following the news as closely as he can. He's convinced, knowing Black Bear, that the investigation will produce a ton of violations and find that some of them contributed to the deaths of the miners."

"That's interesting," Jessie said, "and a real silver lining about your dad. That must be a relief to your mother. Is that your news? Or is there more?"

"There's a whole lot more," Sam said. "The feds and the state are each doing their own investigations. They're crawling all over the mine and talking to everyone they can. They mean to get to the bottom of this. And our office is looking into it to see if there might be some criminal conduct involved. Pete Gage, my boss, has made me the lead Assistant on the investigation."

"That sounds intense. Big-time and exciting. You always wanted to help miners and their families, and now you've got your chance."

"Wait, there's more," Sam said. "Pete says if this thing goes to trial, it will be my case."

"Wow! That will be a ton of pressure. Does it make you nervous?"

"Sure, a little. But I've tried enough cases now that I'm very confident. And if the evidence is there, I intend to nail that bastard George Rafferty."

Jessie just smiled. Sam knew she was happy for her, and very proud of her. This was big stuff, and it seemed to make them even again. It might have moved Sam a little ahead, but not with Jess making partner early.

"So that's the big news from Charleston. What's your second item?"

"Pudge, the friend I mentioned this afternoon. Not Pudge *per se*; he's real enough, but he may only be the symptom that made me think about the larger issue." Jessie then told Sam about her dinner with Pudge in Mobile, their holding hands, the gentle kiss. Jessie and Sam knew each other's soul, and Jess left nothing out. She followed that up with a chapter-and-verse reprise of her long and sleepless night.

"All this leaves me with a couple of questions I can't talk about with anyone but you. That's why I really needed to see you, Sam, to get your take. I don't want to be dramatic, but there may be some life choices to be made here."

"What the hell are you talking about? You're scaring me!"

"The first question is whether Jimmy's screwing around. You know him. Do you think he is?"

"I worried about that a little. Remember, I mentioned it at your place when Chris and I visited? Jimmy travels so much, and he has such a good way with people, that it caused me to wonder. What you think is much more important than what I think though. Where are you on this? If you knew he was, would you want to divorce him? Is that what you mean by life choices?"

"Oh, God no. My reference to life choices was less cosmic than that."

"Meaning?"

"Meaning if he's screwing around, why shouldn't I? Starting with Pudge."

They both laughed heartily, thoroughly enjoying the moment. Sam couldn't resist teasing Jessie. "You'd like that, wouldn't you? Pudge, I mean."

"You bet I would."

"But you're not going to, are you?"

"No."

Sam had been thinking about Jessie's initial question the whole time they'd been talking. She did worry about all of Jimmy's time on the road, away from Jessie and subject to life's temptations. She knew he could charm anyone he wanted. But then she thought about his faithfulness to Miss Yale when he and Jessie were at Stanford, and she was reassured. Jessie may have been having her doubts right now, but she and Jimmy were good, as she had told Sam on Q Street.

"Jess," Sam said. "You asked me whether I think Jimmy is screwing around. No, I don't. I don't think he ever would."

"Thanks. That means a lot to me."

They each ordered a limoncello and chatted about other things. Before they left Emilio's, Jessie asked Sam about Chris. "Do you ever wonder about him? Are you guys good?"

"Do I wonder about whether he's screwing around? No. Are we good? Yes, I think we are. I might not have said that a few years back. I went through a patch of wondering what we were doing, living our boring lives. I wondered whether I could have done better, maybe held out for someone more exciting. It took me awhile, but it finally came to me that I was projecting. I didn't want to take responsibility for my own boring life, so I blamed Chris for it. I remember lying in bed one night, watching him sleep, and thinking he may not be Mr. Excitement, but the little pecker is rock solid. He would literally lie down for me. You can't ask for more than that."

Jessie smiled. "That's good to hear. One last question—how about you? We've talked about my fantasies. Do you ever think about screwing around?"

"No. Chris is my guy."

Back at the hotel, they had a glass of Courvoisier and slipped into bed. This time, their lovemaking wasn't driven by excitement or despair. Nor was it unexpected. They both knew it was coming, and they eased into it like the old pros they were. It was soft and gentle and lingering and intimate, and it lasted all night long.

Sam wondered later that day, as she had on other occasions, if she was a lesbian or, more accurately, bisexual. She was no expert in the behaviors that qualified a person for one category or the other. But she didn't think she was either, because several things were true. She had never been with a woman other than Jessie. She wasn't attracted to women and didn't think about being with them. She didn't even think about Jessie in those terms. She was perfectly content to be with Chris and looked forward to being with him. The armchair psychologist in her said this wasn't about sex or lust or gender, but about love. It was a uniquely Jessie thing. Sharing their bodies as well as their hearts and souls and secrets was the most complete affirmation of what they felt for each other.

That was Sam's third time with Jessie. There were two more times before they arrived at that terrible passage, years later, when their innermost thoughts, fears, doubts, suspicions, and maybe even convictions, made it impossible for them to share anything.

CHAPTER TWENTY-FIVE

Kate wasn't surprised when a deputy from the Bath County Sheriff's Office called and wanted to meet. After all, she knew Jason Worthy well, very well, and it was reasonable that the authorities would want to ask her about him and about their relationship. They would also figure out that she was at Justice Hill early in the morning on April 9, the day Jason died. Maybe they already knew that. They surely did if they had talked to that nosy neighbor—what was her name, Mrs. Dawkins?—who spent all her time watching the road through her living room window. Jason hadn't liked Mrs. Dawkins because he was a private person and she always seemed to be checking up on him. Kate was glad to tell the sheriff's office what she knew.

The dog was in the yard when Angelo pulled up to the modest rambler on Dinwiddie Street. "Hey, Slouch," he called, and the dog playfully ran to him. He spent a minute nuzzling the big guy.

"I can see you like dogs," Kate said from the front door. She was blond and beautiful.

"Yes, I do," Angelo managed to answer. "I grew up in Bath County. It's very rural there. We always had two or three dogs, mostly hounds and retrievers."

"Then we're off to a good start," Kate said. "Please come in."

It was a gorgeous spring day, and they sat on Kate's back porch, overlooking the garden. She brought Angelo a cup of coffee and poured herself an iced tea. "I wish the yard were larger," she said. "Slouch is a big boy, what they call a giant breed. He had a lot more room to run around at Justice Hill and even at Jason's house in Bethesda."

She was very forthright, Angelo noted. Her guard wasn't up at all. She didn't seem reluctant to talk to him or concerned about having been at Justice Hill the morning Jason was killed. If she had anything to do with his death, she was painting a stunningly good portrait of innocence.

"Why don't you just talk for a little while?" Angelo said. "Tell me about your job at Watson Worthy."

"Sure," Kate replied. She told Angelo about her background and her interest in forests and public lands. She had gone to law school to develop the skills that would help her get laws passed to protect those magnificent places. Her being at Watson Worthy was serendipitous; a law school professor friend knew a former senator, Paul Jenkins, who was starting a legislative practice there, and the professor advised her to go to Watson and work with Paul. He said a few years with Paul would give her a solid grounding in legislative work, and she would then be well-positioned to take a Hill job with a Senate or House committee of jurisdiction if that's what she still wanted to do.

"How did it work out for you?"

"I was at Watson Worthy a little over four years. It was a good experience both personally and professionally. Working with Paul Jenkins was everything my professor friend had thought it would be. Paul was in the Senate for three terms before joining the firm, and he really knew his way around. I worked largely but not exclusively on environmental legislation. I got to draft legislation, attend committee hearings, form relationships with committee staffers, see what the paid lobbyists do, basically observe all aspects of how laws are made. I liked the firm as a whole and working with Paul was invaluable."

"Did you work with any of the other partners?"

"Two others in the legislative group. No one outside the group. My interest was in doing legislative work, and that was the deal I cut with the firm when I came in. I wasn't a general associate."

"Then you never worked for Jason Worthy, I take it?"

"That's correct."

"We've been told the two of you had a relationship that lasted for some time." Kate nodded. "How did that come about?"

"There was a firm dinner one night. I guess I had been there a few months at the time. The business part of the dinner was a presentation by the legislative group. I had a role in that. The firm was trying to showcase our practice so the litigators would know what we did, and in keeping with the theme, the dinner was held at one of the House office buildings, Rayburn, I think. After the dinner, seven or eight of us went to Bullfeathers for drinks. Jason was in the group, and so was I. We enjoyed a little banter back and forth. It was a group setting, but you can still tell when something sort of clicks with someone, right? A week later, Jason invited me to lunch. He said it was part of an effort he was making to meet the new associates, but I knew better."

"And things went on from there?"

"Yes, but I was resistant at first. Jason had a reputation for chasing women, and I wasn't interested in being a notch on his belt. Besides, he was one of the name partners, and I was a junior associate, even though I was a few years older than most of the others. It just didn't feel right."

"But?"

"But the Jason I was getting to know, through that first lunch and one or two others, didn't match up with his reputation. He was a really nice guy, and it turned out we had several common interests."

"Such as?"

"Contemporary art, for one thing. Good wine, particularly Italian wine. And we both loved dogs. He had Slouch, of course, and I told him all about Pete, who was my best friend in my forest ranger days. And you know, despite his reputation, he never tried to put a move on me."

"When did it start to get more serious?"

"Oh, I don't know," Kate said, throwing a tennis ball that Slouch neatly retrieved. "A few months in, I guess. It was hard, having a 'friendship' with a senior partner. People at the firm know. They talk. Nothing was going on, but we didn't want to feed the rumor mill. We didn't go out on dates because D.C. is a small town in many ways, and you never know who you'll see—or who will see you—at a restaurant or bar. One day, he suggested we spend a weekend at a place he had in western Virginia, Justice Hill. He said I would have my own room, and he promised he would behave. I was wary, but I said yes."

"Why?"

"I liked him and wanted to get to know him better. That wasn't possible in D.C. I don't like going out just to go out. Life is too short to waste that way. I only had two serious relationships before Jason, and both had started slowly, as friendships, and then grew into more. That was what seemed to be happening with Jason. I'm a pretty good judge of character, and I had come to believe the Jason everyone else knew wasn't the same Jason I was getting to know. Besides, having been a ranger, I knew I could take care of myself if it ever came to that."

"How did the weekend go?"

"It was lovely. That was the first time I met Slouch, and I fell in love with him." Kate looked out at Slouch, who was playing quietly with the ball. "You can see why."

"Yes, I can. He's a great dog. How about the Jason part of the weekend?"

"He was charming, generous, and a perfect gentleman. His house is unbelievable, and down-to-earth comfortable. He calls it a log cabin, but it's much, much more than that. I guess you've seen it. We took long walks in the woods. He has a hundred acres or more, but it doesn't really matter because his property backs up to a national forest, and the woods just keep going. It reminded me of my time in Idaho. We visited the local towns, which were charming. I love the outdoors and had the best time. After dinner in Hot Springs, we went back to Justice Hill and had a glass of brandy. I was tired, and after a second brandy, I said good night. He kissed me on the cheek and told me to sleep well, and we went to our separate rooms. There was no funny business."

Angelo kept the conversation going without being specific, as Scott had urged. "What happened after that?"

"I woke up the next morning to the smell of fresh coffee. Jason was cooking bacon and eggs. It was another joyful day, doing nothing, being together. For dinner, Jason put out a lovely spread of veal chops, a delicate pasta with spinach, and a superb bottle of Tignanello. We relaxed on the sofa after dinner, enjoying a glass of a bourbon Jason liked, Widow Jane. It all felt so comfortable. I reached over and took his hand. We sat quietly for a time, and I told him I didn't want to sleep alone that night. That's how it started."

"And it continued, I take it?"

"It did. We were a couple. Not an ordinary couple because we didn't want to be an issue at the firm. We didn't go out in D.C. I'd go over to his house every now and then, but most of the time we spent together was at Justice Hill. We were there a couple of weekends a month. We loved it there."

"How well did you know Jason?"

"I guess as well as anyone knows the person they live with. My sense was that I knew him pretty well. He had a private side to him, and I saw that sometimes when we were with other people. He would shut down if anyone tried to get too close or asked him a question he thought was personal. But I always felt he was open with me. I trusted him."

"What assets did he have? I'm asking because that may indicate who might have had a motive to kill him."

"Jason's life was the law firm. That's where his money came from. He had some investments, mostly mutual funds, I think, because he said he didn't have time to study the market and mutual funds had managers who did that. He had a 401(k) account through the firm. And he had Justice Hill and his house in Bethesda."

"Any other properties?"

"Not that I know of."

"Did he have a will?"

"I haven't a clue."

"Did he have any relatives?"

"He had a brother somewhere, but he wasn't sure where. They hadn't spoken in years."

"Did you talk much about the firm in your time together?"

"Sure. We both worked there, knew the same people, and had an interest in the place. We delighted in sharing the gossip we heard in the halls. You know, who was doing who and like that. But he always respected our different positions at the firm. He didn't talk to me about other partners, or which associates were doing well or badly—the issues it would have been inappropriate for a partner to talk to an associate about. He was very loyal to the firm and always very professional, despite our relationship. I admired that."

"Did he talk about other women?"

"Are you delicately trying to ask about his screwing around with other women at the firm? That was common knowledge, or at least common gossip. But no, he never talked to me about it. He was sweet, and loving, and we were in a monogamous relationship. That's what I cared about."

"Then I take it neither of you was seeing anyone else during your time together?"

"I certainly wasn't, and I have no reason to believe he was either. As I say, we were a couple. I had moved some clothes and personal effects to Justice Hill, enough so I wouldn't have to pack every time we went there. It was our special place. We spent our Thanksgivings and Christmases there. We were together, and we were very happy."

"Did you ever talk about getting married?"

"Abstractly, yes. We talked about marriage as an institution. We didn't talk about it in terms of our getting married. Jason had had a bad marriage experience and didn't want to get married again. I didn't care one way or the other. I was more interested in our being together, and we did talk about that. He bought me a diamond ring once. He called it a together ring. It was so sweet and captured what I wanted out of our relationship. I loved the sentiment."

"It sounds as if you had an unusually good thing going. When, and mostly why, did it end?"

"It ended last year. In the fall, which made it doubly sad for me because that's when it had started, in the fall. I've never been completely sure why, and I had no indication it was coming. One day, out of the blue, he told me there was another woman. I was shocked. The clear message was that we were done."

"Did you know who it was?"

"No, and I never asked. We were at Justice Hill when he told me. I assumed it was someone out there, someone local."

"What did you do when he told you? Was there a conversation?"

"I left. There was no conversation. I was deeply hurt. If a man tells you there's another woman, you know what he means. There's nothing to talk about, is there? You know what you need to know. You didn't have what you thought you did. I just left."

"How did you leave?"

"We usually drove out together, but as it happened, I had driven separately on this occasion. Jason had gone out a few days early, but I couldn't leave work as soon as he did."

"Did you go back into the house before you left?"

"Just for a second. I had to grab my bag and wanted to say good-bye to Slouch. I also left his ring on the living room table. I certainly didn't want it anymore."

"When did you leave the law firm?"

"I gave my notice the next day. I didn't want to see Jason, I didn't want to be around him, and I wanted to be gone when the talking started."

"Did you have another job lined up?"

"No, but as you know, my long-term interest was in working on the Hill. This was earlier than I had planned, but Paul Jenkins was very kind and offered to help me get a job with the Senate Committee on Energy and Natural Resources. It took four months, but he pulled it off. That's where I am now. It's a great job."

"What did you do during the four months off?"

"I took a part-time job as a receptionist. It obviously didn't fit my career goals, but I needed to make some money. It wasn't a lot of money, but Paul was optimistic about the Senate job, so I wanted something I could get in and out of easily."

"Have you seen Jason since, or talked to him?"

"He called me in early April. I didn't answer the phone, and he left a message. He said he had made a terrible mistake and wanted to get back together. He asked me to call him."

"And did you?"

"No. He had hurt me very badly. I was still angry with him and didn't want to see him or talk to him. I ignored his message."

"Kate, this next part is difficult. Mrs. Dawkins, Jason's closest neighbor, told us she saw you driving away from Justice Hill around 6:30 on the morning Jason was killed. Were you there, and if so, what were you doing there?"

"I had been at a meeting at the Homestead the day before. It included dinner, and we stayed overnight. Since it's nearby, I sent Jason an email from the Homestead, saying I would be stopping by Justice Hill early the next morning to pick up a necklace I had left there. It had been my mother's, and it was important to me. I still had a key to the house, and told Jason I would let myself in, pick up the necklace, and leave. I asked him please to stay in his room while I was there. I told him I didn't want to see him."

"Did you hear back from him?"

"No."

"And that was why you were at Justice Hill the following morning, the day he died?"

"Yes. When I pulled up to the house, Slouch was barking like crazy. He was howling and crying. He sounded frantic. I rushed in and saw Jason on the living room floor. He was all cut up and clearly dead. The scene was grotesque. There was nothing I could do, and I left. I took Slouch with me."

"Did you call the police?"

"No. I should have, but I didn't. Everything about Jason and Justice Hill was painful to me. I just didn't want to be in the middle of this. Besides, I was pretty sure Mrs. Dawkins would be all over it."

Trying to end on a lighter note, Angelo said, "You know, you could get in trouble for taking Slouch. Some might say you stole him."

"I wasn't going to leave him there, in misery and without anyone to feed him or care for him until finally he was picked up by the pound. Besides, Jason knew how I felt about Slouch. He always told me that if he got hit by a bus, I could have Slouch."

She reflected for a moment. "It's funny," she finally said. "Slouch is the only good thing I got out of knowing Jason Worthy."

CHAPTER TWENTY-SIX

Several months after her Staunton getaway with Sam, Jessie received unexpected news that would alter the course of her life. Karen had asked her to dinner. The spring was genial in 2007, and Karen opted for an alfresco event at L'Auberge Chez Francois, a lovely spot in the tony suburb of Great Falls. They met at the restaurant and were seated at a private table in the pleasant side garden.

Karen had little use for social gatherings or small talk. A dinner invitation from her was a rarity, particularly at a venue as relaxed and far away from the business community as Chez Francois. Jessie wondered what the occasion was as she wound her way northwest on Georgetown Pike, tracking the Potomac River to Great Falls. She had recently updated Karen on all pending Sand Ridge litigation, none of which was at a critical stage. She concluded this must be about something new. One thing was certain: regardless of the setting, this was a business dinner. Karen didn't do social dinners.

They opened with a crisp Dom Ruinart champagne. Whatever Karen's agenda, she wasn't rushing into it. Then it was seared *foie gras*, beautifully paired with a sauternes from Doisy-Daene. The uncharacteristic small talk continued. Jessie could only wonder where all this was going. She found out during her opening sip of La Conseillante, a seductive merlot-based beauty from Pomerol that the sommelier had assured them would enhance their entrée selections.

"I have some exciting news, and it presents a career-making opportunity for you," Karen said. "That's why I wanted us to have a very special dinner. The setting has to be just right for these things." Karen was playing it to the hilt.

"First, the news. Sand Ridge has acquired a new company in the energy space. If fits beautifully with our other companies and will shine brightly in our growing galaxy."

"Who is it?" Jessie asked.

"Black Bear Mining Company," Karen said proudly. "They're in Charleston and operate seven coal mines in West Virginia. The company is owned and managed by George Rafferty, a self-made man and an industry leader."

Jessie's heart sank. She had difficulty breathing. Whatever this was going to mean for her, it wouldn't be good. She needed time to figure out how to react. She decided the best course, for now, was to listen, learn, and say as little as possible.

"From our perspective," Karen went on, "Black Bear is promising in all respects but one. They had an unfortunate explosion at one of their mines last October, and several people were killed. The matter is being investigated by federal and state authorities. That's a problem for the company, but it isn't a problem for Sand Ridge because we carved it out in our acquisition negotiations. Under the agreement, Black Bear will cover all expenses and retain all liabilities associated with the explosion."

"Nicely done," Jessie said, trying to keep the conversation going without giving voice to the negative thoughts running through her head, all of which converged into this: *Like hell I'm going to work for the company that killed my father.*

"Thank you," Karen said, taking Jessie's compliment at face value. "Even though Black Bear will be absorbing the costs, it's in our interest to help them get out of this as cleanly, quietly, and inexpensively as possible. That brings me to the opportunity this presents for you. There will be a boatload of crap coming down when the investigations finish. Black Bear will be charged with violations, scores or maybe even hundreds of them. George Rafferty assures us they did everything by the book, but the public outcry will, as a political matter, require a hefty serving of violations and fines. The public relations problems will be enormous."

Jessie nodded. She was only half listening. Her mind was elsewhere, in overdrive.

"The larger issue is that there may well be criminal charges. That often happens with workplace accidents where people die. There might even be charges against George, although it's hard to imagine they'd stick because he's a straight-up guy and a stickler for safety. In short, there will be a ton of legal work. It will require close coordination. The work will be intense and all-consuming. But this is a 'bet the company' case, and Black Bear needs the best lawyering it can get. You'll be a partner soon, Jessie. I want you to lead and coordinate the defense. If you perform as I know you will, the rewards to you and Watson Worthy will be off the charts."

Jessie went through the motions for the rest of the dinner. She was in a deep, dark hole with no way out, and things got worse with every word out of Karen's mouth. She knew Sam would be heading up the prosecution, if there was one, and now her main client and major booster had asked her to lead the defense. *No way*, she thought—she wouldn't represent Black Bear, and she wouldn't take on her best friend in very public, very nasty, take-no-prisoners litigation. But how could she not? Instinctively, she knew everything she had worked for was at risk if she said no. It was too much to lose. She couldn't say no. But she couldn't, and wouldn't, do this. Where was the way out? She couldn't find it. She needed time to think.

She laid the problem out to Jimmy when she got home, thankful he wasn't on a business trip. He had a calm demeanor and an analytic mind. Talking it through with him helped settle her down.

"Obviously, this is your life and your call," Jimmy said. "Let me just tell you how it looks to me. I love you, and I guess that means I'm not an objective observer. But I am more objective than you are. First question: When does Karen need your answer?"

"She's not expecting an answer. She's assuming I'll do this, as I would in the normal course. In her mind, she's given me the assignment and I've accepted it. Things will move forward until I stop them. The burden is on me to do that."

"It's Thursday night. Is anything going to happen before Monday?"

"No, it shouldn't," Jessie said. "Are you thinking what I think you are?"

"Yup. I've got flexibility tomorrow. Let's get out of here early and head down to the cottage for the weekend. We can relax down there and chew our way through this thing in a less pressured way. Hopefully, we'll come up with a plan."

The "cottage" was in fact a small barn they had bought three years earlier and converted into a three-bedroom house. It was outside Charlottesville in the town of Crozet. They had put time and effort into the conversion and were delighted with the result. They loved the place, with its big stone fireplace, heart-pine floors, oriental rugs, leather furniture, and contemporary art. They loved sitting on the back deck, enjoying the firepit in the cooler months and being mesmerized year-round by the cedar grove and running brook below. It was an escape from their crazy, busy everyday lives, and they went whenever they could.

They arrived at the cottage the next afternoon, and Jessie immediately felt better. They gave themselves over to the tranquility of the place, had a quiet dinner in town, and left Jessie's problem for the next day. It only came up once, when they were sitting at the firepit.

"I assume representing Black Bear is a nonstarter for you," Jimmy said. "I know there's also the question about litigating against Sam, but that issue goes away if you don't represent Black Bear."

"Yes, that's right," said Jessie. "If I don't represent Black Bear, that takes care of the Sam issue. And I just can't represent Black Bear. That would be disloyal to my family and all the people I grew up with in Owl Hollow. Sam would never forgive me, and I couldn't blame her. It would end our friendship. I can't be that person."

"You're not that person, Jess. That's why I love you."

"But it's so much to give up. It's everything."

"Let's talk about it tomorrow. It'll keep until then."

They took it up the next day over pulled pork sandwiches and red potato salad from their favorite deli. They had also picked up a decent red, a big one, from one of the vineyards in neighboring Barboursville. Tasting it, Jimmy remarked, "This isn't half bad. It's not as good as what my folks make, but it works."

He looked over at Jessie, assessing her. "Shall we talk?" he asked.

"Yes, we have to. It was a good idea to come down here. I'm in a better place, and I'm ready to work through this."

"Let's try to narrow things down a bit. We agreed last night that you're not going to represent Black Bear. That leaves us with the questions of who to tell and how to deliver the message."

"Yes," sighed Jessie. "Those are the right questions. They're big ones."

"Before we get into them, let me ask this. If this thing goes south, what's the worst that can happen?"

"I'm sure my making partner this year is out the window. Karen's supporting my partnership, in fact she's driving it, but she's a vindictive person. I don't see her continuing to back me if I tell her no."

"But Jason's on your side, right? As is Pudge? They're the name partners at the firm. Wouldn't this be their call?"

"It really boils down to whether Jason would put me up without Karen's support. It would be his decision because most of my work is for Sand Ridge and he's the responsible partner. Pudge would be supportive, no doubt, but he'd defer to Jason and properly so."

"How do you see it playing out? If Karen turns on you, would Jason stand up to her?"

"He might give it a half-hearted shot, but if push comes to shove, he won't buck her. Karen's business is too important to him. As I said before, she's vindictive, and Jason knows that."

"So, what would that mean?" Jimmy asked thoughtfully. "Presumably, you'd have to wait a couple more years to make partner. Or would you have to leave the firm?"

"I don't think I'd have to leave the firm. I've done good work there, and my saying no to this assignment might anger Karen, but it's not dishonest or immoral. I can't see them forcing me out. But now that I've been counting on making partner this year, it would be hard for me to wait two more years. There are other complications as well. Karen almost certainly wouldn't want me working for Sand Ridge anymore, which would mean I'd have to find work elsewhere and develop a new champion in the partnership other than Jason."

"What a mess," Jimmy mused. "Essentially starting over in year six would be tough, and if you stopped working for Sand Ridge, everyone would know something had gone down between you and Karen. It's still a relatively small firm. Losing your name partner sponsor wouldn't be pretty either. Doesn't sound like much fun, all in all. Would you want to stay under those circumstances?"

"I honestly don't know. There are great people there. I've learned how to be a lawyer there, and a good one. I have a place there. It's a lot to give up. But on the other side, I'd be seen as damaged goods. If I left, I'm not sure I'd want to go to another law firm. I'd have to think about that. If I didn't, it would mean a pay cut."

"Fortunately, we're in a position to absorb it. Let's take that issue off the table and focus on how we manage this to come out with the best result."

"I'm all ears, Jimmy. I've been racking my brain and coming up empty."

"Let's talk about process and then the message. Do you have the conversation with Karen? Or do you have it with Jason and let him manage it with Karen?"

"Karen," Jessie said unequivocally. "I give Jason a heads-up, and maybe Pudge, too, since he's a name partner and a friend, but Karen is the principal. I have to have the conversation with her."

"I agree. And when do you have it?"

"Monday. This isn't going to get better, or easier, by putting it off."

"Agreed. That leaves the message itself. The best way to have a hard conversation, in my judgment, is to be direct and honest. Go right at it, be sure she understands your decision is compelled by the unique personal circumstances at play here, and you would love to do this work if that were not the case."

"I think that's exactly the right approach," said Jessie.

"You know, Karen may be vindictive, but I have to believe most people in this world, deep down, are empathetic and decent. We're all human beings, and that gives us the ability to understand each other. If she gets why you can't do this, as a matter of deep and very personal conviction, maybe this will all work out. She knows how hard you've worked for her in the past. She knows the results you've delivered. She knows you've never begged off an assignment before and never will again. Maybe she'll give you a pass this one time."

"Let's hope so," Jessie said, kissing him softly. "Thanks for helping me through this. Thanks for being here for me."

She felt better. But then she thought back to what Karen had said at the end of their celebratory dinner, and back to Pudge's story. She loved Jimmy's optimism and humanity, but he didn't know Karen. This wasn't going to be easy.

CHAPTER TWENTY-SEVEN

Monday morning came too soon. Jessie was in the office at first light. She went to see Pudge. He was an early bird and would be the most sympathetic of the three people she had to see today. She filled him in on her dinner with Karen and the course of action she had settled on.

Pudge listened attentively, with evident discomfort. "Ouch," he said when Jessie finished. "Karen isn't going to like this one bit. Having said that, I think your decision not to take this representation is the right one, and I admire you for it. You're also handling it exactly the right way. I'll be pulling for you."

"Thanks, Pudge. Your support means a lot to me."

Jason was her next stop. She went to his office when he arrived forty-five minutes later. After hearing Jessie out, he just sat there, staring out the window. He was looking for a solution that wouldn't come.

"I don't know what to say," he finally offered. "I understand the position you're in, and I honestly can't fault your decision. With most people, this would go down, hard maybe, but it would go down. But Karen, well, Karen isn't most people. You know that."

"Any suggestions?"

"Is there any chance you'd reconsider?"

"No. I won't represent Black Bear."

"We all make choices in life. You've got to do what's right for you. Good luck. Let me know how it goes."

After leaving Jason's office, Jessie called Karen's secretary and requested an urgent meeting. Karen had an opening at 11:00. She was agitated when Jessie arrived.

"What's wrong? It's not like you to want to meet on a moment's notice unless there's a problem. Is there a problem? What's going on?"

"I can't do it, Karen. I'm sorry, but I just can't."

"Can't do what?"

"I can't represent Black Bear Mining. My father worked at Merriman No. 3, a Black Bear mine, his entire adult life. He was badly injured in a roof fall. He broke his back and lost a leg. He died a few years later because of complications from those injuries. There's reason to believe the accident was caused by Black Bear's negligence."

"I see where you're coming from, and I know how hard it is to lose a parent. We all try to find someone to blame. But I think you're being harsh in choosing to blame Black Bear. We had extensive conversations before the acquisition, and George Rafferty satisfied us, beyond any doubt, that the safety of the miners is Black Bear's highest priority."

"I'd like to believe that, because I would take this representation in a heartbeat if I possibly could. But I grew up at Merriman No. 3, living in a Black Bear company town. My friends and neighbors were Black Bear miners and their families. Several of the miners carried injuries, some quite nasty, from working in the mine. I would do anything for you, and I appreciate everything you've done for me, but I can't do this."

"I wish you'd take some time to reconsider. This is a big opportunity for you."

"It wouldn't make any difference. This is too deep and personal. I can't do it."

"You can't or you won't?"

"Both. I'm sorry."

"Then we're done," said Karen. "I warned you never to cross me."

"I'm not crossing you. I absolutely would do this if I could. But I can't betray my father's memory and the people I grew up with."

"I don't want you handling any matters for Sand Ridge, now or in the future. I'll call Jason and have him transition you off all Sand Ridge cases immediately. Good-bye, Jessie."

"I'm so sorry, Karen." There was no reply. Karen had swiveled her chair around and was on the intercom, telling her secretary to get Jason Worthy on the phone.

Jessie didn't return to her office until early that afternoon. She needed time to decompress, to collect herself. She wanted to call Jimmy, but before doing so, she had to be alone, to take a long walk, to think. That had gone as badly as she feared it would. *Let's hope*, she thought, *that it won't be even worse when it all gets sorted out.* She was sick at heart, yet oddly at peace. She had made a hard choice and done the right thing. Whatever was to come, she could live with herself.

When she reached Jimmy, all he could say was, "I feel so badly for you. I didn't think anyone could be that heartless. Come home early tonight. I'm going to pour some alcohol in you and take you out to dinner."

When she went to see Jason, he quickly said, "I've heard all about it."

"Does she have any give, or will she in time?" asked Jessie.

"Not an inch. She's transferring all your Sand Ridge work and pulling her support for your partnership. I tried to talk sense into her, but she wouldn't hear it. She views your refusal to represent Black Bear as a personal attack on her."

"But it isn't, not at all. I tried to make that clear."

"I know. But there are some things in this world you can't fight, and Karen's one of them."

"Is she pulling her partnership support for this year, or forever?"

"Forever, I'm afraid. And it's worse than that. She wants you out of the firm."

"What? I can't believe it. Is there anything you and Pudge can do to stop it? This is your firm, not hers. You founded it and you run it."

"I haven't talked to Pudge yet, but we're in a tough position. You're a terrific lawyer, one of the best we've ever had, and you've given the firm—and Karen, for that matter—your heart and soul. But Karen is pissed and she's vengeful. Sand Ridge accounts for about twenty percent of the firm's business. If Karen takes the work elsewhere, it will hurt a lot of people here. I'll talk to Pudge, but from my perspective, the best we can do is give you three months to find something else. And needless to say, we'll give you strong references. I'm sorry. I wish there were a better solution, but I don't see one."

In a daze, Jessie went to see Pudge. She quickly brought him up to date. He was sympathetic.

"Unfortunately, I think Jason's analysis of the situation is right. If the firm suddenly lost twenty percent of its business, we'd have to lay some people off, people who depend on us. I hate it that we, and mostly you, are in this situation because of Karen's irrational behavior. There will be payback for her pettiness and hatred someday. I believe that and devoutly pray for it. But in the meantime, let's talk about the predicament we're in and try to find the best way out."

"I'm sorry to be putting you and the firm in this position, Pudge. I truly am."

"You shouldn't be sorry for acting on principle. This is Karen's doing, not yours. Look, I have no doubt I could get Jason to agree to six months instead of three, and we could sell it to Karen without risking the loss of her business. That would take some pressure off you. But what I keep wondering is why you would want to stay here, even for six months. There will be a lasting stench to this thing. Everyone here will know about it. Some will admire what you did, some may blame you, many will pity you. This place won't be the same for you, and my guess is you'd hate every minute you were here. You're a first-rate lawyer with a terrific record, and you could have your pick of law firms. Why wouldn't you want to do that instead?"

"I don't know, Pudge. This is all so sudden, I just don't know what to think."

Jessie talked to Jimmy that night. She resigned from Watson Worthy the following morning. Then she drove down to the cottage to think about what she would do with the rest of her life.

CHAPTER TWENTY-EIGHT

Sam was working hard when Jessie called. The federal Mine Safety and Health Administration was investigating the Rebel Yell explosion and had a long way to go. They had gotten a late start because toxic gases were present in the mine for several weeks after the explosion. Sam was following their investigation with interest, but she had her own investigation to worry about. MSHA was looking into safety violations that might have occurred; it would assess civil penalties for the violations it found. On behalf of the US Attorney's Office, Sam was looking into criminal charges.

Jessie's news diverted Sam from her work preoccupation. She was shocked and upset. Jessie had had a few days since leaving Watson Worthy to digest the change in her life and was actually calmer than Sam was. Sam didn't have time for this, not right now, but she made the time to spend a day with Jessie. She would always be there for her.

This wasn't a leisurely visit, and they jumped right into Jessie's situation when Sam arrived at the cottage. Being a lawyer, and a litigator at that, Sam pushed Jessie to look into some sort of a claim against the law firm, or Karen, or both.

"There's no basis for a claim, you know that," Jessie said, laughing at Sam's instinct to take her side no matter what.

"Why not? You suffered a wrong, and wrongs are redressable in the courts. Surely you can figure out some theory or other." Sam was laughing too. They both knew it was bullshit.

"This is just one of those things. I happened to get stuck with a weirdo for a client. She must have had some bad things happen in her life to make her as paranoid and narcissistic as she is. I just have to move on. Besides, I don't want to burn any bridges with the firm. They've been good to me."

"They've been good to you? You were a star, and they were too gutless to stand up for you. They told you to leave."

"There were reasons for that. I understand where they were coming from."

"What are you going to do?"

"I honestly have no idea. My job right now is to figure that out, and I plan to take my time doing it. Fortunately, I have that luxury because Jimmy's doing well. He's been wonderful through all of this, by the way."

"Good to hear. Are you going to be looking at law firms, either in Washington or maybe here in Charlottesville?"

"I don't know. I'm not sure I want to practice law anymore. I'll think about it, and maybe do some interviewing, but I'm two-for-two having bad experiences at law firms, even though the second one was great until it wasn't. In the big firm model, you're a cog in a machine. In the smaller firm model, management can't protect you from a screwy client with an outsized say. I know I can't generalize because Karen is one of a kind and what happened to me likely wouldn't happen again. But it's all left a bad taste in my mouth. Maybe it's time to try something else."

"Well, you have to figure it out. As lovely as the cottage is, the Jessie Macaulay I know isn't going to be content just sitting here."

Suddenly, Jessie had an inspiration. "You know what I might want to do? I might like to be a judge."

"You can't just be a judge. Someone has to elect you or appoint you or something. Do you know how it works?"

"Not a clue. I just thought of it. It might be fun to be a judge."

Things had a way of working out for Jessie. She had an unexpected call a few weeks later. No one was offering her a judgeship, but her question about what to do next was about to be answered. When she picked up the phone, she heard a woman's voice.

"Jessie, this is Nell Richmond. I'm the dean of the law school at the University of Virginia."

"Yes, Dean Richmond. I know of you. You have a fine reputation."

"Why, thank you, and please call me Nell. You, too, have a fine reputation. I reached out to an old and dear friend yesterday, Pudge Watson. I have an important position to fill, and I thought Pudge might have some ideas. Indeed, he did. He thinks the world of you. He says you're one of the finest young lawyers and litigators he knows, and, furthermore, that you happen to be between jobs right now. I wanted to see if we might get together to talk about it."

"I'd love to, Nell. If I'm a good lawyer, Pudge has to take some responsibility. I worked on several cases with him, and he was a brilliant teacher. He's also a wonderful guy." To say nothing of a good kisser, but Jessie left that part out. "What is the position you're trying to fill?"

"Professor Ed Barnett has taught courses in evidence and trial practice for many years now. He has quite a following and is an icon at the school. Ed told me recently that he plans to retire, and this coming academic year, beginning in August, will be his last. I'm looking for someone to assist him, to co-teach his courses if you will, starting in August, with an eye to taking them over the following year."

"That sounds fascinating. I'd love to hear more about it."

"Good," said Nell. "I have to warn you, Ed will leave big shoes to fill."

Jessie tried on Ed's shoes when August came around. They were big, but she would grow into them.

CHAPTER TWENTY-NINE

Dr. Emma Mancini had done her part. Now it was up to the rest of the team. Two more weeks had passed. It was early May. *At least we won't have any more "April" poetry,* Scott thought with a grin as he headed off to catch up with Deputies Tom Mahaffey and Angelo Jones.

He started with Angelo. "Did you talk to Kate Strange? And?"

"I did. She's a very nice lady. I got to know Slouch too." Angelo then described his conversation with Kate in detail. He talked about how she and Worthy met, how the relationship developed, how they spent a lot of time together at Justice Hill over a period of almost three years, and how things ended.

"So, what are your major takeaways?" Scott wanted to know.

"First, she was at Justice Hill the morning Worthy was killed. And she had a key to the place."

"That's important," Scott interrupted. "So far, we haven't been able to place anyone else there. And her having a key could explain why there were no signs of forcible entry."

"Second, she loved Worthy and was deeply hurt when he ended the relationship. That punches the motive card."

"Go on," urged Scott.

"What else can I say? Those are big things. I don't think she did it, though."

"Because?"

"Because she just doesn't seem the type that would kill someone. She has to know what it looks like for her, but she wasn't at all defensive. She was very cool. She's a tree hugger, for God's sake. Tree huggers don't kill people."

"Don't be too sure about that, hotshot. You're too young to remember this, but there was a time when tree huggers, the ones on the fringe anyway, would drive timber spikes into redwood trees, far in so they couldn't be seen. They were trying to injure people who were cutting the trees or sawing the logs. I remember one guy was seriously hurt when his band saw hit a metal spike and exploded. The point is this: anyone who has a cause, or a motive, and believes in it deeply, is capable of doing things you wouldn't think possible. We need to stick to hard evidence."

"Fair enough," Angelo said. "On the hard evidence front, Kate told me she went to Justice Hill to pick up a necklace she had left there. It had been her mother's, and it was important to her. She went that morning because she had been at a conference at the Homestead the day before. The conference was followed by a dinner, and the attendees stayed overnight. I contacted the Homestead, and what she says checks out. She was a registered guest at the conference and had a room for the night. She checked out of the hotel, in person, at 6:15 the next morning."

"That does show she was in the neighborhood," said Scott. "It also shows she left the hotel after the murder was committed. It's not an ironclad alibi, though, because she could have left the hotel in the wee hours, killed Worthy, and then returned to the hotel in time to clean up and check out at 6:15."

"It would have taken someone very calculating to do all that in order to provide an alibi," Angelo commented. "She doesn't strike me as the type."

"Here we go again with the heartstrings," Scott countered. "One of these days, you'll learn that premeditated murders are done by calculating people. By the way, we also don't know why she went to Justice Hill in the morning, other than taking her word for the necklace story. You got anything else?"

"Just one thing. She said Worthy was a bourbon drinker. He liked a brand called Widow Jane. That doesn't mean he didn't also like single malt scotch, but it does cast doubt on the theory that he was a regular Laphroaig drinker. To me, that increases the likelihood that whoever visited him that night brought the Laphroaig."

"Good work, Angelo. We'll make a deputy out of you yet. Tom, what's new at your end?"

"Well, we still don't have matches for the hair sample or the partial fingerprints on the box cutter. That's because we don't have any suspects. Or maybe we do now, based on Angelo's report. Do you think we can get DNA and fingerprint samples from Kate without issuing a subpoena?"

"Well, since Deputy Jones is such good buddies with her, he could pay her another visit and try to leave with a paper cup or a napkin or something else she's tossed out that has her DNA and fingerprints on it. They do that on TV, so it must work. Or he could be straight up and ask if she would give us those samples so we can rule her out as a suspect. He says she isn't defensive, so it might work."

"She isn't defensive, but that would get anyone's antenna up," Angelo said. "I'd prefer to do it that way, though, rather than trying to take something surreptitiously. What if it doesn't work? What if she says no?"

"Then we're no worse off than we are now. We can always go the subpoena route. What else, Tom?"

"We're making slow progress on the chain saw. Hammersmith uses serial numbers that are ten digits long. The serial number on the saw next to Worthy's body was really old. The last two digits are totally worn away, and the third-to-last is partially worn away. It looks like a 3 or an 8. The people at Hammersmith are trying to match their shipping records against the digits we know in the serial number on our saw, plus the possible combinations for the digits we don't know."

"When we're talking two or maybe three unknown digits, that's a lot of possible combinations," Scott observed.

"Yes, but not as many as you might think. They have records of the serial numbers on the saws they made, and they didn't use every possible combination of digits. So, they only have to check the possible combinations of digits they actually used. It's still a lot of combinations, but it's not unmanageable."

"How long a process is this? What do they know so far?"

"They're down to nine possible serial numbers that might belong to our saw. In other words, the serial number on the saw that killed Worthy will be one of those nine numbers."

"And where does that get us?"

"Four of those numbers were on saws shipped to Georgia, two were on saws shipped to West Virginia, and the other three went to Pennsylvania, Kentucky, and Virginia."

"Meaning the saw that killed Worthy was bought thirty or thirty-five years ago by someone in one of those states?"

"Yup. And it could have been sold, or stolen, or loaned out many times between then and now. It could literally have gone anywhere before ending up at Justice Hill. Still, it's a starting point."

Scott smiled. "Better than a poke in the eye with a sharp stick. Good work, Tom. Given where the murder occurred, I'd start digging into the sales that went to Virginia and West Virginia."

CHAPTER THIRTY

There are many ways to get hurt in an underground coal mine. As workplaces go, a mine is a uniquely hostile environment.

Imagine working in a tunnel several hundred feet below the surface of the earth. It is black, pitch-black. There are some lights where machines are at work or equipment is located, but otherwise, the only light source is the cap lamp attached to a miner's hard hat.

Imagine the downward pressure from the millions of tons of earth above, trying to collapse the tunnel. Roof falls are the number one killer of coal miners. Controlling the roof so it doesn't fall is a tremendous engineering and safety challenge. In a "room and pillar" mining operation, large pillars of coal are left in place to support the roof. In the rooms, which are open areas where the mining has been done, large roof bolts, which operate something like toggle bolts, are used at frequent intervals to hold the roof together and keep it from falling.

Imagine a workplace so large that it extends for miles in every direction. It is like a street map of Manhattan, a grid with avenues running north-south and streets running east-west. The city blocks where buildings would be in Manhattan are pillars of coal. The streets and avenues are entries; these are the open spaces created by mining the coal.

In most mines, there are railroad tracks that run here and there to move men and equipment. There are large conveyor belts that carry the coal from the working faces where it's mined to an outside location where it will be processed. There is enough electricity in the mine to power a small city. The mining activity generally runs three shifts a day, seven days a week.

In room and pillar mining, the method used at Rebel Yell, the tunnel is made by long machines called continuous miners. They scrape the coal seam in front of them using large rotating steel drums with tungsten carbide teeth. They can mine five tons of coal a minute. As the coal breaks loose and falls, it is scooped by large gathering arms onto an internal conveyor belt that moves it to the rear of the machine, where it transfers to a shuttle car that will take it to the conveyor belt to be carried out of the mine.

The working faces, where the continuous mining machines scrape the coal from the seam, are particularly dangerous. The scraping process generates clouds of highly explosive coal dust that floats in the air before settling. It also liberates methane, a gas that is even more explosive. A spark generated in the mining process can easily cause methane to ignite, which in turn can ignite the coal dust and intensify the explosion.

Roof falls are the number one killer of coal miners, but they take their victims one or two at a time. Mine explosions usually cause multiple fatalities. They frequently leave miners trapped, sometimes for days, while rescue operations frantically try to reach them before they run out of air.

The federal mine safety laws exhaustively regulate all aspects of underground coal mining, but their comprehensive and detailed focus on minimizing the risk of mine explosions is notable. They impose numerous ventilation requirements to isolate the methane from possible ignition sources. They require that rock dust, an inert substance that neutralizes the explosive qualities of coal dust, be generously applied to the roof, ribs, and floor of the mine and maintained to within forty feet of the working faces. They mandate a complex and overlapping system of pre-shift and on-shift examinations to test for methane and other hazardous conditions. If methane is found at certain levels, all equipment must be shut off; at greater levels, miners must be withdrawn until safe levels are restored. These examinations are generally made by shift foremen, whose reports must be reviewed and countersigned by the mine foreman. The records must be kept on the surface of the mine for at least a year.

On February 27, 2008, the federal Mine Safety and Health Administration issued its long-awaited report on its investigation of the explosion at the Rebel Yell Mine. It was a damning indictment of Black Bear Mining Company. In all, MSHA issued 296 violations and assessed civil penalties running into the millions of dollars. Some of the violations were silly, like having an inadequate supply of toilet paper. Some were serious but unrelated to the explosion, like improper spacing of roof bolts. But most of the violations, including the fourteen that were issued as flagrant, related to Black Bear's ventilation practices, rock dusting, and methane testing and control. The report concluded that eleven of the flagrant violations "either caused or directly contributed to the explosion that took the lives of five miners on October 13, 2006."

The seven-hundred-page report held back little in excoriating Black Bear "and its management at all levels, including the highest levels," although it never mentioned George Rafferty by name. It said that MSHA had investigated hundreds of mine disasters and had never before encountered "the reckless and cavalier disregard for the safety, and indeed the very lives, of the miners" that existed at Rebel Yell. Undergirding that disregard, it continued, was a "deeply ingrained culture that weighed productivity and profit far more heavily than the well-being of the employees who worked in the Company's mines." The failures of management were so pervasive and pernicious that this tragic result was "almost inevitable."

The specifics were equally detailed and devastating. The ventilation plan, which MSHA had approved, was not being followed, and the practices Black Bear was using were "hopelessly inadequate and inappropriate for a gassy mine like Rebel Yell." Rock dust had been applied but "much too sparsely and in many places, it was at least twenty feet farther from the working faces than the law requires." The mine foreman and the shift foremen appeared to regard the pre-shift and on-shift examination requirements "as optional rather than mandatory." There was evidence that reports of examinations were often filled out in the mine office "as a paper exercise, without the actual examinations having been made." There were also irregularities in the countersignatures of the mine foreman, suggesting that some "catch-up signing had been done" after the explosion but before the investigation began.

It was a dire assessment that painted a picture of negligence, to be sure, but more than that, of a chronic and willful disregard of the mine safety laws. Herschel Watts, the highly respected and straight-talking head of MSHA, did not back down when he was interviewed about the report on national television. When asked to sum up his views about the operation at Rebel Yell, he said, "It was shameful. There are many responsible coal operators out there, but our investigation showed that Black Bear isn't one of them. In my opinion, heads should roll, and there are some people who ought to go to jail."

That was where Sam came in.

CHAPTER THIRTY-ONE

Sam was leading the investigation, but the US Attorney himself, Pete Gage, was right there with her. They were more convinced than ever that Black Bear's wink-and-a-nod approach to compliance with the mine safety laws was directed by George Rafferty, and they badly wanted to take him down. The problem was that George was smart; he knew how to cover his tracks. He was like the head of a mob family. He didn't give direct orders, but his lieutenants, many of whom had been with him for years, knew how to interpret what he was saying. They knew what he wanted done, and they did it. The system worked well for George because he maintained deniability.

The same could not be said for his stooges at Rebel Yell. Mark Livingston, the mine foreman, was definitely going down. So were shift foreman Lefty Williams and one of the section foremen, Paul "Chicken Legs" Mulhern. All three had been implicated, again and again, in the interviews Sam's office conducted of some eighty Rebel Yell miners. Sam had participated in some of those interviews, but most were done by her investigator, Rick Jackson.

The miners they talked to all lost friends in the explosion, and some were among the lucky ones who were in the mine but managed to get out. They knew about the practices at Rebel Yell, how safety was sacrificed for coal production, and they were not about to cover up for management now that the chickens had come home to roost. Five of their friends had paid the ultimate price, and management's bill was due. Telling Rick and Sam what was really going on at the mine, they believed, might finally cause things to change for the better.

The interview notes told the story. Rick had learned shorthand early in his career and he typed his notes up to read like transcripts. Sam looked at his interview notes for miner Sam Stalworth.

JACKSON: What's your job in the mine, Sam?

STALWORTH: I'm a shuttle car operator.

JACKSON: Did you ever get instructions or guidance from your section foreman?

STALWORTH: Yes sir. He always told us run the coal, run the coal, run the coal.

JACKSON: What did that mean?

STALWORTH: Keep on mining. Our job is to mine as much as we can.

JACKSON: Did he ever instruct you about safety practices?

STALWORTH: No sir. He didn't seem to care so much about that. I remember one time I told him I needed to stop loading coal because the rock dust was too far back, and we needed to give it a chance to catch up.

JACKSON: What did he say to that?

STALWORTH: Run the coal. Don't worry about that, just keep on running coal.

JACKSON: Who was your section boss?

STALWORTH: Chicken Legs.

JACKSON: Is that Paul Mulhern?

STALWORTH: Yes sir.

JACKSON: Why do you call him Chicken Legs?

STALWORTH: Everyone does. That's his name. I'm not for sure why. I guess because he walks like a chicken.

JACKSON: The instructions you got from Mr. Mulhern to just run the coal, do you know if that was his idea, or did it come from higher up?

STALWORTH: I'm pretty sure it came from higher up. My buddies who worked on other sections were getting the same instructions from their bosses.

Sam put Stalworth aside and picked up the notes of Rick's interview of continuous miner operator Harold Miller.

JACKSON: You've told me that shift foreman Williams didn't always make his pre-shift examinations. What do you base that on?

MILLER: He's supposed to make those examinations within three hours before the shift change. But he was on the surface with us instead of in the mine. He rode in on the mantrip with us when the shift started. So, he couldn't have made the exams.

JACKSON: How many times did that happen?

MILLER: Lots of times. It was common knowledge. Lefty would even admit it, he'd say it was all bullshit, and he'd laugh about it.

JACKSON: But there are records showing he made the examinations.

MILLER: I don't know about the records, but he didn't make the examinations.

JACKSON: Do you know whether the mine foreman, Mr. Livingston, knew that Mr. Williams wasn't making the examinations?

MILLER: I'm pretty sure he didn't care. Mark Livingston used to tell the section bosses, hell, he used to tell all of us, that the law requires MSHA to inspect our mine four times a year. We have to be on our best behavior when the inspectors are here, and we have to be sure our records show we're doing the things we're supposed to be doing. When the inspectors aren't here, we run the coal.

JACKSON: Were those his exact words, "We run the coal"?

MILLER: Yes sir, that's what he said. He also told us at one meeting in 2006, a couple of months before the explosion, that we were getting great tonnage out of the mine, and if we set a new productivity record for the year, we'd all get bonuses.

JACKSON: Do you know who made the decisions about productivity bonuses? Was that Mr. Livingston? Or Mr. Rafferty?

MILLER: I'd say it was Mark. I never heard anything about it being Mr. Rafferty.

Most of the other interview notes read the same way. The miners were willing to testify at trial. Sam could easily get convictions of Mark, Lefty, and Chicken Legs for, at a minimum, willful violations of mine safety laws and falsification of records. The challenge was to tie their misdeeds to George Rafferty. He was the one Sam wanted. These guys were only doing his bidding. Sam knew it, but she couldn't prove it. She had to get these guys to flip on George, either by offering a sweet plea deal or, if necessary, granting immunity.

Chicken Legs Mulhern would be the easiest to break, but the one Sam really needed was Mark Livingston. He was a longtime coal miner and had been the mine foreman at Rebel Yell for eleven years. He would have had the most exposure to George, and he was the one George would most likely have confided in. He had been with George for many years and would know him far better than Chicken Legs or Lefty did. By the same token, he was into this thing the deepest and, given his close relationship with George, it was reasonable to assume George had taken good care of Mark and his family. Now it was Mark's turn to take care of George, and he would go the extra mile to do that. Turning him would not be easy.

Sam had to crank up the heat.

CHAPTER THIRTY-TWO

Bill Picken was a different man. The investigation into the Rebel Yell explosion, coupled with Sam's investigation into possible criminal charges against Black Bear and George Rafferty, had given him focus and brought him back from the living dead. He had stopped drinking altogether. He now got up each morning, showered and shaved, ate breakfast, and went to work. He had taken a job managing a McDonald's franchise. Having been a section foreman in a coal mine, he found that running a burger joint was easy. It was also fun.

Sam tried to think of what it was about the investigation that had jolted her dad out of his endless slide. She had told him long ago that Big Joe's accident was Black Bear's fault, not his. He was wallowing in a sea of guilt and self-pity at the time and brushed off her comment. But he had thought about it, she believed, and had come to the point of finding it credible. After all, he knew who George Rafferty was, and he knew how Black Bear operated.

Then when Rebel Yell blew up and the investigations started, Bill was energized. He felt he had a personal stake in the outcome. If MSHA determined that the miners' deaths weren't just an accident but were in fact caused by Black Bear's pattern of disregarding safety requirements, then maybe the same held true for Big Joe's accident. Maybe it wasn't his fault after all. If that were so, he had wasted years of his life and put his wife through hell because he had incorrectly seen Black Bear's safety lapses as his personal failure.

Bill read the seven-hundred-page MSHA report on the explosion three times. He read it with a highlighter and made notes in the margins. He often nodded as he read, noting the similarities between the MSHA findings and his own recollections of how Black Bear had operated at Merriman No. 3. When he finished his third reading, he knew the report as well as the MSHA people who wrote it. He saw the Herschel Watts interview on television and cheered him on, feeling an angry pleasure that, finally, someone had the guts to call out Black Bear and George Rafferty for what they were. Most of all, he felt vindicated, and alive.

Bill was Sam's biggest cheerleader as she worked to put together her case against George Rafferty. She couldn't talk to Bill about the case, but she found it useful to hear his stories about Black Bear's practices at Merriman No. 3, like the lavish weeklong vacations at George's hunting preserve that were given to reward productivity, or the time he shut his section down because of a high methane reading and was chewed out by the mine foreman for doing so, or the many times he and others were ordered to lie to the MSHA inspectors to make everything look rosy. It was good stuff and confirmed Sam's belief that she was right to be on George's tail. She couldn't use Bill as a witness because the things he knew happened long ago at a different mine, and she wouldn't have put him in that position anyway. But his input was a valuable road map of Black Bear's approach to coal mining. It provided solid leads about questions she should ask the Rebel Yell miners as she was building her case.

Sam loved having her dad back and experiencing his resurrection. She was particularly grateful that it gave Chris the opportunity to know the Bill Picken she had known growing up, and not just the shell that he had been ever since she and Chris first met. Chris and Bill turned out to have some things in common, hard work and military service among them, and they actually became great friends.

Sadly, the new and improved Bill Picken arrived too late for his wife to enjoy for very long. That great lady died in the summer of 2008. After years of unbearable sadness and strain, she was able, through God's grace, to know the joy of her husband's rebirth before she departed. Whatever the medical cause of her mom's death, Sam believed she died of being plumb worn out.

There was a small gathering in Blacksburg to remember her, to celebrate her life and honor her death. Jessie and Jimmy came down. As a nice touch, Jessie's mother, Jessie Farrell Spaulding, came from Owl Hollow. She and Bill had not seen each other since Big Joe's accident. It was a poignant moment.

"Thank you for coming, Jessie," Bill said, taking her hand. "I'm sorry I wasn't there for Big Joe's service. He was the best man I've ever known."

"It's all right, Bill," she said. "Yes, my Joe was a good man and a hell of a lot of fun. Joe and I loved your family, and I wanted to be here today."

"You're very kind. I haven't been much of a friend. I've stopped blaming myself for Joe's injuries, but it's taken many long years. I know I put all of us, and especially my wife, through enormous difficulty and pain for a long time. I can't apologize enough for that."

"We're all so pleased you've come out the other end. You look great! I'm sorry Joe isn't here to see you, but I'm sure he's watching from somewhere."

They talked on, enjoying their reunion. Bill was reminded of the close friendships in Owl Hollow, none closer than the friendship between the Spaulding and Picken families.

Bill and Jessie Farrell Spaulding kept in touch after the service ended and everyone went their separate ways. The hole created by the death of a spouse is not easily filled, but the loneliness is occasionally addressed by joining forces with an old and trusted friend. In the spring of 2009, Jessie's mother and Sam's father were married. It seemed a little weird, but not totally. She sold the house in Owl Hollow, smiling at the memories as she walked out the door for the last time. Protesting that he was "too old for this stuff," Bill paid three students at Tech to help him move the Spaulding family belongings to his place in Blacksburg.

The move would be more consequential than Bill could have imagined.

CHAPTER THIRTY-THREE

It took a few months before Mark Livingston agreed to roll over on George Rafferty. The grand jury had indicted Livingston, along with Lefty Williams and Chicken Legs Mulhern, on two counts: willfully violating mandatory mine safety standards and making false statements and certifications in records required by the Mine Safety and Health Act. It had also indicted Livingston on the additional counts of bribing a public official and conspiring to violate mine safety laws. All three of the men were looking at prison time, Livingston more than the others because of the extra charges.

Sam didn't expect to have to go to trial in the Williams and Mulhern cases. She didn't push hard to turn them because they couldn't give her enough to get Rafferty. In all likelihood, they would plead out, and Sam would recommend a reduced sentence, something on the order of a year in prison. She wasn't out to crucify them, but their guilty pleas were important. With those in hand, George Rafferty would go to trial in a context where willful violations and falsified records by Rebel Yell's management had already been established.

Livingston was a different story. Sam thought he could bring down Rafferty. She had added the extra charges in his case because they got her closer to Rafferty. She had solid evidence that Livingston had bribed, or attempted to bribe, an MSHA inspector named Bill Bevans. There was a good likelihood that he had done so at Rafferty's direction, or at least with his knowledge. She charged Livingston with the conspiracy count because she believed he was working with Rafferty, or at his direction, to violate mine safety laws; until she had grounds to indict Rafferty, she was treating him as an unindicted coconspirator. He wasn't named in the Livingston indictment, but everyone knew the unindicted coconspirator was Rafferty.

The charging power of a US Attorney is a formidable weapon. The indictment comes from the grand jury; it wears the mantle of fairness because the grand jurors are ordinary citizens who act on the evidence before them. The catch is that the only evidence before them comes from the prosecution. The defense is not allowed to give evidence or even be present at the proceedings. It is a one-sided affair, a rigged system. As long as Sam acted with integrity and within reason, the grand jury would indict on two counts if that's what she asked for, and it would indict on ten if that's what she wanted. She could easily secure grand jury indictments on a number of counts that, upon conviction, would add up to a lot of prison time.

Mark Livingston was looking at a lot of prison time. Like many in his position, he had talked a good game when he was questioned by Sam's investigator, and even later when he was indicted. He was uncooperative and, at times, belligerent. Sure, he had known George and worked for him for a long time, but George stayed out of it and let Mark run Rebel Yell. Mark wanted the mine to be productive and took pride in it, yes, but that was secondary to making sure it was safe. He didn't know George all that well, but he knew him well enough to know he felt the same way. No, he had never heard George direct anyone to violate any law, let alone a law that was there to protect miners. Mark didn't know anything bad to say about George, nothing at all, but just to be clear, he wouldn't rat him out even if he did. He wasn't that kind of a guy.

Mark had softened noticeably now that his trial date was only three months off. He was almost sixty years old, with a wife he loved, two grown children, and five very cute grandchildren. If things went badly at the trial, he could spend more than twenty years in prison. He would come out an old man, some of his best years having been taken from him. And things would go badly at the trial, in all likelihood, because the charges against him were legitimate and there were lots of people out there who would be eager to testify against him.

So, like many in his position, Mark directed his lawyer to reach out to the prosecutor and see if anything could be worked out. He did know a few things, actually, more than he had let on earlier. He even knew a few things about George. If it was George the prosecution wanted, he could help with that, assuming he was treated fairly and didn't have to go to prison.

The negotiations began, and a month later, Mark signed a cooperation agreement. He promised to be fully forthcoming, truthfully answer all questions the prosecution asked of him, provide the prosecution with supporting documents and other evidence, and withhold nothing. Sam agreed to recommend a reduced sentence, assuming he lived up to the deal. The specifics would be determined later and would depend on the quality of his cooperation and the evidence he provided. He would have to do some prison time, but if all went well, Sam would only require him to plead guilty to one count. If he delivered George's head on a platter, she might go so far as to recommend that most of his sentence be in the form of probation and community service.

When Mark was finished talking, Sam felt she had George Rafferty by the short hairs. Her only concern was the troublesome gap between George's actual words and Mark's understanding of them. Mark was 100 percent sure about what George was telling him to do even if George didn't use the exact words. When the time came for trial, Sam would have to prep Mark very carefully and trust the jury to see what was really going on.

Mark believed there wouldn't be many sources of testimony against George because he was private and careful. He controlled his meetings well. He had an all-hands meeting at each of his seven mines once or twice a year, usually around Christmas and the Fourth of July. Those were generally rah-rah meetings; apart from the seasonal platitudes, George would inevitably thank the miners for their hard work and tell them it was important to mine a lot of coal because that's what paid the bills.

He met with the section foremen and senior managers once a quarter. He waved the flag, but he had the senior managers do most of the talking. They knew the message he wanted to instill, and they gave it. It boiled down to keep running coal and don't get sidetracked by things that don't matter. The senior managers stressed the importance of records, how they must be up-to-date and perfect and show that everything required by the law had been done. They said they would tell the section bosses when MSHA would be coming so they could be sure the records were in good shape. They said the safety operation had to look good when MSHA came around because that was the best way to keep running the coal and paying the bills. George wasn't saying these things, the senior managers were, but he was standing by their side, and that made them his words. That's what the senior managers thought anyway.

George met with Mark and the other mine foremen once or twice a week. Those meetings were always one-on-one. George was more open then because it was a tightly controlled and loyal group. In his oblique way, he told the mine foremen how to manage things and what messages and incentives to give the miners. He always went over the production figures with the mine foremen; sometimes, he offered praise, but with or without praise, the message was always to get more tonnage out of the mine—that's what he was paying for. And he paid generously. Mark had gotten several bonuses for production.

Sam picked up on that. "Did he ever give you a bonus for your safety performance?"

"No."

"You said he would review the production figures with you. Did he ever review safety statistics?"

"No."

"Did he ever talk about workplace injuries, and what you could do to avoid them?"

"Never. He only cared about one thing. Run the coal."

"Did he ever tell you, or did you ever hear about his telling anyone else, to violate a safety standard?"

"Many times."

"Give me an example."

"Sure. He and I were in the mine one time, up near a working section. The roof bolting and rock dusting weren't keeping pace with the mining the way the law requires, and the section boss wanted to slow down so they could catch up. The boss radioed me to get the OK. George heard him and shook his head. He just muttered that we don't have time for this shit."

"What did you do?"

"I told the foreman no. Keep running coal."

"That's not what George said, though."

"That's what he meant."

Sam switched the subject. "Let's go back to something you said earlier. You said you told the bosses you'd let them know when MSHA would be coming so they could get their records in shape. How could you know that? The inspections are required to be made without advance notice."

"I bribed an MSHA inspector, Bill Bevans, to give me a forty-eight-hour heads-up when MSHA was going to be coming."

"Why Bevans?"

"I knew him fairly well. He wasn't a gung ho kind of guy about his job, and I knew he always needed money. It wasn't a hard sell."

"Did George tell you to bribe him?"

"Not Bevans specifically, but yes. He was annoyed one day when we had a surprise inspection and got written up for our records not being up to date. He wasn't happy about the civil penalties we'd have to pay. He was bitching to me about it and said, 'It sure would be nice if we could figure out when MSHA was coming. There are other things I'd rather do with the money than pay civil penalties.'"

"He didn't say you should bribe MSHA."

"That's what he meant. He was telling me to figure out a way to get advance notice, and he'd give me a bonus for it."

"How can you be so sure?"

"I've worked for him a long time. Besides, I got us advance notice, and he gave me a bonus."

George Rafferty was a bad guy, but proving it would be hard, as Sam had always known. Thinking out loud, she mused, "I wish there was some way we could make this come to life. You're describing it well, but it would really help to give the jury a better picture of how he talks, how he uses innuendo and suggestion to get things done instead of giving direct orders."

Mark Livingston looked at Sam and smiled. Then he said, "Would tapes help?"

CHAPTER THIRTY-FOUR

While Sam was working her tail off to make the world a safer place for miners by getting George Rafferty off the street, Chris was being Chris and achieving success through hard work, practical advice, putting himself in his clients' shoes, charging reasonable fees, and being a good and caring guy. He was now one of the most sought-after small business lawyers in Charleston.

He was in his office one morning, cleaning up some odds and ends before meeting with a potential new client. She arrived at 9:30 sharp. "I'm Ellie DiFranco," she said. "Thanks for making time for me."

"Sure, Ellie. I'm Chris Lloyd. Can I get you some coffee?"

They settled into the two well-used easy chairs in Chris's office. He didn't like talking to clients across a desk.

"I know you're busy," Ellie said, "so I'll get right to the point." She told him about her small but successful business. "I'm working on a logo and a slogan, and I want to get them trademarked so they're protected. Can you help me with that?"

"Yes, I can, and I'd be happy to. But may I ask why you're coming to me? I do this work, but I don't specialize in it."

"I've become frustrated with the lawyer I've been using," Ellie said. "Nice guy, but no sense of urgency. I call him for help, and it can be two or three days before he calls me back. That's not working for me. I need to move faster than that. So, I've been looking around for a new lawyer. One of your clients,

Esther Montero, is a good friend. She thinks you're great and suggested I give you a try."

"That's nice of Esther. I'll have to thank her for the referral. Now, let's talk about what it is you want to do."

"Sure, but can I get myself another coffee first? I'll get you one too."

Chris pretended to be looking at her business card, but he was watching Ellie as she organized two more coffees. She wasn't beautiful, but she was striking, with close-set eyes and dark brown hair that fell to her shoulders. She seemed businesslike and had a nice way about her.

They got into the specifics of her issue and laid out a plan and timeline for going forward. They agreed to meet again in two weeks.

As Ellie got up to leave, Chris said, "I knew a guy named DiFranco once. He wasn't from around here, though. He was from Virginia somewhere. He was a good guy. His name was Joey."

Ellie stared at Chris in disbelief. "Joey was my husband," she finally said. "He was killed in Iraq."

Now Chris stared in disbelief. Finding himself, he quietly said, "I'm sorry. This is too unreal. I was in the jeep with Joey when we hit the IED. I got out of it with a limp. I've always felt guilty that I lived, and Joey died. I'm sorry, Ellie. I don't know what to say."

There was nothing to say. The shock was overwhelming. They exchanged a brief but heartfelt hug, two people who would always be bound by Joey. Then Ellie left, and they each grappled with their own thoughts as they pondered this astounding development.

Chris didn't share this with Sam. He would have told her if she had asked him, but she didn't know to ask. He wasn't a secretive person, with one exception. He never talked about his time in Iraq. It was too painful. Sam knew, of course, that his injury had been caused by an IED, and he had once told her there was another soldier in the jeep who had been killed. It was his way of saying how lucky they were. But he never mentioned the other guy's name or said anything else about him, and Sam didn't ask. She didn't want to put Chris through that because she knew how hard he was trying to forget Iraq, so that he, so that they, could look forward.

Inevitably, Chris and Ellie developed a bond that went beyond their lawyer-client relationship. It wasn't romantic, but they shared something that was uniquely theirs. They shared memories of Joey. Together they could keep him alive. Their friendship evolved over time, but Sam didn't learn about it until much later.

CHAPTER THIRTY-FIVE

Angelo made good time driving from Bath County to Arlington. Kate had agreed to meet with him but asked that they do it on the weekend so she wouldn't have to miss work. He pulled up to her house at 2:30 on a Saturday afternoon, half an hour early. She wasn't home, and rather than sit in his car to wait, he took a walk. Kate lived in a nice neighborhood, filled with modest, well-kept homes. People were outside, mowing lawns, tending gardens, chatting with friends, playing with dogs. *This is how families live,* Angelo thought. *I can't wait until I have a family.*

As he neared her house, Kate and Slouch were coming toward him from the opposite direction. They had been on a walk too. Slouch was panting and thirsty. Kate was radiant. "I love walking Slouch around the neighborhood," she said. "He's a real crowd-pleaser. Everyone stops to say hello."

"Thanks for seeing me again, Kate."

"Happy to. Are you making progress with your investigation?"

"We are, and that's why I'm here. But may I ask you a personal question first? I just took a walk myself. This is a nice neighborhood, but it's all families. Why does a single person like you choose to live here?"

She seemed taken aback by the nature of the question, but she answered, "Most single people live in apartments, but I don't care for apartment living. I like having a yard."

"I'm sorry, I shouldn't have asked. It's none of my business. I was just curious."

"Besides, I have a family," she said. "Slouch is my family." There was just a touch of possessiveness in her voice.

This had started badly. Angelo was trying to figure out how to get things back on track. He couldn't, so he jumped right in.

"We are progressing with the investigation, and I'd like to ask your help. We have hair samples from the murder scene. They were near Worthy's body. There was also a box cutter that the killer used on Worthy. We found partial fingerprints on it. We know you were there the morning he was killed, and we'd like to eliminate you as a suspect if we can. Would you be willing to give us DNA and fingerprint samples?"

"That sounds ominous," Kate said. "*Am* I a suspect?"

"You're a person of interest. You were there. We'd like to rule you out as a suspect."

"I'm enough of a lawyer to know I should stop talking to you at this point. I should get a lawyer before saying anything else or giving you any samples. But I'll give you samples because sooner or later, one way or another, you're going to get them anyway. The thing is, I doubt they'll eliminate me. They may even implicate me. But they won't prove anything."

"Why is that?" Angelo asked.

"Because I lived at Justice Hill, on weekends anyway, for almost three years. My clothes are still there. I was there the morning of the murder. It's entirely possible the hair samples you found came from my head."

"And the box cutter?"

"If that's the box cutter Jason kept in his gadget drawer next to the bar, I probably used it ten times while I was living at Justice Hill. To open packages, that sort of thing. I used it once to slice up a pizza we had made. My fingerprints will certainly be on it."

"Those are valid points, for sure. Thanks for agreeing to give us samples. My hope is they'll exonerate you."

Angelo collected the samples and was getting ready to leave. "Just a few more questions if you don't mind," he said. "You told me you and Jason drank bourbon together at Justice Hill. Are you a bourbon drinker?"

"I prefer single malt scotch. Jason was a bourbon guy, though, so that's what we drank when we were together."

"I see. One final thing. When you stayed at the Homestead before going to Justice Hill, were you there all night long?"

"Yes."

"Can anyone corroborate that?"

"You mean did someone share a room with me? No, absolutely not."

Angelo felt badly when he left. He had done what he had to, but he didn't like it. Hurting people, particularly nice people, didn't come naturally to him. Maybe he should think about a business career after all.

It didn't take long for the lab results to come back.

CHAPTER THIRTY-SIX

The trial in the government's case against George Rafferty was set to begin on September 21, 2010. At Sam's request, the grand jury had indicted Rafferty on three counts: conspiring to violate federal mine safety laws, conspiring to bribe a public official, and obstruction of justice. The first count was the big one, because it would let the prosecution show that Rafferty directed a wide array of willful violations. Sam would focus on the flagrant violations involving ventilation, rock dusting, and the falsification of records, all of which MSHA concluded had "caused or directly contributed to" the deaths of the five miners. She had no evidence that Rafferty had personally committed violations or engaged in bribery, but the conspiracy counts got her to the same place. The obstruction charge was more direct; she believed she could prove Rafferty had instructed miners to lie to federal investigators and withhold documents from them.

Sam had wanted to charge Rafferty with substantive crimes like reckless endangerment or maybe even manslaughter. Those are sexier than charges of "conspiring to violate safety standards," but crimes under state law were outside her remit. Her job was to prosecute violations of federal law. The Mine Safety and Health Act is limited in the conduct it criminalizes, and Sam had to do the best she could with what she had. She contented herself in thinking that would be enough to take Rafferty down. The charges might sound a little tame, but she knew she could provide drama.

The Honorable Dylan Forrester would preside at the trial. He was a good draw. Of the several judges in the Southern District, Judge Forrester was generally regarded as the most fair-minded and least political. He had grown up in Morgantown, the son of a history professor and the head librarian at West Virginia University. He went to law school at Duke, then returned to Charleston to practice law. He had never been in politics and had no apparent ties to the mining industry.

Sam's opposing trial counsel would have been Jessie if she had not stood up for what she believed. Instead it was Jessie's former boss, Jason Worthy. Sam knew all about Worthy and didn't like him as a matter of principle. She never completely bought the excuses Jess made for him. She thought Worthy should have done more to stand up for her friend. So now Sam had two people whose asses she wanted to kick: George Rafferty and Jason Worthy.

Sam wanted to win this trial more than she had ever wanted anything in her life, and she prepared intensely. In the weeks leading up to the trial, she and her team selected and organized the documents they wanted to use, prepared their trial exhibits, worked with their witnesses on their testimony, and carefully analyzed the pool of potential jurors. The hours were long, and Sam's temper was short. Chris was a saint, God love him. He was there when Sam needed him to be, and he stayed away and gave her space when that was her preference.

Sam knew what the prosecution had to show and was relentless in putting together a case that would show it. They had to tell the jury, and the general public, that the rampant and outrageous disregard for safety, the overt flouting of the laws enacted to protect miners, the brazen emphasis on production at all costs, and the corresponding de-emphasis on safety—all of it was the culture at the Rebel Yell Mine. That culture was inspired and paid for by George Rafferty. He was its architect and head cheerleader. It was his proud creation and true design.

Jessie called Sam the night before trial to wish her well. Chris and Bill were in the courtroom on opening day, seated together. After that, Chris came by when he could, but he had his own job to do. Bill had a job too, but he took vacation for the two weeks the trial was expected to run and was in the courtroom every day, cheering Sam on. It was too far to drive from Blacksburg and back on a daily basis, but Bill took a room at an inexpensive hotel near the courthouse. He wasn't about to stay with Sam and Chris when she was in trial.

It took two days to select and seat the jury. Sam was happy with ten of the twelve jurors. She had misgivings about the other two, for different reasons.

Juror number six was Dasha Lee, an eighth-grade teacher at a public school in a poor section of Charleston. She answered all the questions put to her as part of the jury selection process without raising any red flags, she had no preconceived notions about the case, and she thought she could be fair. There was nothing disqualifying about her. That was what bothered Sam. She seemed a little too perfect.

There are two types of challenges a trial lawyer can make in picking a jury. She can challenge any potential juror for cause, and the potential juror will not be seated if the judge believes he would not be impartial. Where no cause exists to warrant a challenge but, for whatever reason, the trial lawyer doesn't want a potential juror seated, she can use a "peremptory" challenge to strike him. If she's a defense lawyer, for example, and believes people who wear blue suits are hard on defendants, she can use a peremptory challenge to strike the potential juror in the blue suit. The catch is that the number of peremptory challenges is limited. In the case against George Rafferty, the government had six.

Sam had no basis to challenge Dasha Lee for cause, and she ultimately decided not to use one of her precious peremptory challenges to strike her. Dasha Lee was seated.

Juror number eleven was Rufus Baines. Sam had a big problem with him. He struck her as a George Rafferty kind of guy, a little too sure of himself, a little too lacking in values. There was nothing tangible to warrant a challenge for cause, and Sam had already used her six peremptory challenges to strike other potential jurors. She would have to live with Rufus Baines.

On day three, with the jury in place, Judge Forrester asked for opening statements. This was Sam's case, but Pete Gage badly wanted a piece of it, and they agreed that he would make the opening statement for the United States. How could Sam argue with that? Pete was her boss, and it was his call. More importantly, he was a brilliant trial lawyer. He would do an excellent job and set the tone for the trial.

Pete's opening was masterful. He said the prosecution's evidence would show the jurors how the explosion happened, but more importantly why it happened. The tragedy of any death is compounded, he went on, when that death didn't have to happen, as was the case five times over here. And yet, he proclaimed, the deaths of the five miners, though unnecessary, were "almost inevitable," as the federal investigators had found. And why? Because of one man's greed. George Rafferty's insatiable hunger for money caused him to disdain the laws that protected miners because they got in the way of his shoveling money into his shuttle cars. He couldn't allow that, so, through his words and actions, he directed and encouraged his employees to disregard the laws and just keep running coal. What we need is more tonnage! That was his mantra, and it became the culture at Rebel Yell. It's harsh but true to say that Rafferty's lust for money made him indifferent to the safety of his employees and so, tragically but inevitably, five of them gave their lives on October 13, 2006. Such a tragedy, so unnecessary. All so Rafferty could make a little more.

"After hearing all the evidence, ladies and gentlemen of the jury," Pete closed, "I believe you will be outraged and disgusted by the defendant's conduct. Through the evidence, you will see what he did and why he did it. He ordered and orchestrated many dangerous violations of law, and five miners died as a result. This didn't have to happen."

There wasn't a sound in the courtroom as Pete took his seat next to Sam. He had done well, and they were both bursting with pride. They were off to a good start.

Finally, Judge Forrester said, "Do you wish to make an opening statement, Mr. Worthy?"

Rising to his feet, Jason replied, "Yes, Your Honor. I will be brief."

"Ladies and gentlemen," he began, addressing the jury, "what happened at Rebel Yell was a tragedy. We can all agree on that. And if we could take that terrible day back and live it over, I know we all would. No one feels that way more than my client.

"As you listen to the prosecution's case, I want you to remember one thing: context. I want you to think about who the witnesses are. And I want you to think about where their testimony is coming from.

"Who are the witnesses? They are miners at Rebel Yell. They were friends of the men who died. Some of them almost died. Where is their testimony coming from? They are angry. They are looking for someone to blame. That is understandable.

"What is not understandable, and what the evidence will not support, is putting the blame on my client. You will agree if you listen carefully to the evidence. Listen closely to each witness and ask yourself, did he testify that Mr. Rafferty *told* him to violate the law? Did he testify that Mr. Rafferty *told* him to bribe a mine inspector? Is there any evidence that Mr. Rafferty actually *ordered* or *directed* a single violation of law? Or did the orders come from others? If you listen carefully, I think you will conclude that any orders to disregard the law were given by people who have already pleaded guilty to that charge, people like Mark Livingston, the mine foreman at Rebel Yell."

It was brief but effective. It went straight to the heart of the prosecution's biggest weakness.

Sam called her first witness. Trials quickly develop a rhythm, and this was no exception. Sam used her witnesses to establish a culture of greed and a disregard for safety, and Worthy used his cross-examinations to show, as his opening statement had foreshadowed, that it wasn't traceable to Rafferty.

Sam's first witness exemplified the pattern. Using the MSHA investigation report, Herschel Watts set the stage by testifying to the facts and causes of the explosion. After qualifying him as a mine safety expert, Sam asked him for his observations about the safety practices and attitudes at Rebel Yell.

"We found a shocking disregard for safety," Watts testified. "The absence of basic compliance was appalling, the worst I've ever seen."

"What accounted for that, in your opinion?"

"Management always sets the tone, for good or bad. The situation we found at Rebel Yell could only have existed because that's what management wanted."

Worthy's cross-examination was short. "When you attribute the situation at Rebel Yell to management, are you referring to George Rafferty?"

"He was a part of management, in fact he was management, so yes."

"And yet your report didn't mention him by name, did it?"

"No, it did not."

"Is that because you couldn't tie the situation directly to Mr. Rafferty?"

"We didn't have specific proof that he told anyone to commit violations or lie to federal investigators, no. But he had to be involved. He ran the company. This couldn't have happened without him."

The trial days went on, and the pattern was the same. Sam called Bill Bevans, the former MSHA inspector who had accepted a bribe. He had been fired when the bribery came to light and was working at an auto body shop. He was facing a trial of his own.

"Mr. Bevans, when you were an inspector for MSHA, were you ever offered a bribe by Rebel Yell?"

"Yes, I was."

"What was it for, and did you accept the bribe?"

"Mark Livingston offered me five hundred bucks a month to give him a forty-eight-hour heads-up before any inspection at his mine. I needed the money and I took it."

"Do you have any knowledge as to whether George Rafferty was involved in ordering or approving the bribe?"

"George was a hands-on guy. He was at his mines every day, looking into their operations and staying active. He had to be involved. No way Mark did this on his own."

When his turn came, Worthy asked, "Mr. Bevans, do you *know* that Mr. Rafferty ordered or approved the bribe, or are you just assuming that because he was an active manager?"

"I don't know it for sure, but I know it because he had to have been."

"Did you and Mr. Rafferty ever have a conversation about the bribe?"

"No."

"Did Mr. Livingston ever tell you that Mr. Rafferty wanted advance notice of the inspections, or that he wanted Mr. Livingston to offer you a bribe?"

"No."

"Did Mr. Livingston ever lead you to believe that Mr. Rafferty even knew about the bribe?"

"No, I can't say that he did. But he had to have known."

The prosecution's direct case entailed several days of testimony by Rebel Yell miners. Yes, safety conditions at the mine were terrible. Yes, the miners had complained about them. No, the complaints hadn't changed anything, but they did cause a couple of the complaining miners to get chewed out for getting sidetracked and not sticking to the business of running coal. That was always the emphasis, running the coal. Yes, the miners had been directed to ignore safety regulations, many times. It was almost a daily occurrence. Those orders had come from their bosses. No, they had never been directed by Mr. Rafferty himself, but that's not the way things worked. They got their orders from their bosses. Mr. Rafferty didn't give orders to the miners. He had other things to do. But he was in charge, he was the *Man*. All of this had to come from him.

When the trial day ended on Tuesday of the second week, Sam took stock of where things stood. She was exhausted but had the adrenaline to keep going for as long as it took. In her judgment, the government's evidence was going in well. The only defense being put up was the one she had always feared: Rafferty was smart enough to use the right words and not use the wrong ones, with the result that no one could tie anything to him directly.

Sam thought about the jury. By their body language, the ten jurors she was happy with at the outset seemed to be validating her assessment. They were buying what she was selling, that there was no way in hell George Rafferty wasn't at the bottom of this. They saw right through the hyper-technical defense Worthy was putting forth. They didn't care whether or not the actual words were there. It was obvious what was going on. George was in this up to his rosy-red keister.

For that matter, juror number six seemed to be on board. She was attentive and bright, and she seemed receptive to the prosecution's witnesses. Maybe Sam had been wrong about her. Juror number eleven troubled her, though. He troubled her a lot. He seemed much less interested in the direct evidence than he did in Worthy's cross-examinations, and twice Sam had caught him rolling his eyes when the prosecution scored a key point. It only took one juror to prevent a conviction. This was the juror to worry about. And Sam was worried. Damn, she should have used one of her peremptory challenges to get rid of him.

As the final day of the prosecution's case approached, Sam felt they were in good shape, but a conviction wasn't in the bag. This was like the tenth round of a heavyweight fight: when it's too close to call, you can't afford to play it safe. You have to go for the knockout.

Sam had one witness left: Mark Livingston.

CHAPTER THIRTY-SEVEN

Mark was in a box. He went back a long way with George Rafferty and still felt loyalty to him. His problem was that he felt a greater loyalty to himself. He didn't want to see George go to prison, much less be a part of putting him there. But he couldn't have it both ways. He was either going to help put George in prison, or he was going to prison himself. Of all the concerns Sam had, putting Mark on the stand wasn't one of them. He had been solid since he signed the cooperation agreement. He wasn't going to cross her now.

"Good morning, Mr. Livingston," Sam said, and the testimony of her final witness began. After taking Mark through his background, experience, and responsibilities at Rebel Yell, she asked him about his relationship with George Rafferty.

"I've worked with George a long time. He was my boss, but he was also my friend. I like him a lot, and I don't want to see anything bad happen to him."

"Then why did you sign a cooperation agreement with my office and agree to testify against him?" The jury was going to learn of Livingston's cooperation with the prosecution one way or the other. Sam preferred to bring it out herself, rather than have Worthy present it as if it were a deep, dark secret she was trying to hide.

"I didn't want to and resisted it for a long time. I consistently protected George when I was questioned by the investigators from MSHA and also from your office. I told lies to protect George. I took responsibility for things he had told me to do. I finally realized the more I lied to protect him, the more I was hurting myself and my family. I don't want trouble for George, but I don't want to hurt my family either. I got to a point where I could see that coming, and I just couldn't do it."

"What does the cooperation agreement require you to do?"

"Tell the truth and hold nothing back."

"And is that what you're doing today?"

"Yes."

"Did Mr. Rafferty tell you to lie to the investigators?"

"Yes, he did."

"Can you recall his exact words?"

"We were talking one day after the explosion, just the two of us. We all knew a big investigation would be coming. And we knew conditions in the mine weren't the best from a safety standpoint. The politicians were screaming, and there was no question the investigators would come after management. And George says to me, 'We can't let that happen, Mark. They'll be coming after me hard. We have to cooperate, but we have to do everything we can to put the best light on things. We have to keep the mine running.'"

"I listened carefully to what you just said, Mr. Livingston, and I didn't hear Mr. Rafferty tell you to lie to the investigators."

"That's what he was saying. In the language we both understood, it's exactly what he said. He was telling me to lie to the investigators."

Sam and Mark went through several examples of orders Livingston had given to section bosses and miners to violate safety standards. Usually, the violation was committed by simply disregarding the legal requirement. In some cases, it was the ordered falsification of records to show that required safety examinations had been made when in fact they hadn't.

"In each of those cases, did Mr. Rafferty direct the conduct that you ordered?"

"No, not all of them. In the early years, yes, but as time went by and I came to understand what George expected of me, I didn't need to be told. I acted on my own."

"Believing you were acting on Mr. Rafferty's wishes and directives?"

"Knowing I was. It was the culture of the place."

Perfect, Sam thought, and moved on to the bribery of Inspector Bevans. "Please tell the jury how that came about."

"We had a surprise MSHA inspection. Our records were in terrible shape and we got crucified. The violations that were written up were going to cost Black Bear a ton of money in civil penalties. George was pissed. He said to me, 'Mark, don't you wish there was some way to know when the inspectors are coming so we can be prepared when they get here? I sure do. That way, we could find a better use for the money than paying all these damn penalties.'"

"What did you understand that to mean?"

"He was telling me to find a way to get advance notice of the MSHA inspections. He was telling me he'd give me a bonus if I did. I understood my orders. I bribed Bill Bevans, and we got advance notice of future inspections."

Sam baited the trap. "But those weren't Mr. Rafferty's words."

"It's what he meant. I can prove it because it's what happened. I bribed Bevans, we started getting advance notice, and I got a bonus. But more importantly, it's exactly what he said in the language we always used."

"Please tell the jury what you mean by that."

"Sure. The reason some people don't understand that George is giving orders is because they're looking at what his words mean in plain English. But George and I, and his other bosses, spoke a different language. We used English words, but they had different meanings. You learned the language when you worked for George for a while."

"Can you give some examples?"

"When George says, 'Wouldn't it be nice if someone could find a way,' the meaning in Georgespeak is 'I want you to find a way and get it done.' When George says, 'That's a nice idea, but we have to keep the mine running,' he's saying, in our language, 'Run the coal and ignore anything that gets in the way.' When he says, as he did to me before the investigators came, 'We have to cooperate, but we have to do everything we can to put the best light on things,' he's saying, 'Do whatever you have to but make this go away.' There are no moral limits on that instruction. We are to lie, to withhold, to intimidate, whatever it takes. If George says, 'I'd like to put that money to better use,' he's saying, 'You'll get a bonus for getting this done.' This is the language

George uses to communicate with us. It is real and we understand it, just as you understand and communicate in English."

Sam thought Mark had done well. She thought the prosecution was ahead on points but needed the knockout. That was going to come in the form of two tape recordings Mark had made of conversations he had with Rafferty. Sam carefully began to walk Mark through the process of laying the foundation for the first tape she intended to introduce.

Worthy was on his feet. This wasn't his first rodeo. He had been given the tape in discovery and was concerned that it might support Livingston's testimony about the "different language" he and Rafferty used. It put Worthy's carefully crafted "he didn't use the words" defense at risk. "Objection!" he shouted. "Where is this going, Your Honor?"

"Counsel will approach," said Judge Forrester, and Worthy and Sam went to the judge's bench for a sidebar. Judge Forrester wanted to hear their respective positions, but in order to avoid prejudice, he did so out of the jury's hearing.

Sam explained what the tapes were about and made a proffer of evidence, stating what the tapes would show if they were admitted. Worthy objected to their admission on two grounds: first, that Rafferty didn't know he was being recorded, and second, that the proffered foundation for the tapes was inadequate to assure their reliability. Judge Forrester didn't make formal rulings on the objections, but it was clear he was more troubled by the foundation issues than by Rafferty's lack of knowledge. He circumvented the issue by asking, "Ms. Picken, are these tapes of conversations about which Mr. Livingston has already testified?"

"Yes, Judge," Sam answered quietly. They were still in sidebar.

"Do they add anything new?"

"Not substantively, Your Honor, but they are important because they allow the jurors to hear the words directly from Mr. Rafferty's mouth. This case is about whether his words mean something other than what they seem to say, and the jury will be better able to assess that by hearing him say them."

"That's a nice argument, Ms. Picken, but this is a thorny area, and since the tapes don't add anything new, I'm going to disallow them. Counsel will return to their seats."

Sam was not surprised by Judge Forrester's ruling, nor was she disappointed. She had offered the tapes in good faith, believing they would achieve the very result Worthy feared. But she recognized that the tapes showed Rafferty communicating just as Livingston and the other witnesses had described, nothing more and nothing less. It was entirely possible the jury would not be impressed if it heard them. In that sense, their exclusion could actually be helpful. Knowing there were tapes and seeing the defense strongly object to their admission, the jury might believe there was more to them than there actually was. Sam hoped the jurors would feel they had been denied important and damning evidence.

"Ladies and gentlemen of the jury," intoned Judge Forrester, "counsel and I have just had a private discussion about whether certain evidence offered by the prosecution should be admitted. My ruling is that it should not. The jury will disregard anything it heard prior to the sidebar about certain tape recordings made by Mr. Livingston, which I have determined to be inadmissible."

Fat chance the jury will disregard what they heard, Sam thought. *The tapes aren't in evidence, but they're in the heads of the people deciding this case.* Sam snuck a peek at the jury box. Jurors six and eleven were both engaged, a good sign.

"Please call your next witness, Ms. Picken," Judge Forrester said.

"We have no more witnesses, Your Honor. The prosecution rests."

"All right," said the judge. "This is a good time to break for lunch. We will resume at 1:30."

To the surprise of no one, Worthy advised the Court that he would call no witnesses. This was a case about whether George Rafferty had ordered or directed certain illegal activities. Through various witnesses, the prosecution had put on evidence of several instances in which Rafferty had given such orders and directions. There were only two ways to counter that evidence. One was through the cross-examination of those witnesses, and Worthy had done a good job of getting them to admit they had never heard Rafferty give those orders in so many words, despite their testimony that they were acting at his direction. The other was to put Rafferty on the stand to rebut the evidence directly. That wasn't going to happen. Every defense counsel knows how risky it is to let the defendant testify and expose himself to cross-examination, and those risks are intensified with a defendant as arrogant and volatile as Rafferty.

Worthy's assessment was that he had, through his cross-examinations, done enough chipping away to create reasonable doubt about whether Rafferty had given the orders, and that was all he needed. There was no call for a Hail Mary. Rafferty would remain silent.

With this development, the court adjourned early that afternoon. Worthy and Sam made their closing arguments the following morning, and the case went to the jury.

CHAPTER THIRTY-EIGHT

The end of a trial brings an odd sense of joy mingled with letdown. As with college students after they take an important test, a lawyer experiences a range of thoughts and emotions: anxiety, analysis, self-assessment, and second-guessing. *Do I want to talk about it with others? Or should I just forget about it? How did you answer question seven? Do I really want to know? Will knowing make me feel better or worse? Will not talking about it make me feel better or worse? How do you think the cross-examination of witness X went? Did I prove the elements of the crimes? Do you think I connected with the jury? Do I want to know what you think? I do if it will make me feel better, but otherwise, I'd rather not.*

The self-torture doesn't matter. It's just passing time. What you did is done, and you can't change it. The professor, or the jury, will grade your performance in due course. And then you'll have your answer. The grading may be fair, or it may not be fair. It doesn't matter. Either way, you'll know how you did. You won or you lost. You put that bastard George Rafferty away, or you didn't.

Bill was ecstatic. He hugged Sam and wouldn't let go. "How did my little girl get to be so smart?" he asked. "You showed 'em, you really did. You put it to Black Bear and that miserable Rafferty. Big Joe would be so proud of you, just like I am."

Chris was there too. He had come for the closing. He hugged Sam and said, "Good job, babe. You worked hard and did great. I'm proud of you." Coming from Chris, that was raw emotion.

Well, that was two votes, but unfortunately, neither Bill nor Chris was on the jury. These were views Sam treasured but couldn't credit because they were analyzing with their hearts and not their heads.

She took Pete Gage's assessment more seriously. He, too, wanted a conviction, badly, and like most lawyers who construct an argument, he strongly believed in the prosecution's case. But Pete was a realist. He had learned there are always things at work that can't be seen. He said, "Nice job, Sam. There's more than enough evidence to convict, and I'm optimistic. Whatever happens, you worked your heart out, and you represented the people well. Thank you. I'm proud of you."

"Thanks, Pete, and thanks for giving me this opportunity," Sam replied, thinking about what he had said. He was "optimistic," which is what she also felt. That beats the alternative, but it's well short of "It's in the bag" or "We crushed 'em." Sam wondered if he was worried about juror number eleven, Rufus Baines, as she was.

Now the waiting began. Time goes slowly when you're waiting for the jury to give you your grade. Sam knew nothing was going to happen this afternoon. Tomorrow was Friday, and the jury would have all day. She hoped they would come back with a verdict so this wouldn't hang over her all weekend.

You go through the motions, waiting for a jury. You find things to do, though your heart and mind aren't in your busywork. Friday came and went with no result, and Judge Forrester sent the jurors home for the weekend.

Sam and Chris managed to get through a very long Saturday and Sunday. He took her out to a nice dinner, though she was too preoccupied to be good company. He paid some bills and raked some leaves. She reorganized the kitchen shelves. They rattled around like two quarters in an empty soda can.

Monday came and went with no result. Sam was worried. It shouldn't be taking this long. Was the delay a good sign for the prosecution? She didn't think so. More likely, it meant there was a holdout. Rufus Baines, probably. She cursed herself for not having used one of her peremptory challenges to strike him. *Stupid. That was really stupid.*

At 11:00 Tuesday morning, the foreperson sent Judge Forrester a message that the jury was deadlocked. He met with them and said he understood the difficulty of working through the issues and reminded them of the importance of the case. Then he sent them back to deliberate further. At 2:30 that afternoon, the jury requested the transcript of Mark Livingston's testimony. Sam's agony continued.

They got the call to return to the courtroom early Wednesday afternoon. The jury was back, and the court would be in session. Sam's heart was racing. When all were seated and the court was called to order, Judge Forrester asked the foreperson if the jury had reached a verdict.

"We have not, Your Honor. I'm sorry to report that we are hopelessly deadlocked."

Sam knew what that meant even before the ritual played out. She had failed to get a conviction, and the court would declare a mistrial. They would have to do it all over again, if that was Pete's decision.

On each of the three counts, the jury hung at eleven votes to convict and one to acquit. As was her right, Sam requested the court to poll the jury. That is a process by which the jurors have to stand up in open court, one by one, and state whether or not they agree with the reported result. A juror will occasionally change his or her vote in that setting, but it doesn't happen often. Sam didn't expect that, but she needed to know which juror had let George Rafferty off the hook. In her heart, she knew it was Rufus Baines. She needed to hear him say it.

To her surprise, Dasha Lee, juror number six, was the lone holdout. Rufus Baines had voted to convict on all three counts.

Judge Forrester declared a mistrial. He thanked the jurors for their service and dismissed them. The case was over.

In the coming weeks, the US Attorney's Office would have to decide whether to retry the case before a new jury. That would be Pete's call. Sam's hatred for George Rafferty was still there. Her desire that he spend many years in prison was stronger than ever. She just wasn't sure she could go through this again.

Sam had gotten her grade from the jury. Dasha Lee had given Rafferty a pass, for now anyway. It's a game of winning and losing, and Sam had lost. She took it very hard. She was utterly deflated.

Chris hurt too. He hurt for Sam. He took her losses harder than his own.

Bill Picken was pissed.

CHAPTER THIRTY-NINE

"What've you got, Tom?" O'Hanlon barked.

"The hair samples are a match," said Tom Mahaffey. "The hair we found next to Worthy's body is Kate's."

"And the prints on the box cutter?"

"They match too. We can't say with certainty they're Kate's prints because they're only partials and there aren't enough points of contact for them to be conclusive, but every contact point on the partial is consistent with the prints Angelo got from Kate."

Angelo didn't like where this was going and tried to head it off. "This doesn't prove anything. There are perfectly legitimate reasons why her hair would be found at Justice Hill and her prints would be on the box cutter. She lived there. It was her home."

"What are you, her defense counsel now?" Scott said mockingly. "Easy there, big guy. It's going to take a lot more than this to charge her, but we got the samples to see if we could rule her out as a suspect, and we can't. She's still in the pool. In fact, she has the pool to herself, so far anyway. We haven't been able to identify anyone else to throw in there with her."

"But Scott, I just don't see—"

O'Hanlon cut Angelo off. "Save it, hotshot. Look at what we know, not what we feel. She had motive and opportunity. She was there—we have a witness who saw her leaving the scene, her hair and prints place her there, and she admits she was there. That's not nothing."

"How about the Laphroaig? And the propofol?"

"Well, she told you she likes single malt scotch whiskey. Worthy had called her and said he made a mistake and wanted her back. Maybe she went over with a peace offering, with the intention of getting him drunk and killing him."

"They drank bourbon together. Why would she bring scotch?"

"Maybe it was symbolic, maybe it was her way of telling him some things would have to change if she went back. Hell, I don't know. I'm just speculating, but it isn't ridiculous, not without anyone else even in the pool."

"And the propofol?" Angelo asked, looking for anything to grab onto.

"You got me there, kid. Maybe she was a medic in Afghanistan or something. Maybe she was an endoscopy nurse somewhere along the way. There are a lot of holes we have to fill. And you should be out there filling them instead of arguing with me."

Angelo was undeterred. "How about the chain saw piece of this? Where would she get a chain saw? How would she know how to use it?"

"That one's easy. She was a forest ranger. She was a smoke jumper. A chain saw is a tool of the trade for those people. She's probably used a chain saw more than you've brushed your teeth. Where did she get it? I don't know, eBay, maybe? A yard sale? She might have kept one from her ranger days. Why are you asking me these questions, anyway? You should be out there investigating and finding answers. And hopefully finding something that will solve this crime."

Tom had been sitting quietly, listening to this exchange. Now he weighed in. "She might have gotten a chain saw on eBay or at a yard sale, but I don't think the saw that killed Worthy was from Kate's ranger days."

Scott whirled around in his chair. "What do you know that you haven't told us, Tom?"

"Hammersmith has eliminated the saw that was shipped to Virginia. It's ninety-five percent confident the saw that killed Worthy was one of the two that went to West Virginia."

"Do they know which one?"

"Yes, they think so, but it doesn't really matter. Both of the saws were shipped to the same buyer."

"C'mon, Tom, you're killing me. Out with it! Who was the buyer?"

"Black Bear Mining Company. The saws were shipped to the Merriman No. 3 Mine."

CHAPTER FORTY

The town of Woodstock lies near the northern end of Virginia's Shenandoah Valley, hard by the seven horseshoe-shaped bends of the Shenandoah River's north fork. It is flanked by the Blue Ridge Mountains to the east and the Allegheny Mountains to the west. A friendly town of about five thousand people, it is the county seat of Shenandoah County.

Woodstock was settled primarily by Germans who came down from Pennsylvania. One of them, Jacob Muller, founded the town as Muellerstadt, or "Millerstown," in 1752. The name was changed to Woodstock in 1761.

The Woodstock area is rural, and roots run deep. The families of some of the old German and later Scotch-Irish settlers have lived there for generations. There is a resulting frequency to some surnames that aren't found in many other places. The family farm is still an important fixture, though there are fewer of them. The citizenry is less indigenous than it once was, as city people have moved to the area to retire or enjoy a second home. There are more vineyards now.

One is easily seduced by the lush green pastures, limestone ridges, and meandering streams that characterize the area. The people are honest and hardworking, and they exhibit the refreshing patriotism of small-town America. The parades and other community gatherings are well-attended, as is the annual county fair. People love the outdoors, enjoy hunting, and support the Second Amendment. They are neighborly and look after each other.

Interstate 81 bisects greater Woodstock and has spawned a strip of fast-food places and the inevitable Walmart. If one can put that aside, along with the oversupply of thrift shops and auto parts stores, Woodstock has much to offer. There is a historic courthouse, a small hospital, and a military academy. In the downtown area, which is "old" Woodstock, there is a movie theater, a brewpub, an art gallery, a museum, a library, and a tattoo parlor. Most importantly, there is a wonderful restaurant, the Woodstock Café, that serves delicious food and wine in a warm and comfortable setting. Geographically and socially, the Café is Woodstock's heartbeat.

Around the corner from the Café, at 127 Court Street, are the law offices of Picken & Lloyd, LLP. Sam and Chris set up shop there in 2011. It was a big change for them, but after the Rafferty trial ended so devastatingly, Sam knew she was done with being a prosecutor. She was also done with Charleston.

The loss—a mistrial isn't technically a loss, but Sam took it that way—affected her as Big Joe's accident had affected her father. She blamed herself, totally and unequivocally. She felt she had let Pete down, along with the entire office, the community of Owl Hollow, and miners and their families everywhere. To say nothing of Jessie. She ran away to hide her shame. She didn't turn to alcohol and, thanks to Chris, she didn't give up on life, but otherwise, she was every inch her father's daughter.

Sam needed to change location and she wanted to do something different. Chris was well-established with his firm and client base and Sam knew moving would hurt him, but he brushed it off. He said he could do corporate work for small businesses almost anywhere, and as long as they were together, he was good. They decided to start their own firm.

Woodstock was an emotional preference more than a business decision. In their early years in Charleston, Sam and Chris went there once for a long weekend. They stayed on the river, at the Inn at Narrow Passage. It was scenic, peaceful, and restorative. They returned twice, and they vowed that if they ever left Charleston, they would live in Woodstock.

From a business perspective, Woodstock ended up making a certain sense. It is thirty miles southwest of Winchester and thirty miles northeast of Harrisonburg along I-81. Both are substantial communities that abound in small businesses. Chris thought he could draw clients from both locations—he was an experienced small business lawyer, and his rates would be lower than those of the "big city" lawyers in Winchester and Harrisonburg. Sam would handle the litigation side of the practice. As the county seat, Woodstock has the courthouse and is the litigation center, so she was bound to pick up some work just by being there. The cases would be different from what she knew, and she would be on the defense side, but litigation is litigation. The clients Chris attracted would be likely sources of work for Sam as well.

They knew starting a business would be hard. They knew they would have a lean year or two as they worked to build a reputation and a client base. They also thought it would be fun, building something together. It never occurred to them that they could fail; they were good lawyers, and their self-confidence was high.

The venture turned out better than they had expected. Sam was fascinated to see Chris in action. He was so thoughtful and caring. It was easy to understand why clients loved and trusted him. And in his understated way, he had a talent for bringing in work. In their second month, he managed through a former client in Charleston to arrange a pitch to a group of doctors in Winchester who operated as the Jubal Early Medical Group. Somehow, he reeled them in. They became a stable source of corporate work for Chris and, in due course, they also threw off litigation that Sam handled.

She did her part too. She volunteered to work with community groups and charitable causes as a way of meeting people and generating business. In just a few months, she was representing an insurance broker in Woodstock, a builder in nearby Edinburg, a small IT business a little farther away in Mt. Jackson, and three of the local wineries. Whenever her clients came to her office to meet, she introduced them to Chris, and he did his Chris thing, gaining their friendship, then their confidence, and finally their business.

They broke even after six months and were actually making reasonable money at the end of their first year. In September 2012, eighteen months after opening their doors, they gave up their rental apartment and bought a house in the Spring Hollow Estates development west of town. It was one of the smaller houses, but it sat on two acres, had three bedrooms and two baths, and most importantly was their very own.

Life was good. Then Sam had a call from Pete Gage, and the past came rushing back.

CHAPTER FORTY-ONE

"Hey, Sam, I hope you're doing well," Pete said. "We miss you at the office."

"I *was* doing just fine, but getting this call makes me nervous. What's up?"

"You didn't lose the Rafferty case. Dasha Lee, the juror who voted to acquit, was bribed. I thought you'd want to know."

"Whoa! What are you talking about, Pete? This is out of left field. Slow down and fill me in."

"The trial ended two years ago, but it didn't end for me. I kept thinking about it. It didn't sit well. Lee was a teacher, and teachers are supposed to be intelligent people, right? And teachers aren't generally inclined to side with rich people who don't take care of their employees, right? There was plenty of evidence that Rafferty didn't give a hoot about his employees. So why would an intelligent person, a teacher, not see through Worthy's technical defense? It was pretty obvious what was going on. Everyone else on the jury got it. Why would Lee miss it, and side with a scumbag like Rafferty?"

"Maybe she thought even scumbags should get a fair shake," Sam offered. "Maybe she had an expansive view of reasonable doubt and just didn't think we had nailed the case down tightly enough."

"Nah," Pete said. "That doesn't work for me. The Lee vote just didn't add up. It kept eating at me. I've been surprised by jurors before, but this felt different. I couldn't let it go. After six months, I decided to learn more about Ms. Lee."

"Meaning you put a tail on her?"

"Yeah, your old investigator, Rick Jackson. He always thought you got screwed, and he went after it with a vengeance."

"Good old Rick," Sam said, smiling. She had always liked him, and apparently, he felt the same about her. She was grateful.

"Yeah, good old Rick. This was in May of last year, 2011. Rick went to the school where Lee teaches, picked up the tail, and followed her home. Guess where she lives?"

"Tell me."

"Kanawha Overlook. Can you believe it? Kanawha fucking Overlook!"

"That's the luxury apartment building on the riverbank, isn't it? The one that advertises rents starting at two grand a month for a studio?"

"That's the one," Pete confirmed. "But it gets better. Rick wanted the specifics, so he buddied up to the lady at the reception desk. After a few minutes, he asked her about Dasha Lee. He got the old 'I can't talk about the tenants' stuff at first, but he stayed with it and soon she couldn't talk enough about the tenants. It turns out Lee lives in a two-bedroom river view apartment on the ninth floor. The monthly rents for those babies are six large."

"How does she swing that on a teacher's salary?"

"Exactly. Rick checked up on her. Single, never married. Her parents are of modest means and live in Wheeling. Her car is paid for. She has credit card debt, but nothing out of the ordinary. She has a checking account with an average monthly balance of nine hundred bucks and change. The apartment doesn't fit. It makes no sense."

"And?"

"And Rick went back to the apartment and asked to see the building manager. He wouldn't talk to Rick about the tenants as a policy matter. He changed his tune, though, when Rick said he was from the US Attorney's Office and was investigating a possible crime."

"What did Rick learn?"

"That Lee had been living there since the previous October. She was a good tenant who lived quietly and never caused any trouble. She paid her rent promptly every month."

"Did she pay by check? Where did she get the money?"

"That's where it gets interesting," Pete said. "Her rent checks came in the mail. They were drawn on an account at the Sundowner Bank of Baltimore and signed by a John Wiggins."

"Who's he?"

"We still don't know. We've been looking and can't find such a person. The bank account is real, though, and it pays the rent for Lee's apartment each month."

"Did you talk to the bank?"

"We tried to, but they made us do it the hard way. Privacy and all that, you know. We had to subpoena the bank records. It took some time. We finally got them earlier this year."

"What did they show?"

"The account is in the name of a company called Rose Hill. It doesn't have a physical address or a website. It appears to be run by Wiggins. He's the only authorized check signer."

"Was there a phone number for the account?"

"Yup. We called it. No luck. A voice told us it wasn't in service."

"When was the account opened?"

"October 2010. The same month Dasha Lee moved into her fancy apartment."

Sam shook her head in disbelief. "That was the month after the Rafferty trial."

"Quite a coincidence, isn't it?" teased Pete. "But it isn't a coincidence. There's more."

"Let's have it," Sam said, urgently.

"The account was opened with a hundred-dollar deposit, but $500,000 was wired in shortly thereafter. Later that day, Wiggins transferred $300,000 to a bank in the Cayman Islands. The remaining $200,000 was left in the account to fund the rent payments."

"Is there any activity in the account other than those payments?"

"Nope."

"Where did the $500,000 deposit come from?"

"It came from a bank in Charleston. The account belonged to one George Rafferty. Ever hear of him?"

"Bingo," Sam said. She was smiling. "Now you've got a new charge to bring against Rafferty, bribing a witness. He seems to like that bribery stuff. Where do you go from here?"

"We'll charge Lee and keep looking for Wiggins."

"And Rafferty?"

"We can't do anything about him. He died last week. Heart attack, apparently."

CHAPTER FORTY-TWO

Jess and Jimmy spent Thanksgiving with Sam and Chris in 2012. They had only been in their house for two months, but it was in good shape. Sam was thrilled to have a place, finally, that she could invite Jessie to without feeling embarrassed. When she offhandedly mentioned that to Chris, he just shook his head and readied the Whistle Pig. He had gotten an extra bottle. It wouldn't do to run short with Jimmy there.

Just for fun, they also invited the folks—Jessie's mother and Sam's father. There were many positives about the move from Charleston to Woodstock, and one was the increased closeness to family. Blacksburg was only a three-hour drive, and Crozet less than half of that. Jessie and Sam got together every two or three months, often in Staunton, which shortened the drive for both of them and also brought back memories.

There was much to be thankful for that year, even more than the usual abundance. As the group sat down to Sam's beautifully roasted (if she did say so herself) sixteen-pound turkey, procured from a local farmer, Sam raised her glass and said, "I'd like to propose a toast." Because the occasion called for something special, she and Chris had splurged on a magnum of 1989 Haut Brion, which would be showing beautifully. Sam looked at the deep purple in the glass and made a silent vow to keep her toast short so they could get into the wine.

"Actually, two toasts. The first is to family. It is so good to be with all of you. Thank you for coming." Glasses were clinked, the "hear, hears" were said, and sips were taken. A moment of appreciative silence followed. "Man, that's good," Jimmy said, almost in prayer.

"And now," Sam continued, "to my best friend, the Honorable Jessie Macaulay. May she rule fairly and always in my favor. We're so proud of you, Jess!" Everyone stood and raised their glass to Jessie, who beamed from ear to ear. "HEAR, HEAR!" Bill said, and they all clapped for a good long minute.

Jessie had been teaching law for five years. She was a natural and had become an institution in her own right. The work and the slower pace of Charlottesville, and Crozet, agreed with her. She and Jimmy still had the house on Q Street, but he was spending more time in Crozet, with Jessie. It was a good time in their lives.

Then, early in 2012, a judgeship vacancy opened up on the Charlottesville Circuit Court, following the unexpected death of Judge Delehanty. Dean Richmond had called the governor, a longtime friend, and suggested that Jessie would be a superb replacement. In relatively short order, on the governor's recommendation, Virginia's General Assembly elected Jessie to fill the seat. She would be a trial court judge. She would start after the Thanksgiving break, in early December.

As she passed the candied yams, Sam said, "Five years ago, you told me you wanted to be a judge, but you didn't have a clue how that was going to happen. And somehow, it has. It's awe-inspiring how good things keep finding their way into your lap."

There was happy banter at the dining table, as everyone dug into their meal. Jessie One, as Sam had taken to calling Jessie's mother (she couldn't call her Mom, and there was already a Jessie in her life), couldn't stop smiling. "Just one thing, though," Sam went on. "If you think I'm going to call you Your Honor, forget about it."

It wasn't long before the Honorable Jessie Macaulay rose to offer a toast of her own. "To my best friend, Sam Picken, who can finally sleep nights now that the record has been set straight. We all knew you nailed Rafferty, Sam. Congratulations!"

Sam smiled and said, "Thanks, Jess. It does take away some of the disappointment and the hurt."

Bill asked what they were talking about. With everything else going on, Sam hadn't had a chance to fill him and Jessie One in on Pete's call. Now she did, in detail.

"Well, well," he said. "I knew there was something wrong when the case ended in a mistrial. You kicked butt in that courtroom, and it just couldn't have ended the way it did. I'm not surprised Rafferty was behind it. The man has no soul and no bottom."

"Had no soul and no bottom, Dad. Rafferty's dead."

"Hallelujah," he exclaimed. "Now I'd like to propose a toast. Chris, be a good lad and break out some of that Pig stuff you and Jimmy drink." Sadly, the Haut Brion was gone. Happily, "that Pig stuff" was a suitable chaser.

Five glasses of Whistle Pig magically appeared. Bill stuck to water and raised his glass high. "To the death of George Rafferty," he said. "May that rat bastard burn in hell."

"That's not nice, Sam," Jessie One chided.

"I know, but it's how I feel," he rejoined.

"I'll forgive you this one time," she said, smiling. "But who are you going to hate now that George is gone?"

"Why, this Wiggins guy. He was in on the bribery with Rafferty, wasn't he? He was part of taking away Sam's rightful victory. I'll hate him, and it won't be hard."

"If they ever figure out who he is," Sam cautioned.

"Surely that won't be difficult. That juror they bribed, the Lee woman, she must know who he is."

"She doesn't. Pete talked to her after she was charged. She told him her only contact was with a woman named Dana."

"Did she say how the bribe went down?" asked Jimmy.

"Yes," Sam said. "Lee had a visit from Dana right after the first day of jury selection. At that point, a number of potential jurors had been eliminated, and there was a strong likelihood Lee would be empaneled. Dana was well-dressed and well-mannered, and she was driving a Mercedes. She told Lee she had a proposition for her that would change her life. Lee asked her who she was, and Dana said it didn't matter. She said, 'Let's take a ride,' and drove Lee to Kanawha Overlook. She showed Lee the apartment and said it could be hers, rent free, for three years. She could move in right after the Rafferty trial was over. All she had to do was vote not guilty, and that would be easy to do because there would be reasonable doubt. There was always reasonable doubt. Lee was excited but troubled. She had tried to live an upright life, which was hard at times without much money, but she had tried. Dana said she didn't need an answer right then, that Lee should take her time and think about it. Her vote would be her answer. If she voted not guilty and stuck to it, she could move into the apartment the week after the jury was dismissed. The apartment manager would be expecting her, and the rent would be covered. Lee never saw Dana again."

"Did Pete and his people ever figure out who this Dana was?"

"Yes, and surprisingly, her name actually was Dana. Dana Cropper. She worked in Rafferty's office. Her title was manager of special projects. She was Rafferty's fixer."

Everyone was into it now. "Did Dana confirm Lee's story?" asked Jessie.

"She did, down to the last detail."

"Did she know who John Wiggins was?"

"No. She hadn't even heard the name. Her only job was to contact the apartment manager if Lee voted not guilty and have him get the apartment ready; she was to tell him someone else would call him about the rent payments. Whatever the arrangements were for the rent, George handled them himself."

"And the dead tell no tales," Jessie said. "So, the mysterious John Wiggins is in the wind. Is there any chance Dana was lying and she really is Wiggins?"

"No. Dana's been charged for her role in this, and until her trial comes up her actions are being closely monitored. No indication she's involved with the rent payments. Besides, she lives and works in West Virginia, and the rent checks are coming from Baltimore."

Suddenly, Sam had a new thought. "Jessie," she said, "you know Jason Worthy well. Is there any chance he could be involved in this, or even know about it?"

Jessie thought for a long moment. "No, I don't think so," she said. "Jason's a secretive guy, and there's a lot I don't know about him. But bribery? That's not his style."

"Are you sure?" Bill asked. "I watched that guy every day during the trial. There's something wrong about him. Can't put my finger on it, and he dresses up nicely in his lawyer suit. But he's a wrong kind of a guy."

CHAPTER FORTY-THREE

Terry Gomez lived just outside the Beltway in Merrifield, Virginia. Each weekday, she walked her youngest child to the school bus at 7:23, then took the Metro into Washington. She arrived at Watson Worthy at 8:30, a little ahead of Jason. He texted her when he was five minutes away so she could have hot coffee on his desk when he got in. She accompanied the coffee with the *Charleston Gazette* the morning after George Rafferty died.

The story of Rafferty's death was front-page news, just below the fold. Jason took off his coat, sat down, and had a sip of coffee. It was piping hot with a touch of cream, just the way he liked it. He picked up the paper and smiled.

Jason had fought hard for Rafferty and kept him out of jail, but he didn't like the man. Deep down, he knew the allegations against him were true. He was all about money and wasn't going to have his miners wasting time on safety crap when they could be running coal. He was clever, though, Jason had to give him that, the way he maintained deniability by never giving a direct order. *Guys like that, the world's a better place without them,* Jason thought. *Rest in peace, shithead.*

Jason was smiling for another reason. There were lots of people he didn't like, but he didn't care whether they lived or died. What made George different was that he had something on Jason. He and he alone could tie Jason to the bribery of Dasha Lee. What's more, he was vindictive enough to use it as leverage against Jason for as long as they both lived. Well, that hadn't turned out to be very long, had it, so Jason was smiling. With George Rafferty's death, Jason was essentially home free. He sat back to enjoy his coffee and reflect.

In Jason's mind, he didn't bribe Dasha Lee. Someone else did that; Jason didn't know who except it had to be someone who worked for Rafferty. Hell, Jason didn't even know the Lee woman. He knew who she was, of course, and had spoken to her as a member of the jury when he was addressing the jury during the trial, but he had never actually met her. He hadn't paid her, either. The only thing he did was write a rent check once a month, using someone else's money. That didn't seem so bad. But he did know about the bribery. Not at first, not before the trial, but when it hit him between the eyes and he couldn't deny what was happening, he did nothing to stop it. He was part of making it all work. And George could have fingered him and would have without a moment's hesitation if it had served his purposes.

Why had he ever agreed to do it? Jason asked himself for about the fiftieth time. He had always prided himself on his legal ethics. He had played it straight throughout his entire legal career. Why had he said OK that night, a couple of days before the trial, when George asked if Jason would do him a favor? It had seemed innocent at the time. George had said he might need someone to handle some administrative matters for him after the trial was over. If Jason was willing, he would be well-paid for his troubles.

Then the trial ended. George was ecstatic about the outcome. Jason, too, was pleased; he knew he had performed well. They went back to George's office for a celebratory drink.

"I'd like to talk to you about that administrative work I mentioned before the trial," George said. Jason nodded, and George continued, "I want you to open a bank account that has a check-writing feature. It shouldn't be in your name, and it shouldn't be a West Virginia bank. Open it with a hundred dollars. Tell me when you've done that and give me the account and routing numbers. Within two hours after I hear from you, I'll wire in a deposit of $500,000. Leave $200,000 in the account. You'll need it to write a check for Dasha Lee's rent each month. The other $300,000 is for you. You did well, and I want to express my gratitude. This is apart from your firm's normal billings, of course."

There it is, Jason thought. *I didn't win the case after all. Rafferty bought a juror. I should say no right now, stop this thing in its tracks, and blow the whistle. It's the right thing to do. But I can't do it now, not when I've been drinking. I need a clear head to think this through and take action.* He decided to wait until the next day.

The issue seemed cloudier in the morning. Jason made good money as a partner at Watson Worthy, but he lived well and generally spent what he made. He saved a little each month and invested it in mutual funds. He wasn't worried about his retirement because that was way down the road, and anyway, his 401(k) would take care of it. But he had put a lot of money into Justice Hill in 2007; although he loved the result, he was in significant debt when the project ended. Then the 2008 financial crisis hit. Everything went south, the mutual funds, the 401(k), and even his earnings from the firm. Everything but his debt. It was all temporary, he knew; he was confident the economy would bounce back.

Two years had passed since then, and things weren't coming back as quickly as expected. The debt from the Justice Hill work was a killer. Jason knew he'd gulp it down, somehow, but he still owed $150,000 and couldn't seem to get over the hump. Now George Rafferty was giving him $300,000 as a bonus for doing a good job at trial. That was a lot of money. He could pay off his debt and have enough left over to make a down payment on another apartment building for the Rose Hill portfolio. That was attractive. He decided to think on it for another day.

The thing was, Jason rationalized, the money was a bonus for the work he'd done. He couldn't see anything wrong with accepting a bonus. George hadn't tied it to the rent checks, though Jason was fairly sure there was a link. Anyway, what was wrong with writing a few checks? Dasha Lee had been bribed, but Jason hadn't made the bribe and wasn't paying it, at least not funding it. He was only writing checks. That was purely ministerial. If it was wrong, he tried to persuade himself, it was only borderline wrong.

And there was one other thing, a big thing. Jason was getting tons of credit for winning the Rafferty case. That was nice in its own right, but it also meant future business for him and his firm. If he reported the bribery, it would tell the world that he didn't really win the case. The future business would vanish.

Each day, it became easier to put the decision off, and to rationalize, until one day, Jason said the hell with it and opened an account at the Sundowner Bank of Baltimore. Since some of the proceeds were going to buy another apartment building, which Jason had decided to call The Yellow Rose, he opened the account in the Rose Hill name. John Wiggins would sign the checks. There was a separate Rose Hill account at another bank, so Jason took steps to make the Sundowner account largely invisible by using a post office box address and a fake phone number. Jason believed his only real risk was George.

Now that risk was gone. It had been almost two years since Jason opened the Sundowner account. There had been no trouble, though for a time he had feared there would be. Several months ago, the US Attorney in Charleston had somehow uncovered the bribery scheme. Dasha Lee and the woman who had allegedly offered her the bribe had both been charged. They had almost surely talked, and the US Attorney must have obtained copies of the rent checks. That meant the Sundowner Bank and John Wiggins were known to the authorities, yet nothing had found its way back to Jason. Dasha Lee and the other woman clearly didn't know who was making the payments. *I have to hand it to Rafferty,* Jason thought. *I didn't like him, but he was one smart dude. No one in his world knew anything except what he told them, and he didn't tell them anything.*

Jason mentally gave himself one agenda item before turning to his legal work. He would close the Sundowner account today. That would make the trail to him even more obscure. He could do it now that he didn't have to worry about George. Dasha Lee wouldn't need the apartment much longer anyway, as she was probably going to jail. And if she did, too bad. She had accepted a bribe. She shouldn't be rewarded for that. What could she do anyway? She didn't know who was writing the rent checks.

There was still a balance of $59,000 in the Sundowner account when Jason closed it. He knew what he would do with the money. Kate Strange had changed his life. He would buy her a diamond ring.

CHAPTER FORTY-FOUR

The summer of 2014 was steamy, but Chris was refreshingly cool as he called the meeting to order. Sam had to admit she was proud of the little pecker. He had gotten himself elected mayor of Woodstock, and he was now bringing together the town's civic and business leaders to review his goals for the coming year. His major push was to continue and even accelerate the effort to attract small retail businesses, particularly high-quality shops and restaurants, to Woodstock. That would add buzz and bring money to the town, and more money would enable even greater advances.

Sam and Chris had dinner at the Café Saturday night, as they usually did. The meals there, particularly the pasta dishes, were exceptional. The owners, a young couple, were delightful. He was the chef and ran the kitchen. She ran everything else. It was a first-class operation, the kind Chris wanted more of in Woodstock.

This was an unusually nice dinner, not because it marked any special occasion or event, but because Sam and Chris were in lockstep and felt such pride in what they had accomplished. She lifted her glass of chardonnay and said, "Congratulations, Mr. Mayor." They drank, then he lifted his glass and said, "And to you, Sam, because like everything else, we did this together."

Over a fine meal and a delightful Amarone, they relived their three and a half years in Woodstock. Coming here had been a good decision. They had never been happier. They were now one of three go-to law firms in town and were living comfortably. More importantly, they had earned the respect and affection of the community. Their dinner was a celebration of their achievements, and even more, their blessings.

There was a rhythm to their lives. Chris typically began his day with coffee at the Café. It was an easy way to support his favorite client and interact with townspeople who also came for an early coffee. Chris understood the value of a quick hello here, a private word there, and perhaps some gossip across the way. The morning ritual invariably put him in a cheerful mood, occasionally yielded useful information, and generally started the day on a good footing. He then went to the office and was in before 8:00. Being mayor of a small town like Woodstock is important, but it doesn't pay the rent. Chris still worked hard at his day job.

At any given hour on any given day, he could be found working in the office, visiting a client, conducting a closing, handling town business, or attending a civic or charitable event. In his world of variables, only two things were fixed: the daily morning coffee at the Café, and his half-hour call with Ellie DiFranco on the second Tuesday of each month.

Chris and Ellie hardly saw each other anymore, not since Chris and Sam had moved to Woodstock. In fact, Ellie had also left Charleston. Her father had died, and she wanted to be closer to her mother. Chris helped with the legal niceties of getting her business reestablished in Virginia.

"It's funny," Ellie had told Chris at the time of her move. "Joey and I went to Charleston to get away from our parents. We thought having some distance between us would be a good thing. And I guess it was, but then before you know it, we're a little older, and the folks are a little older, and suddenly they don't seem so bad. Maybe it would be different if Joey were here, but I look forward to seeing my mother now. It means so much to her and, honestly, it means a lot to me too."

Their monthly phone calls were important to them both. Joey was the bond, and they remembered him in every call. Ellie liked to tell Chris Joey stories, because it was a way of recalling and reliving their time together. Chris hadn't known Joey well but had instinctively liked him. It was fascinating to have him come to life through Ellie's eyes.

Ellie had asked Chris once how Joey had died. His hesitation told her he didn't want to go back to that day. "He died bravely," was all Chris would say. She let it go.

Their friendship was rooted in Joey but grew larger. Initially, they shared stories about childhood days, college experiences, favorite movies and songs, and places they wanted to go. As trust increased, they moved on to more personal matters. They talked about values, dreams, and fears. Chris told Ellie about Sam, how she had grown up in a coal mining town with her best friend, Jessie, and how they had gone on to college and then law school. He told her about Sam's trial of the Rafferty case and her disappointment at the way it ended, only to learn later that a juror had been bribed. He told her about Woodstock and their life there.

One day, Ellie asked Chris to name the three biggest loves of his life.

"Sam, Sam, and Sam," he replied.

Tears came to Ellie's eyes. She took a moment before speaking. "There was never anyone else?"

"Never."

"That's so great, Chris. You're a lucky guy. I hope Sam's as proud of you as you are of her."

"She hasn't said it, but I think she is. We don't really talk much about personal stuff."

"How can you not tell each other how you feel?"

"I don't know. It would be weird and make us uncomfortable. We're proud of each other, and we know we don't want to be with anyone else. That means a lot. At least it does to us."

"You'd do anything for her, wouldn't you?"

"Yes, I would. Anything."

It was years after Chris met Ellie, and quite by accident, that Sam learned about her. As she tried to understand what drove their friendship, she came to realize it was a mutual need. Ellie needed someone she could talk to about Joey, someone who had known him and cared about him. Chris needed someone he could talk to about Sam, much as Sam could talk to Jessie about him. Ellie became his Jessie.

In time, Sam understood Chris and Ellie's friendship because she could relate to it in a very personal way. She understood it was more than a friendship. It was actual love.

CHAPTER FORTY-FIVE

Jason knew it was a mistake as soon as he did it. Maybe he had known even before he did it. Kate was a woman of substance. If he ended their relationship, she would never come back.

Kate had been the best part of his life. They had so much in common: art, food and wine, reading, walks in the woods, dogs. Slouch, certainly Slouch. She loved the big guy as much as he did. He always told her Slouch was hers if something happened to him.

He had thought about Kate constantly since their breakup last fall. He thought back on their time together, smiling as he remembered. She had a way of pushing him intellectually, and Jason liked that. But she did it without putting him down, and she never tried to make him into someone he wasn't and didn't want to be. He liked that too. They were easy together. They were good.

Still, things were beginning to seem routine. Three years was a long time, almost as long as Jason had been married to Jennifer. It wasn't as exciting as it had been at the beginning. Jason was a guy who needed excitement, and he had scratched that itch in his marriage to Jennifer. She had scratched a similar itch, and it all came crashing down.

Jason had learned from that experience. Things were different with Kate. He had been faithful since their first time at Justice Hill. It was easy because she held his interest and they were so good together. With Jennifer, well, there was no comparison. Then it had been two beautiful young people who were good in bed saying, "Well this is cool, let's get married," without having a clue what that meant. Kate was so different. She knew who she was.

The itch had started last fall, the fall of 2015, as a sense of everydayness was settling in. He had gone to Justice Hill a few days early to meet with a contractor who was restoring the old springhouse at the back of the property. Kate couldn't get away but would drive down to join him on the weekend.

On his second night at Justice Hill, Jason couldn't find anything to eat. He headed over to Snead's Tavern, a perennial favorite, to have something at the bar. Ollie, the bartender, was an old friend and would be good company. He would give Jason the scoop about what was going on in Hot Springs.

Pulling out a bar stool, Jason greeted Ollie.

"What's up, my man?" said Ollie. "Good to see you. Are you alone tonight?"

"So far," Jason replied. "Maybe my luck will change."

They both laughed. Jason and Kate were regulars at Snead's, and Ollie was fond of her. "I'll have a margarita on the rocks while I'm waiting," Jason said. "Plenty of salt."

"Patron Silver OK?"

"Let's do it, my friend."

As Jason enjoyed his second margarita and waited for the best burger in Bath County to appear before him, he felt a gentle hand on his shoulder. The touch was warm, definitely feminine. He turned to see an attractive young woman smiling at him.

"Excuse me," she said. "I'm sorry to bother you, but someone said you're the owner of Justice Hill. I love that place, and I wanted to introduce myself."

"I am," Jason replied. "And it's no bother at all. I've heard all of Ollie's jokes, and I'm ready for some grown-up conversation."

They sat at the bar for the next three hours, sharing drinks and stories, getting to know each other and liking what they saw. Ollie frowned but kept his distance; he knew this wasn't his business. He had seen it before, but he had thought, and hoped, that things were different with Kate in Jason's life.

They left together and went to her place. Their lovemaking was good, so gentle and slow and then urgent, then gentle again, and tender. Jason was in heaven. She made him feel interesting, and adored, and it was anything but routine. He had missed that feeling. He wanted more of it, and they saw each other the next two nights.

When Kate got to Justice Hill the following day, Jason told her he had met another woman. He knew it was a mistake, but he couldn't help himself. He wanted more of that feeling that he was the most desired man in the world. Kate didn't say a thing. She just walked away. That was the worst part.

The affair lasted a few months. By mutual agreement, they always stayed in, either at her place or his. Neither wanted to be seen in public. She had a business in town and didn't want to be talked about. He didn't want to be seen with another woman so soon after Kate. People knew Kate and liked her, and they wouldn't think well of him for quickly starting in with someone else. As the affair inevitably began to feel routine, Jason realized how much he missed Kate. He ended it in March.

Sitting alone one night at Justice Hill in early April, listening to music and drinking Widow Jane, Jason thought about Kate. The Eagles were singing *Desperado*. They were singing it to him.

> *. . . why don't you come to your senses?*
> *You been out ridin' fences for so long now. . .*

God, he missed Kate. He picked up the diamond ring she had left on the coffee table. He turned it over in his hand, remembering. What had he done?

> *. . . it seems to me some fine things*
> *Have been laid upon your table*
> *But you only want the ones that you can't get. . .*

Why couldn't he let the shiny objects be? Why couldn't he appreciate what was real, what he had with Kate? The feeling of being adored for fifteen stinking minutes just wasn't worth it.

> *Your prison is walking through this world all alone. . .*

He called Kate. She didn't answer. He left a message. She didn't call back.

CHAPTER FORTY-SIX

It was Friday, April 8, 2016. Jason drove out to Justice Hill early. It had been a long week, with an oral argument in the D.C. Circuit Tuesday morning and three rancorous depositions Wednesday and Thursday. He was looking forward to a quiet weekend at his favorite place in the world. No going out, no company, just Jason and Slouch.

The two friends took a long walk in the national forest and got back home as dusk was setting in. Jason gave Slouch his dinner, then took a long, hot shower. It felt good to be here alone. It would be better with Kate, but that was done, and he had to get on with his life.

Rather than open a new bottle of Widow Jane, he opted to finish the one-third-full Laphroaig bottle on his bar counter. It made him think of Kate; she drank Widow Jane when they were together, but he knew she preferred a good single malt. He took a sip as he sat back in the leather recliner. *Not half-bad*, he thought. He was rereading one of his favorite books, Steinbeck's *The Winter of Our Discontent*, and only had ninety pages to go. He wanted to finish it before dinner.

He closed the book at 8:45 and started to roll the pizza dough. He was determined to master making pizza from scratch. He didn't have the hang of it yet, but he was getting close. He had stopped at Whole Foods on the way out and picked up some sausage and a green pepper. He knew there were black olives in the pantry, so he was all set. He poured himself a third glass of Laphroaig. He was starting to feel a nice buzz.

It was almost 10:00, and he was taking the pizza out of the oven when Slouch headed to the front door, wagging his tail. It was unusual for someone to be way out here this time of night, but Slouch regarded whoever it was as a friend. Jason opened the door.

"Hi," the woman said. "Remember me?"

"Of course, I do. I'm just surprised. I didn't expect to see you again."

"We're done, I get that," she said, "but we had a good run, and I'd like to keep our friendship. I brought a peace offering." She handed him a bottle of Laphroaig.

"Funny, that's what I've been drinking tonight. I'm not sure why. But I'm into it now, and I finished what I had, so you've arrived in the nick of time. Please come in."

She gave Slouch a hug while he opened the bottle and poured them each a glass. "I'm glad you came by. I've just made a pizza and it's more than I can eat. Would you like to join me?"

They dug in. She said it was good. He said he needed to work on the crust. She said he was handy in the kitchen, and he'd get it right. He said it was odd to have whiskey with pizza. She said it was good though. He poured them another glass.

After they had each had their fill and given Slouch the leftover sausage, they sat on the sofa and made small talk. Yes, they were both working too many hours. No, he wasn't getting to Justice Hill as often as he'd like. No, she wasn't dating anyone, she wasn't ready yet. No, he wasn't either. Yes, they'd had a wonderful friendship, hadn't they? He refilled their glasses.

She was thinking she hated him for what he did to her. He was thinking she looked good. She was thinking she wanted to get this over with. He was thinking they were done, but maybe they could still be friends. What was the term, friends with benefits? She had come to see him, hadn't she? Hadn't she said she wanted to be friends? He poured two more glasses.

The playlist was working its way through Sinatra's *Only the Lonely* album. "Would you care to dance?" he asked, slurring a little.

She got up. It was definitely slow dancing, actually slow clinging with an occasional stumble. She could feel that he was hard. It was well past midnight, maybe even 1:00. *It won't be too much longer,* she thought. *One more glass and he'll go night-night.* She was still in good shape. He had gotten off to a huge head start, and even if he hadn't, she had always been able to drink most people under the table. Besides, she was on a mission. She had to stay alert.

He was clumsily kissing her neck and her ear. "Let's go back to the sofa," he slurred.

"Aren't you the amorous one?" she teased. "I thought you said it was over."

"I didn't really mean it." His slur was more pronounced. "I've missed you."

Great, she thought. *I'm going to have to fuck his brains out before cutting him up. Oh well, I've done it many times before. This will be the last time. And it's for a good cause.*

"Let me get us some Laphroaig first," she said, buying time and wanting to get some more alcohol into him for safe measure. She looked at her watch as she went to the bar. 1:15. The timing was good. She needed him to be unconscious at 2:00. She took a bathroom break and steeled herself for the next fifteen minutes or, at the rate he was going, maybe the next fifteen seconds.

When she returned to the sofa with two more glasses, Jason was passed out. His mouth was open, and he was lightly snoring. "That's good, sweetie," she cooed. "Sleep tight."

She waited five minutes to be sure he was out. The snoring was louder, but there was no other movement. He was well and truly toasted. Now it was time to go to work.

She reached into her bag and put on the latex gloves. She took the whiskey glasses, put them in the dishwasher, and turned it on. With a damp rag, she wiped down the Laphroaig bottle and left it on the bar. Then she took a moment to recall everything she might have touched and wiped away all possible fingerprints. Good, she thought. That only took ten minutes.

She returned to the snoring Jason. She grabbed him by the ankles and dragged him onto the floor, pulling off his pants as she did. It was a clumsy process, and she bumped the coffee table, knocking a diamond ring to the floor, but she got it done. "There, honey," she said. "You wanted to have sex, so I've taken your pants off for you. And you always liked it on the floor. Let's get it on."

She thought about Slouch. He was sleeping soundly, but she couldn't take a chance on his waking up. She reached into her bag for the syringe with the small dose of propofol and injected the big dog. It wasn't a problem. He was a great dog. She patted him and told him to sleep well.

She returned to Jason and injected the larger dose of propofol into his left arm. It was 1:45. He would be under until at least 2:30, then the propofol would wear off. He'd probably still be out of it from the alcohol, but she knew she had no time to waste. She had to get this done and get out of there.

She went to the gadget drawer next to the bar and grabbed the box cutter. She carved a crude X on his forehead, deep enough to leave a prominent scar that would alert other women he might try to seduce. Then she carved an X across his mouth, a message that women should not buy into his bullshit. Finally, she carved an X on his penis, a last warning in case he ever got that far with a woman again. Somehow, she doubted he would.

Then she went outside and waited. She waited, just in case. It was 2:00. She waited some more. 2:10. Nothing. 2:15. If her accomplice didn't come in the next five minutes, she would have to grab the chain saw she had left on the front porch and finish this herself. It had been a long time since she'd used a chain saw, but she'd been good at it once.

CHAPTER FORTY-SEVEN

Many things could be said about Bill Picken. He was a good worker and an honest man. He had dug a deep hole for himself, but he had pulled himself out. He had confronted his demons and stopped drinking, no easy task. He had rebuilt his life and restored his honor. He was loyal to a fault.

His loyalty to Big Joe Spaulding was the shovel he used to dig his way into hell, and his loyalty to the truth was the ladder he used to climb back out. He had accepted the burden of responsibility for Joe's accident, and it almost ruined him. Then, in his obsession with the Rebel Yell investigation, he sought the truth, for Joe's sake and his own. When the investigation ended and the prosecution of George Rafferty began, his loyalty to Sam was a sustaining force.

One more thing had to be said about him: he could hold a grudge deeper and longer than anyone Sam knew. When it came to the bribery of Dasha Lee and the identity of the mysterious John Wiggins, he put Jason Worthy squarely in his crosshairs and kept him there. He would never forget that Worthy was the man, along with Rafferty, who had wronged his daughter.

It turned out he was right. When Pete Gage learned of Worthy's murder, he saw a flicker of hope that they might finally find John Wiggins. He waited a month so the murder investigation could progress, and then called the Bath County Sheriff's Office. He asked to speak to the officer investigating the Worthy murder and was connected to Angelo Jones.

"I'm Pete Gage," he said. "I'm the US Attorney for the Southern District of West Virginia. I understand you're investigating Jason Worthy's murder?"

"Yes sir," Angelo said. "How can I help you?"

"Several years ago, we brought a criminal case against George Rafferty. It involved an explosion at a coal mine Rafferty owned. Jason Worthy was Rafferty's lawyer."

"I remember reading about it," Angelo said, wondering where this was going.

"The case ended in a mistrial, and a couple of years later, we discovered that Rafferty had bribed a juror. Rafferty's dead, as you probably know, but he had an accomplice that we've never been able to locate. In your investigation of Worthy's murder, has the name John Wiggins ever come up?"

Angelo thought for a minute and then remembered the name. He had heard it from Terry Gomez. "Yes, it has," he said. "Wiggins was Worthy's alter ego. Worthy ran a slumlord operation and created Wiggins to use as a cover. Jason Worthy was John Wiggins."

"Thank you, Deputy Jones," Gage said. "There's nothing we can do about Worthy now, but you've put my mind at rest."

Pete hung up and called Sam with the news. "That son of a bitch," was all she could say.

When Sam called Bill to tell him, he reacted with glee. "I knew I had the right guy. He got what he deserved, right down to losing his leg like Joe did."

When Sam told Chris, he only nodded. He was oddly quiet.

CHAPTER FORTY-EIGHT

Scott O'Hanlon was impatient. The governor was on his case. Two months had passed since Worthy's brutal murder. The people of Bath County were on edge. They wanted the killer found. The media were asking, more loudly each day, why it was taking so long.

"Why the hell is it taking so long?" O'Hanlon roared. "We have to wrap this up, and now! Emma, anything new?"

"You know what I know, Scott."

"Mahaffey?" It was bad when Scott used last names. He didn't use Emma's, but they went back a long way, and he never would.

"The only open item is the chain saw. I called the Merriman No. 3 Mine and gave them the serial number. I asked them to check all their saws and see if it was there. It wasn't."

"I know it wasn't, goddamn it. It was at Justice Hill, cutting off Worthy's leg. How did it get out of Black Bear's possession? Did they sell it? Did someone steal it?"

"They didn't sell it," Tom answered. He was calm, though Scott was anything but. Angelo was scared. He was up next.

Tom went on, "The folks at the mine think someone probably took it home to cut some firewood and never brought it back. They say that stuff happens all the time. They're apparently not very careful about controlling their portable equipment."

"Check it out. Get down there and talk to the miners. Talk to the foremen. Someone's got to know who took it."

"Scott, it was probably twenty or thirty years ago," Tom protested. Scott glared at him. "OK, OK," Tom said.

"Jones," O'Hanlon bellowed.

"Sir," Angelo said, a little too loudly.

"What have you been doing to find a suspect other than Kate Strange?"

"There's no physical evidence that points to anyone else," Angelo said, "so I've been talking to people who might have seen something or heard something. The neighbor lady, Mrs. Dawkins, watches the comings and goings at Justice Hill like a hawk. The only person she can place there other than Worthy is Kate. I've been asking around town, and no one knows of any work Worthy's had done out there since he restored his springhouse four months ago."

"You're not making me happy, Jones," raged O'Hanlon. "Did Worthy have enemies? Did he owe anyone money? What does his secretary say? What do his law partners say? Bartenders know everything—what does Ollie over at Snead's say?"

"Zippo, boss. There were some people who had run-ins with him, but nothing heavy-duty. The tenants at The Yellow Rose in Baltimore don't like him, but they think he's John Wiggins, not Jason Worthy, and anyway, they aren't going to come out to Bath County to carve X marks on him and cut off his leg."

"Yeah, what do those things mean?" Scott asked, picking up the thread. "Why would someone carve X marks on him? Or cut off his leg? That's so odd it must mean something. Revenge, or sending a message, or something like that. We already know Kate Strange was there and hated him. This could have been payback time. Her ring was on the floor, wasn't it?"

"Yes, but—"

"Don't 'yes but' me, Jones. I don't need you being her defense counsel again. Look, I don't like her for this either, but we've got nothing else. What was Worthy doing after he broke it off with her? Who was he dating?"

"No one his secretary knows about. Mrs. Dawkins didn't see any women at Justice Hill after Kate stopped coming. I've asked around town. No one's seen him with anyone else. Ollie said he was talking to a woman at the bar a few months back, and it looked like they were deep into it, but he never saw them together after that. He didn't think it meant much anyway because Worthy was always flirting with women."

"That leaves Kate all alone in the pool," Scott concluded. "Let's review what we've got on her."

"The hair sample and the partial print on the box cutter," Tom said. "And the diamond ring."

"And none of that proves much because she had lived there and left the ring there," said Scott, calming down a bit and trying to trade bombast for analysis. "Still, it's all we have. Plus, she was a forest ranger and a smoke jumper, so she knew how to use a chain saw. Anything else?"

"Two more things," Angelo said reluctantly. "I got copies of her personnel file from her old smoke jumping outfit. It turns out a lot of smoke jumpers are also trained EMTs. Kate was one of them. So, she had at least some basic medical training."

"And would have known how to give an injection," Scott finished the thought. "What else did the file show?"

"Her evaluations were off the charts. She was smart and well-liked, always the first one into a fire. She was fearless. There was one incident where another jumper had bested her at something, and she went out of her way to get even, to make him look bad. Her team leader said it was unnecessary. That was the only ding on her."

"You said there were two things. What was the other?"

"I met with the events manager at the Homestead. He gave me the attendance list for the event Kate went to the day before Worthy was killed. He also gave me the seating chart for the dinner that night. There were seven other people at Kate's table, and I called all of them to ask what they remembered about the dinner and about Kate. One of them, the guy sitting next to Kate, said she left the dinner early and never came back."

"That's about three coincidences too many for me," Scott said. "Pick her up."

"But what about the propofol and the chain saw?" Angelo protested. "We can't tie her to those."

"Pick her up," Scott repeated. "Bring her in."

CHAPTER FORTY-NINE

The Commonwealth of Virginia charged Kate Strange with first-degree murder and brought its case in the Bath County Circuit Court. The defense promptly moved to transfer the case to Charlottesville, arguing that everyone in Bath County knew about the gory killing of a respected member of the community, and it would be impossible for the defendant to get a fair trial there. The defense also argued that Charlottesville would be more convenient for the witnesses, many of whom were expected to be from the Washington, D.C. area. It would not unduly burden the Bath County witnesses, on the other hand, because it was only a hundred miles away.

As it happened, Charlottesville would also be more convenient for the defense. Amos Neale didn't include that in his motion because it wasn't legally relevant, and everyone knew where his office was anyway. There wasn't a judge or lawyer in Virginia who didn't regard the graying fifty-seven-year-old as the premier trial lawyer in the Commonwealth. Amos had an impressive record of victories, including two high-profile cases that had been thought unwinnable. When people in the legal community described him, they used terms like "wily," "superbly prepared," "masterful," and "a brilliant cross-examiner with an eye for the jugular." He was all of these things, but Amos Neale was also a kind and compassionate man.

When Pudge had called and asked him to meet with Kate, Amos said yes as an act of friendship. He wouldn't have agreed otherwise because he didn't need the work and couldn't spare the time. But he and Pudge went back a long way. Amos had been best man when Pudge married his sister Becky so many years ago. They were locked together by the tragedy of her death. Pudge was a decent man and a good friend. Amos would not say no to him. His only question was why the case mattered to Pudge, and he got the answer he expected. "Kate was at my firm. She was one of my people. I know her well enough to know she couldn't have done this. I don't want an innocent person to go to jail, and I know you don't either. Please meet with her, see what you think, and do what's right."

Although the meeting was an accommodation, Amos found himself drawn to Kate and her case. She was smart, open, and genuinely perplexed by the situation she was in. As an elite trial lawyer, Amos had developed a sixth sense about people. He trusted his instincts to an extraordinary degree. He listened carefully to Kate's story, poked gently at an apparent hole here, prodded deftly at a seeming weakness there, and never found reason to doubt her. He had represented many defendants over the years and had never met one in whose innocence he had such an unshakable belief. Against all expectations, he agreed to represent Kate.

Amos Neale's motion to transfer the case was granted without much of a fight. There was token resistance by the Commonwealth, but it evaporated quickly in the face of Judge Kent Franklin's obvious distaste for the spectacle a trial like this would create in Bath County. Equally obvious, spectacle aside, was Judge Franklin's distaste for having this mess on his plate. He granted the motion, and the case was transferred to the Charlottesville Circuit Court, where it was assigned to the Honorable Jessie Macaulay.

Sam called Jessie when she heard the news and wished her well. Presiding over this case would be no easy task, but Sam knew Jessie was up to it. Curious, Sam asked Jessie whether she had thought about recusing herself, given her past relationship with the deceased.

"Sure, I have," she said. "But the fact that I knew Jason has nothing to do with the case. This is about who killed him. I don't know the defendant, and I'm agnostic about her guilt or innocence, so I don't see a conflict."

Her analysis seemed right to Sam. They were both missing the bigger picture.

Chris, Sam, Bill, and Jessie One were keenly interested in the case because of their common hatred for Jason Worthy. At some level, they wanted his killer to get off. That was particularly true if it turned out to be the intelligent and likable Kate Strange, but they felt she couldn't be the killer because she wasn't the murdering type. The charges against her had to be wrong. As interested as they were, they held their tongues around Jessie—this was going to be hard enough for her without their input.

The trial was set to begin on Tuesday, May 30, 2017. It was expected to run for two weeks. Lily Cohen would prosecute the case for the Commonwealth. She had gone to law school at William and Mary thirty years ago and had been prosecuting cases ever since. She periodically threatened to jump to a law firm "to make some money" but never did. The truth was, she loved trying cases for the people, "fighting crime" as she described it, and she was good at it. She was meticulous in laying out facts for a jury. She was pleasant and straightforward in questioning witnesses but would bring the hammer if she thought a witness was not being straightforward with her. She and Amos Neale had squared off twice before. They had each won one and lost one.

The jury was seated with only minor squabbles. Lily and Amos were veterans who knew what they wanted, knew the value of courtroom civility, and knew when to pick their fights. Both were content with the twelve men and women who ended up in the jury box. It was an intelligent and diverse group. The lawyers believed their clients would get a fair and impartial hearing.

Lily Cohen gave a traditional opening argument. She greeted the jury, advised them of their responsibilities, and thanked them for their service. She said the case was about the gruesome killing of Jason Worthy, for which the defendant, Kate Strange, had been charged. She said it would be the jury's job to determine whether the defendant was guilty of premeditated murder. She previewed the evidence she expected to elicit from the witnesses and cautioned that some of it would be difficult to see and hear. She urged the jurors to keep asking themselves, as they listened to the evidence of how the victim had been carved up and cut up, what would motivate one human being to do that to another. She believed the evidence would show that Kate Strange had that motivation and exacted a brutal revenge on Jason Worthy.

Amos Neale sat for a long moment after Lily finished. He picked up his reading glasses from the table in front of him, looked at them thoughtfully, then put them down again. He knew the jury was watching him, and he used the silence and anticipation to elevate their interest. He slowly began to rise when he noticed Judge Macaulay's impatient fidgeting out of the corner of his eye. He moved to the front of the jury box and silently made eye contact with each juror before beginning to speak.

"I, too, thank you for your service," he said. "I'm glad you're here."

Amos spoke slowly as he continued. "Ms. Cohen has told you what she expects to show. She may show those things, some of them anyway. And then I will show you the holes in her evidence. I will show you the weaknesses in her case. And I will tell you what she has failed to show, even though it is necessary for a guilty verdict.

"Ms. Cohen has told you a crime like this one required passion, hatred, raw emotion. 'Motivation' was the word she used. 'Revenge' was the word she used. Watch my client. Listen to the evidence about her. Get to know her. As you do, you will see a person who could not have committed this crime."

Amos thanked the jury and took his seat. There was damning evidence, to be sure. There were also gaps in the evidence, crucial gaps. He had observed Kate and heard her story. He had gotten to know her and could not believe she had done what she was charged with. He was convinced the jury would come out the same way.

Amos would have to see how the evidence went in and watch how the jury reacted, but he thought this might be the highly unusual case in which he broke rule number one in the criminal defense lawyers' manual. He might put Kate Strange on the witness stand.

CHAPTER FIFTY

Lily Cohen called Deputy Sheriff Scott O'Hanlon as her first witness. Scott laid the groundwork, testifying that he had gone to Justice Hill the morning of Monday, April 11, 2016, in response to a call from Jason Worthy's law firm expressing concern about his whereabouts. He gave a detailed description of the scene they had found in the living room, beginning with the extensive quantity of blood that was present. He testified that Worthy's body was naked from the waist down, that X marks had been cut on his forehead, mouth, and penis, and that his right leg had been cut off just below the groin. He testified that a box cutter and chain saw were near the body, as was a diamond ring. He carefully described the steps that were taken to locate hair samples, fingerprints, footprints, and other tangible evidence that might be submitted for testing and analysis.

Amos Neale didn't have any serious questions for O'Hanlon, not at this point, but he wanted to get a feel for the man. "How did you know the victim was Jason Worthy?" he asked.

"I had met Mr. Worthy once," Scott answered. "I knew him by sight. Besides, we were in his house, and the call asking us to investigate came from his law firm."

"I see. We know you found hair samples, some fingerprints, and a diamond ring. Did you find footprints, or tire tracks?"

"No."

"Did you find any other tangible property that you came to consider relevant?"

"Yes, the box cutter and the chain saw. There were also two bottles of a scotch whiskey called Laphroaig. One was empty, and the other was partially full."

Looking at Lily, Amos asked, "May I assume we'll get into the evidence in detail later, either through Sheriff O'Hanlon or other witnesses?"

"You may," Lily answered.

"Then I have no further questions at this time."

Scott was excused, subject to recall. Lily called Dr. Emma Mancini. After reviewing Emma's credentials and walking her through her responsibilities as the Bath County medical examiner, Lily asked her to describe her observations at the crime scene.

"Being a medical examiner is not for the squeamish," Emma answered. "Fortunately, killings are rare in Bath County. We see a fair number of gunshot wounds, mostly caused by hunting accidents. The crime scene at Justice Hill was a sight I hope never to see again. It was a murder, yes, but it was a cruel, violent, and savage murder. There was blood everywhere."

Under Lily's guidance, Emma testified about her findings as to time and cause of death. "Worthy died between 7:00 p.m. on Friday, April 8, 2016 and 5:00 a.m. on Saturday, April 9, 2016. The chain saw severed his femoral artery when his leg was cut off, and he bled out. That was the cause of death. The X marks made by the box cutter were serious but not life-threatening."

"Sheriff O'Hanlon testified that there were no signs of resistance at the scene," Lily said. "How do you explain that in the face of what was clearly a vicious assault?"

"There were two factors that neutralized the victim and overcame his ability to resist." Emma then explained about the Laphroaig and the propofol. She was closely cross-examined by Amos Neale about the properties and uses of propofol and gave the same answers she had given Scott O'Hanlon when he had asked her similar questions.

Eliza Dawkins took the stand next. "Mrs. Dawkins," Lily said, "your house is situated on the road to Justice Hill, is it not?"

"Yes, it is."

"Is there any other road into Justice Hill?"

"No."

"How far is the road from your house?"

"The house is at the road. Well, there's a driveway, but it isn't very long. I would say it's about thirty feet from the house to the road." A photographic image confirming her estimate was shown to the jury.

"Do you have a good view of the road from your house?"

"I have an excellent view of it from the living room."

"Do you spend much time in the living room?"

"Almost all my waking hours. I'm older, and my life is basically reading books, doing needlepoint, and watching TV. I have a favorite chair in the living room, right by the window, and that's where I spend my time."

"Were you at home, and basically in the living room, between April 7 and April 10?"

"Yes."

"Please think back to that time period and tell the jury what traffic, if any, you observed going past your house to Justice Hill."

"Mr. Worthy drove in around noon on Friday, April 8. His dog, Slouch, was with him. I remember it because when he comes out for the weekend, he usually doesn't arrive until evening. The only other traffic I observed was the following morning. It was about 6:30. That girl, Kate, who used to come out with Mr. Worthy, was driving away from Justice Hill, and she had Slouch in the car with her."

"Can you identify Kate as the defendant in this case?"

"Yes, she's seated at the table over there, next to Mr. Neale."

"How can you be sure it was 6:30 when you saw Kate drive away?"

"I'm a creature of habit. My coffee machine is on a timer so that it's ready at 6:30 each morning. I get up at 6:15, wash up, and then the coffee is waiting for me when I get to the kitchen. On that Saturday morning, I had just settled into my living room chair with my first cup of coffee when Kate and Slouch drove by."

There's not too much to be done with this, Amos thought. *Kate admits she was there and left about that time. But maybe I can do a little.*

"Mrs. Dawkins, were you at your house the whole time between April 7 and April 10?"

"Yes, Mr. Neale. I only leave the house on Wednesdays. I go into Warm Springs to shop for groceries and pick up some medications. Other than that, I'm home."

"Do you spend any time in the backyard, or in parts of the house that don't have a view of the road?"

"Not in the backyard, no. If I go outside, I sit on the front porch. It's a sunny spot, and I enjoy it there. I do use the kitchen, and of course the bathroom, but I can see the road from both rooms."

"You testified that you saw Mr. Worthy arrive that Friday around noon and Kate leave early the next morning, and you saw no other traffic. Is that right?"

"Yes."

"I take it, then, that you didn't see Kate arrive?"

"No, I didn't."

"How do you explain that?"

"I saw her leaving at 6:30 in the morning. She must have arrived during the night."

"Would you not have seen her then, or at least heard her car?"

"No. I go to bed at 9:30. I believe in a good night's sleep, so I take a sleeping pill. I also wear eyeshades, so I won't be disturbed. Hardly anything wakes me. It has to be loud, or I don't hear it."

"So, if anyone went to or left Justice Hill between 9:30, when you went to bed, and 6:15, when you got up, you wouldn't have seen or heard them?"

"That's right."

That's a good place to stop, Amos thought, taking his seat. *The jury now knows that anyone could have been out there that night.*

It had been a good day for the defense. The story of the murder was in, and the basics had been established, but there was no evidence tying Kate to it. Not yet, anyway. Amos knew the following day would be rougher. Deputy Angelo Jones, the investigating officer, was up first.

CHAPTER FIFTY-ONE

This was his first time testifying in court, and Angelo was nervous. He was sworn and took the witness chair. Lily took him through his investigation, step by step. He began by covering his interviews of Eliza Dawkins and Terry Gomez. He omitted the parts about Rose Hill and John Wiggins because they weren't relevant and he didn't want to out Terry, but he was otherwise thorough.

Amos Neale made a couple of half-hearted hearsay objections but was overruled. Judge Macaulay observed that he might wish to save his objections until they were past the background testimony. "Very well, Your Honor," Amos said, smiling. He knew she was right.

Angelo's testimony about his first meeting with Kate was detailed. Her relationship with Worthy—how it began, progressed, and ended—was at the heart of the case, and Lily took care that Angelo laid it out clearly and completely. He was doing a good job, and Lily let him tell the story his own way. She interrupted only now and then to fill in a missing piece or make a telling point.

"Deputy Jones, did the defendant call the police after making her gruesome discovery at Justice Hill on the morning of April 9?" Lily asked.

"No. She acknowledged she should have, but said she had painful memories of her time with Mr. Worthy and didn't want to be involved in this."

"Do you recall the exact words she used to describe her feelings toward Mr. Worthy after he told her there was another woman?"

"She said she was 'deeply hurt' or 'badly hurt' two or three times. She also said she was 'angry' at him."

"When you had this first meeting with the defendant, did she seem sorry that Mr. Worthy was dead or emotional about the manner of his death?"

"No."

"How would you describe her demeanor?"

"She was calm and surprisingly open. She wasn't defensive at all."

Amos Neale watched intently. He found Deputy Jones smart and honest. He also had an emerging suspicion that Jones might be too kindhearted for his job and had maybe even developed a soft spot for the defendant. He wondered how he could best use that to Kate's advantage.

"What were the most important things you learned from your initial meeting with the defendant?" Lily asked.

"There were two. First, she was at Justice Hill the morning Mr. Worthy was killed, and she still had a key to the house. That means she had access, and it could explain why there were no signs of forced entry. Second, she was angry at Worthy, which establishes a possible motive for killing him."

"Let's move to your second meeting with Ms. Strange. Please tell the jury when that meeting was and what it entailed."

Angelo explained that the purpose of the second meeting was to try to get a DNA sample and fingerprints from the defendant on a voluntary basis. She had been cooperative. He also learned that her drink of preference was single malt scotch whiskey.

"Did your office analyze the DNA sample and fingerprints?"

"Yes."

"Who made the analysis?"

"Deputy Tom Mahaffey was in charge of it."

"What were the results of the analysis, if you know?"

"There was a match between the DNA sample I obtained from the defendant and the hair sample we recovered at the scene of the crime. There was also a match between her fingerprints and the partial prints that were taken from the box cutter."

Lily then had Angelo describe his efforts to find any other persons who may have been at Justice Hill between 7:00 p.m. on Friday, April 8 and 5:00

a.m. on Saturday, April 9. After he did so, Lily asked, "Would you describe your efforts to identify any such persons as extensive?"

"Yes."

"And were you able to place anyone else at the scene?"

"No. Only the defendant," Angelo said. Amos Neale thought there was sadness in his voice.

It was 3:30 when Lily's direct examination of Deputy Jones ended. After conferring with counsel, Judge Macaulay adjourned for the day. They would resume tomorrow morning at 9:00.

Amos and Kate took a moment to go over the day's testimony. Amos asked if Angelo had said anything she disagreed with. She said no, he had been truthful in recounting their meetings. Amos asked why she had voluntarily turned over a DNA sample and fingerprints. She gave her reasons.

"For what it's worth," Amos said, "I think that was smart. They were going to get them anyway and giving them up voluntarily shows the absence of a guilty mind. And they don't prove anything; I'm sure the jury will understand that."

The court came to order at 9:00 sharp the following morning. Judge Macaulay directed Deputy Jones to take the witness chair and reminded him he was still under oath.

"Good morning, Deputy Jones," Amos began.

"Good morning, sir," Angelo replied.

"Was this your first homicide investigation?"

"Yes sir, it was."

"Were you at the crime scene with Deputy Sheriff O'Hanlon and Dr. Mancini on the morning of April 11?"

"Yes."

"Was there anything about it that made a particular impression on you?"

"It was horrible, you know, really grisly. It was so violent and bloody that Scott thought a man must have done it."

Amos smiled and thought, *Well, that was a nice gift.* "Objection!" Lily yelled. "Sustained," ordered Judge Macaulay. "The jury will disregard that last answer."

"Deputy Jones, what if anything did you conclude about the match of the hair sample found at the scene to the defendant's DNA?"

"It showed the defendant had been at Justice Hill."

"Did it tell you when she had been there?"

"No."

"Did it tell you what she was doing there?"

"No."

"And the fingerprint match, what did that tell you?"

"That the defendant had used the box cutter."

"Did it tell you when?"

"No."

"Did it tell you what she had used it for?"

"No."

"So, based on those two matches alone, you did not conclude the defendant killed Mr. Worthy, did you?"

"No, it's not possible to conclude she killed the victim based solely on the hair sample and fingerprint matches."

I couldn't have asked him to phrase it any better, Amos thought. He had done well with Jones. He decided to shift gears.

"You testified on direct that the defendant likes single malt scotch whiskey. Why does that matter?"

"Because we found two bottles of Laphroaig at the scene. That's a scotch whiskey, and Mr. Worthy had consumed a large quantity of it before he was killed. Since he was generally a bourbon drinker, it appears the killer was someone he knew and invited in, someone who brought him the Laphroaig."

"When the defendant said she liked single malt scotch, did she mention Laphroaig in particular?"

"No."

"Or any other brand?"

"No."

"What connection do you make between the defendant's preference for single malt whiskey and the presence of the Laphroaig at the scene?"

"It's a data point, but not overly meaningful. There are a lot of single malt drinkers out there."

This guy is the gift that keeps on giving, Amos thought. *Time to wrap this up.*

"You spent a lot of time with the defendant, getting her story and her samples. Did you ever have the impression she was hiding anything?"

"No, sir. She was cooperative and forthcoming."

"Did she ever tell you anything that later turned out not to be true?"

"No."

"Did she have a criminal record?"

"No."

"Was there anything in her background that would have shown a disposition to commit a crime like this one?"

"Nothing that I found, sir."

When the trial recessed for lunch, Kate told Amos he had done well with Deputy Jones. "Don't thank me, Kate. That was your doing. You were straight with Jones. He likes you. He wanted to help you as much as he could, consistent with doing his job."

"So, where do we stand?"

"I'd say we're ahead right now. But Deputy Mahaffey's coming up. That means we'll hear about the murder weapon. It's starting to get serious."

CHAPTER FIFTY-TWO

Tom Mahaffey testified quickly and precisely about the hair sample found at the scene. "It was a woman's hair, blond," he said. The jury looked at Kate. Sure enough, she was blond. "The DNA test matched it to the defendant."

He was equally quick in talking about the partial prints on the box cutter. "The prints aren't conclusive because there aren't enough points of contact, but they are entirely consistent with the defendant's prints as far as they go."

"Now let's talk about the chain saw," Lily said, "which Dr. Mancini determined to be the murder weapon. Would you describe the chain saw for the jury?"

"It was a commercial model made by Hammersmith, an older model. They haven't made it in thirty years."

The chain saw was shown to Mahaffey, who identified it as the saw found next to Worthy's body. Lily introduced it into evidence as People's Exhibit 7.

"Did the saw have a serial number on it?"

"Yes. It was ten digits long. Seven of the digits were legible. Two were not. One was partially legible."

"Did you try to trace the history of the saw?"

"Yes, I worked with Hammersmith on that. I gave them what we had of the serial number. By using that information and their own records, they determined that the serial number on the saw that killed Worthy was one of nine possible numbers."

"Were they able to narrow it down any farther than that?"

"Yes, they used their shipping records to identify the buyers of the nine saws. They contacted those buyers and managed to account for eight of the saws, including one of two that were shipped to a buyer in West Virginia."

"Who was that buyer?"

"Black Bear Mining Company. Two of the saws were shipped to its Merriman No. 3 Mine in Owl Hollow."

No one in the courtroom noticed Judge Macaulay tense up, her eyes suddenly alert. They left the witness, just for a second, to glance at the newly admitted exhibit.

"Where are those saws now?"

"One of them is still at the mine. The other is in this courtroom. It's the saw that killed Jason Worthy."

"How did it get from the mine to Justice Hill?"

"We don't know. The portable equipment custodian at the mine thinks someone probably borrowed it and never returned it. The record-keeping at the mine was lax, to put it kindly. I went to the mine and asked around, particularly of the old-timers. Everyone agrees that's what probably happened because miners used to borrow portable equipment all the time, but no one has any idea who it might have been. The records show it went missing more than twenty years ago."

"Do you have any way to tie the chain saw to the defendant?"

"Chain saws have ways of moving around. People lend them to friends, who may lend them to other friends. They get stolen. They get sold at yard sales. Used saws are available at many farm or garden equipment dealers. They're even available on eBay. We can't trace this saw to the defendant or anyone else, but there are a lot of ways she could have gotten it. And she obviously did, because all the other evidence points to her."

"Your witness, Mr. Neale."

Amos rose slowly. He looked confused. "Isn't that a pretty big miss in a murder one case, Deputy Mahaffey?"

Tom started to shrug but caught himself. "Unfortunately, the evidence is rarely one hundred percent perfect. That's the nature of homicide investigations."

"Well, let's see what we have," Amos said. "Were the defendant's finger-prints on the chain saw?"

"No."

"Were anyone else's?"

"No. It seems clear the killer was wearing gloves. But the defendant's partial prints were on the box cutter."

"Ah, yes. The box cutter. The defendant spent a substantial amount of time at Justice Hill over a three-year period, did she not?"

"Yes."

"And during that time, she might have used the box cutter to open a pack-age, or slice a pizza, or carve a jack-o'-lantern, might she not?"

"She might have."

"And in the course of any of those activities, she would have left finger-prints on the box cutter, would she not?"

"Yes, unless she was wearing gloves." Mahaffey was struggling. He should have let it go at yes.

"Do you ordinarily wear gloves to open a package, Deputy Mahaffey?"

"No."

"Well, then."

Judge Macaulay unexpectedly interjected, "There's no need for sarcasm, Mr. Neale. Please move along."

"Very well, Your Honor," Amos said, regarding the judge with a long and curious look. *Where did that come from?* he thought to himself. *I might have been a little sarcastic, but not enough to warrant a rebuke.*

"Wouldn't you agree with me, Deputy Mahaffey, that the hair sample match and the partial prints on the box cutter, standing alone, aren't enough to show that the defendant killed Mr. Worthy?"

"Standing alone, yes, but they don't stand alone. There was the chain saw." Mahaffey was not about to go down without a fight, it seemed.

"Do you mean the chain saw that didn't have the defendant's fingerprints on it, and to which you otherwise can't connect her?"

"Objection," asserted Lily, "counsel is badgering the witness." It wasn't an objection she ordinarily would have made or expected to win. But she, too, had wondered at the judge's earlier rebuke of Amos and decided to test it.

"Sustained," ruled Judge Macaulay. "Please refrain from your sarcasm, Mr. Neale. I've warned you once before."

"I apologize, Your Honor," Amos said, turning back to the witness. "Have you been able to establish any connection between the defendant and anyone at the Merriman No. 3 Mine?"

"No."

"How about between the defendant and anyone at Black Bear Mining Company?"

"No."

"But you've tried, haven't you?"

"Yes, but as I said earlier, there are various ways the defendant might have gotten possession of the chain saw."

Amos decided he'd better stop there. It wouldn't do his client any good for the jury to see her lawyer being scolded by the judge.

He tried to reconstruct events to figure out what had gone wrong. These hadn't been major outbursts, but Amos wanted to understand them. Judge Macaulay had been pleasant and even-keeled throughout the trial and had suddenly gotten prickly. Amos replayed the day's events and couldn't find the reason. He wondered what was eating her.

CHAPTER FIFTY-THREE

Jessie had seen People's Exhibit 7 many times before. Her father kept the chain saw on a hook in the garage in Owl Hollow and used it to cut firewood several times each winter. Jessie had cut firewood with it too. Big Joe taught her how. He waited until she was older, until she was strong enough to pull the starter cord and mature enough to be safe. She remembered him saying, over and over, "You have to be careful using a chain saw, honey. It isn't a toy. You can hurt yourself very badly if you don't keep your mind on what you're doing."

Big Joe had loved that chain saw. He'd smile when he'd fire it up and listen to it roar. "This is a fine piece of equipment," he'd say. "The commercial saws are so much better than the residential ones. This gets us the firewood we need in half the time." Then he'd add, "Hey, Jess, remind me to bring it back to the mine one of these years, will you?" And he'd laugh heartily, like it was the funniest thing anyone had ever said.

But how did the saw get from the hook in Big Joe's garage to Justice Hill? Jessie knew the answer as soon as she asked the question. The dots were all there. All she had to do was connect them. And that was painfully easy.

The saw would have stayed on its hook in the garage after Big Joe died. Jessie's mother might have used it now and then to cut some firewood, but she always would have put it back. She was an orderly person who put things away after using them. She wouldn't have returned it to the mine; she probably didn't know Big Joe had "borrowed" it from the mine, but she wouldn't have returned it even if she did. You needed a chain saw in Owl Hollow, and this was a good one.

The saw would have stayed on its hook in the garage until Bill Picken married Big Joe's widow and moved it, with the other household goods, to Blacksburg. Bill had his own chain saw, Jessie knew that, but you can always use an extra. He might not even have known he was moving it. One of the Tech students who helped him move might have loaded it up. Anyway, when you're moving things, you just move them; you don't take the time to sort through them and leave some behind. You can see what you've got at the other end and try to sell the stuff you don't need. Bill probably wouldn't have sold it though. This was a good chain saw. Big Joe was always bragging about it.

Jessie really didn't want to connect the remaining dot, but it was staring her in the face. She knew how much Bill hated George Rafferty. She knew he had transferred that hatred to Jason Worthy when Rafferty died. She had heard him say it a dozen times around a dozen dinner tables. Bill hated Worthy because he had represented Rafferty and gotten him off, and he had done it by cheating, by bribing a juror. Worthy's cheating had deprived Sam of a victory she had earned. It had damn near ruined her life.

Rafferty had taken Big Joe's leg, and Bill and his family paid a steep price for it. There was nothing to be done about that; Rafferty was dead. But his pal Worthy wasn't. He was as bad as Rafferty, and he was still around. What was it the Bible said, an eye for an eye? Bill had an extra chain saw, and it was a good one.

It was all so clear to Jessie. The Commonwealth was prosecuting the wrong person. Kate Strange didn't kill Jason Worthy. The prosecutors may not have known how the chain saw got from the Merriman No. 3 Mine to Justice Hill, but Jessie did. Bill Picken took it there. He cut off Jason Worthy's leg with it. It wouldn't have taken thirty seconds. In half a minute, Bill exacted vengeance for Big Joe and also for Sam.

Jessie couldn't explain the Laphroaig and the propofol and the box cuts, but those were details. She could explain the murder weapon. She knew who killed Jason Worthy. What was she going to do about it?

She could only see four options. She could go to the authorities with what she knew. If she was right, Bill would spend the rest of his life in prison. If she was wrong, she would have accused him falsely. In either case, she would ruin her mother's life and Sam's as well. And her own, in the process.

She could recuse herself without giving a reason. That would mean a retrial before a new judge. Questions would arise about why the recusal came midstream and not at the outset. The media would instinctively know Jessie had acquired relevant and material information in the course of the trial. They would dig until they found it.

She could remain silent and let the trial play out. So far, there didn't appear to be enough evidence to convict Kate Strange. If she were acquitted, there would be an unsolved crime, and the police would keep looking. Bill would remain at risk, and his family and all they held dear with him.

She could remain silent, stay in the case, and put her finger on the scale. Not much, just an evidentiary ruling here or there, or perhaps a jury instruction to redirect the emphasis. She didn't want the defendant, who seemed like a nice young woman, to be wrongly convicted. Maybe she wouldn't be—that would be up to the jury.

Four options, none of them good. Three put her family at risk. The fourth violated everything she stood for but protected her family. Jessie made her decision quickly.

CHAPTER FIFTY-FOUR

"The people call Mike McAdams," Lily stated, and day five of the trial was underway.

The witness, a rugged-looking man in his early fifties, ran a small sporting goods store in Boise. This was his first trip east of the Mississippi.

"Do you know the defendant, Kate Strange?" Lily asked.

"Yes, ma'am. I haven't seen her for a long time though."

"Do you see her in the courtroom today?"

"Yes, she's sitting right over there. Hi, Kate," Mike said, giving her an awkward wave.

"Please tell the jury how you know Ms. Strange," said Lily.

"We were smoke jumpers in Idaho ten or eleven years ago. I was a team leader. Kate was on my team."

"What skills and training are required of smoke jumpers?"

"Well, you have to be willing to jump out of an airplane, and you have to be trained to do it successfully and under adverse conditions. You have to be in excellent physical condition. You have to be strong enough to carry a hundred pounds of gear and cover considerable distances on the ground with it."

"What are the basic tools a smoke jumper uses in fighting fires?"

"Chain saws and shovels."

"Did you ever see Ms. Strange use a chain saw?"

"Too many times to count."

"Was she proficient at it?"

"Absolutely. Kate was proficient in every way a smoke jumper needs to be. She was as good as any jumper I ever worked with. She was always the first one into a fire. She was fearless. I said so in a personnel evaluation I wrote on her once."

"In that evaluation, did you also relate an incident in which she sought revenge on a fellow jumper who had shown her up?"

"I don't think I said 'revenge,' but Kate was competitive. She didn't like anyone getting the best of her. She took it personally. But that was a long time ago. We were young, and we all took things personally at times."

"Still, you thought it was important enough to put in your report, didn't you?"

"Yes. It was the only flaw I saw in Kate. I wanted her to overcome it. She had a great future, and I didn't want something like that to hold her back."

"Did she have any specialized skills, over and above what you've already described?"

"She had EMT training. That's increasingly important in smoke jumping. You're out there by yourself in dangerous conditions. It's easy to get isolated. It helps to have basic medical training."

"Did that training include giving injections?"

"Yes."

McAdams was a good witness. He hadn't meant to hurt Kate, but he did, just by telling the truth. His testimony answered many of the questions the jury would have. Yes, she was strong. Yes, she knew how to use a chain saw and had done so many times. Yes, she knew how to give an injection. Yes, she had been known to seek revenge on at least one occasion. All Amos could do on cross was to try to limit the damage and adjust the angle of the light McAdams was shedding on Kate. *Keep it positive and short*, he said to himself.

"Let's talk about the incident in which you described Ms. Strange as competitive. You said you wrote it up because you wanted her to overcome it. Did you ever see her act that way again?"

"Never."

"Do you think your message got through to her?"

"I believe so. Kate is very smart. You don't need to beat her over the head to make a point. She came to me after reading the review and thanked me. She appreciated the comment because it revealed something she needed to fix, and she intended to fix it. I don't know how that went because Kate left the team a few months later, but knowing her, I'm willing to bet she fixed it."

Judge Macaulay stepped in. "Mr. McAdams, please stick to the facts in your testimony, and don't speculate about what the defendant might or might not have done."

"Sorry, ma'am," McAdams said.

"You have described Ms. Strange as smart and also fearless," Amos said, trying to revive the chastened man. "How did you rate her judgment?"

"Top-notch."

"How about her ability to keep her head in a crisis?"

"Best of the best."

"Do you have anything you'd like to add?"

"Only that if I went to war, I'd want Kate at my side. They don't come any better."

The next witness, Skip Powell, was an associate at an environmental law boutique in San Francisco. He had attended a wetlands conference at the Homestead on April 8, 2016. He had been seated next to the defendant at the dinner that night. The after-dinner speaker was an old fart who liked to hear himself talk, and Kate had excused herself at 9:45, explaining that she didn't feel well. She didn't return and Skip didn't see her again.

"All true?" Amos whispered to Kate. "All true," she whispered back.

The Homestead clerk who had checked Kate out at 6:15 on the morning of April 9 took the stand. He verified that she had checked out in person. She had not contacted the front desk or room service during the night, and no one had seen her since the dinner. Yes, he knew where Justice Hill was, it was only a few miles away. Yes, she could have left the hotel during the night and returned in plenty of time to check out at 6:15. No one saw her, but the Homestead is a big place, and most of the staff wouldn't have recognized her anyway.

Lily called Dr. Anthony Valenti. "What is your occupation, Dr. Valenti?" she asked.

"I'm an anesthesiologist in Washington, D.C. I have a small office with two other doctors. We work with surgeons at Georgetown and Sibley hospitals and with three endoscopy clinics in the Washington area."

"Do you know the defendant, Kate Strange?"

"Yes, she worked as a receptionist in our office for a brief time in late 2015 and early 2016."

"You're familiar, I assume, with the drug propofol?"

"Yes, of course."

"Do you keep a supply of it in your office?"

"That and several other drugs that we use in the normal course of our work."

"Who has access to those drugs?"

"They're kept in a locked cabinet. We try to maintain tight security, but we're a small office with only a few employees. They're intelligent and responsible, and most have been with us a long time. Besides, the drugs we keep aren't recreational, so we're probably more casual than we should be. Theoretically, any of our employees could access the drugs."

"Including Kate Strange when she was there?"

"Yes."

"Thank you, Dr. Valenti. That's all I have." Lily took her seat.

This isn't going well for Kate, Amos thought. *There's no hard evidence going in, but Lily is making points by piling up the circumstantial stuff.* His only option, once again, was to try to limit the damage.

"Dr. Valenti, do you have any reason to believe Ms. Strange took any propofol from your office supply?"

"No."

"Was any found to be missing from your office while she worked there?"

"No, not that I know of."

"Thank you," Amos said, feeling he had done what he could.

"Redirect, Your Honor," Lily said, getting to her feet. Judge Macaulay nodded. Lawyers don't always conduct redirect examinations of their witnesses. When they do, their questioning is limited to what was covered in the cross-examination.

"Dr. Valenti, you testified that no propofol was missing from your office while the defendant worked there. How often do you inventory your drug supply?"

"Every few months. If we're really busy, it can be longer than that."

"Isn't it possible, then, that propofol could have gone missing while Ms. Strange was there, but it wouldn't have been discovered until later, when you took your next inventory?"

"Yes, that's possible. It may not even have been discovered at all."

"How's that?"

"We're only required to report significant losses to the DEA. That's the Drug Enforcement Administration. They're mainly tracking recreational drugs that are missing in quantity. A small shortage isn't reportable, so we may not even notice it. That's particularly true of liquids, like propofol. A small amount could easily be poured out of a container and go undetected."

That was a dagger, Lily thought. *I'll stop there.* "The people rest, Your Honor."

"It's been a long day," said Judge Macaulay. "Let's adjourn. We'll resume at 9:00 tomorrow morning."

As he thought about the next day, Amos considered the situation. Lily had done a good job. She offered no direct evidence of Kate's guilt, but she had presented a powerful circumstantial case. Kate had been at Justice Hill the morning of the murder. She had a key and let herself in. She had been badly hurt by Worthy and was angry with him. That translated into motive. Her fingerprints were on the box cutter. Her diamond ring and her hair sample were next to the body. She knew how to give an injection and had access to propofol. She was experienced with a chain saw. Checking out at 6:15 the morning of the murder wasn't much of an alibi since there was ample time between dinner and dawn to go to Justice Hill, kill Worthy, and return.

The problem is, Amos thought, *all of that is true. There is nothing to dispute. Kate didn't do this, but the sheriff's office has no other suspects.* He knew the circumstantial becomes plausible when the defendant is the only game in town.

Amos had no choice. He had always believed in Kate. He thought the jury would too. He had to put her on the stand.

CHAPTER FIFTY-FIVE

Sam never knew why Chris liked the damn thing so much, but one of his favorite possessions was a carved wooden grizzly bear he had picked up when they were in Charleston. Preston, as he called it, stood about five feet tall and was rearing up on its hind legs, snarling and reaching forward aggressively with its right paw as if beginning an attack. It was the kind of thing you see guys selling out of the backs of their pickups along country roads. *Kind of cheesy,* Sam thought, *but the little shit loves it.*

The Picken & Lloyd office in Woodstock was a small, two-story frame house. Shortly after they moved in, Chris stationed Preston on the sidewalk outside the door. He had acquired one of those Smokey Bear hats, and he put it on Preston's head when he got to the office each day. He exchanged it for a sleeping cap, one of those long ones that hang down with a puffball at the end, when he left each night. It was a ritual the townspeople came to understand. The Smokey hat meant the office was open, please come in. The sleeping cap said sorry to miss you, please try us again tomorrow.

Sam and Chris worked Saturdays as a matter of course. But on the first Saturday afternoon in June, the sleeping cap went into service early. Bill and Jessie One were coming up for dinner and would stay the night. There was some grocery shopping to do before they arrived.

Their visits were always a joy. Bill was the great guy he had been when Sam was growing up. During his lost years, she never expected to see that guy again. She never thought Chris would get to meet him. Now they were fishing buddies.

It was glorious in the Shenandoah Valley, as June so often is. The air was crystal clear, and Massanutten Mountain to the east and North Mountain to the west were proudly strutting their stuff. It was perfect for a low-key evening on the patio. Chris, Sam, and Jessie One enjoyed a cosmopolitan while Bill, the rising sophisticate, had advanced from water to club soda with lime.

"Dad, I always feel guilty when we're drinking and you're not," Sam said.

"Not to worry," Bill replied. "Whenever I think I'm missing out, I remember that awful place I used to be. I don't want to go back there. Club soda suits me fine."

Chris threw some strip steaks on the grill along with fresh corn on the cob from Adams Apples. Sam had roasted some potatoes and made a nice salad from their garden. To accompany this feast, they had chosen a local cabernet, the award-winning Clio from Muse Vineyards. And, of course, a nice club soda from Schweppes.

They held off talking about the trial as long as they could, although it was on all of their minds. Finally, as they were finishing their steaks, the most innocent among them ventured in. "What does anyone hear about the trial?" asked Jessie One.

"They're about halfway through," Sam offered. "I went over and watched the morning session on Thursday. The deputies were testifying when I was there, describing the investigation and what they found. It seemed pretty routine at that point. Jess was doing a good job."

Jessie One smiled. That last part was what she wanted to hear. Sam had been truthful—she didn't know much beyond what she had said. She had a day job, and it was keeping her busy. Her three hours in the courtroom hadn't caused her to alter her belief that Kate Strange was an unlikely candidate for Worthy's murder.

Chris said he didn't know much, which was no surprise. His various responsibilities didn't leave him much extra time. Besides, it stood to reason that his interest level was lower than Sam's. Her hatred of Jason Worthy was pure because he had harmed her. She wanted his killer not only acquitted but celebrated. Chris hated him, too, but his hatred was derivative. Sam's had to be the greater interest because hers was the greater hatred, right? Also, the trial judge, Sam's best friend, was presiding, and it was an important case. Sam was interested in how she was doing.

"Do you know any more than the rest of us, Dad?" Sam asked.

"I'm afraid not," Bill lied. "I haven't been paying much attention to the trial."

In truth, he had followed the trial closely and had been riveted to it since Deputy Mahaffey's testimony. *The murder weapon was a chain saw that was shipped to the Merriman No. 3 Mine many years ago and then disappeared?* Bill thought. *That was the saw Big Joe "borrowed" and cut firewood with until he died. He always meant to give it back but never did. I got it when I married his widow.*

Mahaffey's testimony caused Bill great anxiety. Things had suddenly gotten personal.

CHAPTER FIFTY-SIX

Amos and Kate did all they could when the trial resumed. She told her story directly, without drama or self-pity. Yes, she had been angry at Worthy. Yes, she had been at Justice Hill the morning of April 9, 2016 and had seen the body. No, she hadn't called the police although she knew she should have. Yes, she had used the box cutter when she used to stay at Justice Hill, but no, not the night Worthy died. No, she had not taken propofol from Dr. Valenti's office, and in fact had never taken anything that didn't belong to her. No, she had never before seen People's Exhibit 7, the chain saw. Yes, she had been in her room at the Homestead the entire time between her April 8 dinner and April 9 checkout, but no, she had no one to corroborate that. No, she had not killed Jason Worthy.

The jury saw the same Kate that Amos saw, a levelheaded, stand-up person who didn't look capable of murder, let alone a gruesome killing like this one. But someone had killed Worthy, the circumstantial evidence said it was Kate, and there was no one else to blame. She hadn't disputed the evidence because it was true. Lily hadn't cross-examined her because it didn't seem necessary. Lily's circumstantial case was intact, and it was strong. The jury would either believe Kate or it wouldn't.

In his closing argument, Amos stressed that all the evidence, taken as true, did not establish guilt beyond a reasonable doubt. The jury could not get from the evidence to a guilty verdict without making enormous and impermissible assumptions. Among them were the assumption that Kate took propofol from Dr. Valenti's office, although he didn't say she had and she denied she had, and the assumption that she came into possession of a chain saw owned by a mining company in West Virginia, although she denied ever having seen it before. The people had not tied Kate to the murder weapon, Amos argued, and that was fatal to their case. "Look at the defendant. You've gotten to know her over the last week. You've heard testimony from her and about her. Can you really believe, beyond a reasonable doubt, that she killed Jason Worthy?"

In her rebuttal, Lily argued that "the defendant may present well and portray innocence, but it is well to remember that she thrived in the violent world of smoke jumping." Lily asked the jury to ponder two proverbs that "have stood the test of time: first, 'You can't judge a book by its cover,' and second, 'Hell hath no fury like a woman scorned.'" She implored the jury "not to be taken in by the innocent cover, but to read the book, and judge according to the evidence."

Judge Macaulay instructed the jury using Virginia's model instructions for criminal cases. Amos had no quarrel with that, but he was concerned with the emphasis she chose to apply in reading those instructions to the jury. She stressed that reasonable doubt is a doubt "based on your sound judgment" after a full and impartial consideration of the evidence. She underscored that the jury "may convict the defendant on circumstantial evidence alone."

Although she read all the words, Amos thought Judge Macaulay's emphasis on select phrases transformed their meaning. He felt the jurors might understandably have believed they were to decide using their best judgment and could convict solely on circumstantial evidence. He felt the reasonable doubt standard had been deemphasized to the point of evisceration. That was a critically important error in a case like this one, where circumstantial evidence was all there was.

Amos asked for a sidebar to state his objection. Judge Macaulay looked to Lily for a response. Not surprisingly, she hadn't noticed anything unusual or improper in the way the instructions were read. Amos was overruled, with the judge chiding him for being overly sensitive. She granted his request that his objection be preserved for the record.

The case went to the jury, which deliberated for a less than a day before convicting Kate Strange of murder in the first degree.

CHAPTER FIFTY-SEVEN

Sam was in the courtroom when the verdict was announced. From what she had seen, it was an outrageous miscarriage of justice. Jessie had not prevented it. Far worse, she appeared to have engineered it. Sam was beside herself. That wasn't the Jessie she knew and loved. Why had she done it? Sam had no answers. She didn't want to see Jess but resolved to write her a pointed letter that evening.

After dismissing the jury, Judge Jessie Macaulay retired to her chambers and slumped in her chair. Filled with relief and shame, she sat, stared, and wept for a full hour.

Kate was placed in handcuffs and led from the courtroom. She looked confused and terrified.

Amos assured Kate that this would get fixed on appeal and then sank into his chair at the defense table. *What the hell happened?* he wondered. *Kate didn't do this. I let her down. Not just me, though—there was something weird going on with the judge. I need to review the record carefully and figure out what it was.*

Angelo Jones sat in the rear of the courtroom and sadly shook his head. *This isn't right*, he thought. He had always believed in Kate's innocence. They had to charge someone because of political pressure, he got that, but he, Scott, and Tom had failed Kate by not finding the real killer. He was disgusted with himself for his part in this travesty. Slowly, he got up to leave. Terry Gomez and Eliza Dawkins had been helpful, and he wanted to tell them what had happened.

Bill was at work in Blacksburg when news of the verdict flashed across the television screen. He excused himself from the restaurant and went to sit in his car. He needed some time alone to process the result of the trial.

He felt terribly for the young woman. He knew she hadn't killed Worthy. But his empathy for Kate was secondary to his enormous relief. His thoughts went back to his two-week stay in Charleston during the Rafferty trial. He and Chris had dinner one night when Sam was working late to prepare for the next day's witnesses.

"I have a present for you in the car," Bill had said to Chris. "It's Big Joe Spaulding's chain saw. It got moved up here from Owl Hollow with his other things. I know you don't need it now, since you and Sam live in an apartment and don't have a fireplace, but you will someday. There's no point in my having two of the damn things."

"Thanks, I guess," Chris said. He certainly didn't need it now, but he couldn't argue with Bill's reasoning.

"There's just one thing," Bill added. "Keep it in your office until you need it. Sam doesn't like chain saws, and you don't have room for it in your apartment anyway."

After they left the restaurant, they went to Chris's office and dropped off the saw. Bill was right; Sam didn't like chain saws. When she was in fourth grade, a friend of hers was accidentally nicked by one, and it left a terrible scar. Sam got physically sick when she saw it.

Bill had been worried ever since Deputy Mahaffey's testimony about the chain saw. He was worried for Chris, whom he had come to love like his own son. Chris wasn't a violent guy, but Bill knew he hated Worthy almost as much as he himself did. There was one other thing Bill knew: when it came to Sam—loving her, protecting her, maybe even avenging her—there was absolutely nothing Chris wouldn't do.

CHAPTER FIFTY-EIGHT

S am fired off a letter to Jessie as soon as she got back to the office. It was short and biting. She was disgusted and let Jessie know it. It was more threatening to their friendship than anything Sam had ever done. But the same could be said about Jessie's conduct. Sam was pissed. The post office was around the corner on Muhlenberg Street. She would drop the letter off on her way home.

You can never find a stamp when you need one, Sam thought. She knew Chris would have stamps, somewhere. He was one of those guys, whatever you needed, he had it. A stapler, an envelope, a deck of cards, some chewing gum, it didn't matter—Chris would have it. She opened the drawer on the right side of his desk. There were the stamps.

There was also a photograph Sam had never seen before. It showed two soldiers in camo fatigues lounging against a jeep. They were hot and sweaty, and their shirts were unbuttoned. Each was holding a can of beer and wearing a broad smile. One was a younger version of Chris. Sam didn't recognize the other, but the handwriting at the bottom of the photo said, "Joey DiFranco and Chris Lloyd, Iraq 2005." She instinctively knew that Joey was the other guy in the jeep, the one who was killed. She looked at Chris and smiled at the goofy little shit in his soldier suit.

Chris was working at home that afternoon. He had a closing the next day and needed some uninterrupted time to review the documents. That wasn't possible in the office. Between his mayoral duties, the telephone, and friendly people popping in to say hello, something was always going on. Sam called him to let him know she was back from Charlottesville and tell him about the verdict.

Chris was stunned that Kate Strange was convicted. His thoughts went to Ellie as he tried to make sense of this development.

He remembered her third or maybe fourth visit to his office back in Charleston. They had gotten over the shock of their discovery and were settling into a strong new friendship cemented by Joey. When their business was completed and she was about to leave, she noticed a chain saw in the corner.

"That's an odd place to keep a chain saw," Ellie observed.

"We don't have room for it in our apartment, and I don't need it now," Chris said. "I'm just storing it here for the time being."

"Let me borrow it for a few days. I'll make something for you," she said, smiling.

"Like what?" Chris asked, returning her smile.

"You'll see," Ellie teased.

"Who could resist that?" Chris said. "Take it. But be sure to bring it back. It was a gift from Sam's father."

When she came for their next meeting two weeks later, Ellie wrestled a cardboard box that looked like a small coffin into Chris's office. "What in the world is that?" Chris asked, laughing.

"I told you I'd make you something. Open it!"

Chris did. He was delighted with the carved grizzly bear that he pulled out of the box. It was quite good. "Wow. Did you make that? I don't know what to say."

"I call him Preston," Ellie said, "but you can rename him if you like."

"Preston?"

"Yes. Like *Sergeant Preston of the Yukon*. Do you remember him from the old-time comic books? It just popped into my head. You know, he was in the Royal Canadian Mounted Police, and there always seemed to be a grizzly in the story."

"Then Preston it is. Thanks, Ellie."

"My pleasure. Anything for my favorite lawyer. By the way, I'll bring your chain saw back next time. It was more than I could manage today along with Preston here."

"Sure. No rush. I won't be needing it for a while."

A few years passed. They were both busy, then Chris moved to Woodstock. It was 2016 before Ellie reached out about returning the saw.

CHAPTER FIFTY-NINE

Sam called Jessie after getting her reply. Given the accusatory tone of Sam's letter, they were both tentative, and the call was awkward, but they managed to schedule lunch for the following Wednesday in Staunton. Sam had made an unwanted discovery since sending her letter, and her anger at Jessie had abated.

Three mornings a week, while Chris was at the Café attending to his ritual coffee, Sam went to the gym. She hated it, but after she got there it wasn't so bad, and she actually felt virtuous after the workout. Then came the best part—she went home, took a hot shower, and had a relaxed coffee all by herself. She checked her emails while enjoying the coffee, so she wasn't being entirely slothful.

On Monday, June 12, Sam had a heads-up call at the gym from a friend at the circuit court involving a case development that was important to one of her clients. She knew her client would want to know about it as soon as possible, so she spent the remainder of her workout mentally composing an email to send when she got home. Great plan, but she couldn't find her laptop at the house and realized she had left it in the office the evening before.

Chris had a desktop computer in the den that he used primarily for town business and other non-law office work. It wasn't password protected, and Sam knew he wouldn't mind if she used it to send her email. They were both careful about respecting each other's privacy, but there were no secrets between them. Her borrowing his computer to send an email wasn't a big deal.

As soon as she powered on, Sam realized she didn't have the client's email address. Her name was Janice Dean, and since Chris also did work for her, Sam went into his contacts to see if he had the address. There were only four entries under D and Janice Dean wasn't one of them. There was an Ellie DiFranco, however, a name Sam didn't recognize. Surprising, since she and Chris talked about their friends openly. *DiFranco? That was the name of Chris's friend in the photograph, wasn't it? The one who was killed in Iraq? Joey DiFranco?*

Sam's curiosity got the better of her. She ran a search for Ellie DiFranco. One email came up. It was more than a year old. On April 6, 2016, Ellie had emailed Chris.

> I want to return your chain saw. You can pick it up on the front porch at JH at 2 a.m. on Saturday, April 9. Your "friend" will be inside waiting for you, immobilized, but only until 2:30. Be there at 2 a.m. sharp—it's important! Let's talk next Tuesday.
>
> P.S. I'll bet Sam will be pleased!
>
> P.P.S. Joey died eleven years ago today. My heart aches.

Sam read it and read it again. It made absolutely no sense. The last part tied Ellie to Joey, though. *She must have been his wife. How does Chris know her?*

What's this about returning a chain saw? I saw our chain saw in the garage when I pulled in this morning. It's the one we bought at Lowe's when we got this house. We didn't need one before then. What's she talking about?

What's JH, and why would Ellie leave a chain saw there for Chris to pick up instead of just sending it to him? And what chain saw? What "friend" will be inside? Why 2:00 in the morning? That's an odd time to do anything except sleep. What's all the skulduggery about? And mostly, why the hell would I be pleased?

Sam's heart was racing. Her mind was racing. *Calm down,* she said to herself. *Just think this through. Let's start with the date. What was happening around April 9, 2016?*

Suddenly, it hit her. People had been talking about that date last week, when she was in Charlottesville at the trial. *Shit! That's the date Jason Worthy was killed!* And then it all came rushing in. *JH is Justice Hill! He was killed with a chain saw!* And then the worst part. Sam would "be pleased." Yes, she was OK with Worthy being dead. *But what does any of this have to do with Chris?*

Sam was coming unhinged. Whatever this was, it seemed very real. This Ellie person sounded like she was involved with Worthy's death. Sam didn't know her, so she didn't care. She had a fleeting happy thought that this would set Kate Strange free. *But what did Chris have to do with it? He couldn't have been involved—not Chris! I'm sure he was here with me that night. He never goes anywhere. He has an alibi. Me.*

Sam went to her 2016 Day-Timer to be sure. She knew exactly where it was because she kept her calendars with their respective year's tax file. She opened it to April. Her heart sank. Chris never traveled, but her calendar said he had been in Lexington the night of April 8 having dinner with a college friend. *I can't alibi him. But if it comes to that, I'll alibi him anyway. I'm not losing this guy.*

The impossible was looking less so. Sam could feel everything starting to slip away. She knew she couldn't talk to Chris about this. What was she going to do, ask him if he killed someone? What if he said yes? Where would they be then? What if he said no? Would she believe him?

Wait a minute. The chain saw. They said at the trial that it had been shipped to the Merriman No. 3 Mine, and then the trail went cold. They thought a miner probably took it and didn't return it. *I wonder if Dad knows who it was. Come to think of it, I wonder if Jessie knows anything about it. She showed me Big Joe's chain saw once when we were girls, even though I didn't want to see it. She said her dad let her use it sometimes, if he was with her and she was careful. Wait, it's coming back to me. She said he had borrowed it from the mine and would have to return it one of these years. She said he laughed every time he told her that.*

Sam was on the phone to her dad. "What happened to Big Joe's chain saw?" she demanded.

"What do you mean?" Bill replied. "Why are you asking?"

"C'mon, Dad, this is important. When you and Jessie One got married, did you bring the chain saw up to Blacksburg?"

"Sam, I don't think we should have this conversation." He knew Sam wasn't accusing him. He knew she was worried about Chris.

"Dad, did you give Big Joe's chain saw to Chris?"

He was silent. She had her answer. And now she understood Ellie's email.

CHAPTER SIXTY

Jessie and Sam greeted each other at their favorite restaurant in Staunton. They hugged each other as they always did. They ordered their usual bottle of rosé. They tried to be as they had always been. But it wasn't working. It felt staged. It was awkward, uncomfortable. Something had changed, something deep and personal. Something essential. They both knew it.

"Sam, I—" Jessie began.

"No, don't." Sam broke in. "I was wrong. There's nothing to explain. I understand now. Thank you for what you did."

Jessie looked up. "Do you?" she asked.

"Yes."

There was a strained silence. "I don't want this to affect our friendship."

"No, neither do I."

It was too late. Their friendship was already different. And they couldn't even talk about it. They couldn't take the risk.

Jessie had concluded that Bill Picken murdered Jason Worthy. She had abandoned her oath of office, her values, and everything she stood for to help him get away with that murder. What else could she do? She did it for Bill, more so for her mother, and mostly for Sam. She did it to protect them and preserve the relationships that were their everything.

It had never occurred to Sam that her dad killed Jason Worthy. She had concluded it was Chris, and that Jessie knew it. Why else would Jess have acted against all of her principles? She did it to protect Chris, to protect Sam, really, because she knew Sam couldn't live without him.

Jessie couldn't talk to Sam about her father being a coldhearted killer, and Sam wouldn't have wanted her to. What would that conversation look like? Where would it go? And Sam couldn't talk to Jess about the savage act Chris had committed out of revenge. He did it for her, and she couldn't hate him for it. But Jessie might not see it that way. Not many would see it that way. It was too intimate and intense to talk about, even for Jessie and Sam. What would they say? Tell me, what's it like living with a man who cut off another man's leg with a chain saw? How could they ever again be who they were?

Then there was the price Jessie had paid to protect Sam. It was too high. She might come to resent Sam for what she had given up. Even if she didn't, Sam would never be able to repay it. They were uneven. They could never be even again.

They weren't the people they had been. The goodness and nobility of their younger selves were gone. They had made compromises. They had fallen from grace. For the first time, they had secrets. If they weren't who they had been, how could their love be what it was?

CHAPTER SIXTY-ONE

Angelo Jones called Terry Gomez to close the loop. He thanked her for her help and told her about the verdict. She was gracious about the former and incredulous about the latter. "I don't know how that could have happened," she said, "But I'm telling you right now that girl didn't do it. Either she had a lousy lawyer, or someone bought someone off."

Angelo laughed. "Well, she didn't have a lousy lawyer. I don't know about the second part. I watched most of the trial, and there were times I thought Kate was too honest for her own good."

"Yes, she's honest. She's also kind. I hope she wins on appeal. She didn't do it."

"Thanks again for your help, Terry."

"Sure. By the way, I work for Pudge Watson now. He asked for me after Jason died."

"How's that working out?"

"Night and day. Pudge is a good guy through and through."

"I'm happy for you," Angelo said.

Then he called Eliza Dawkins. He would visit her since she was local, but he didn't want to drop in unannounced. The answering machine said she was away until Friday, June 16. He called that day, and they made an appointment to meet the following Monday afternoon.

As Angelo drove the now-familiar twisting road to Eliza's house and Justice Hill, he thought about all that had happened. He felt heartsick about Kate's conviction. He knew she didn't kill Worthy. *How did we miss the real killer? There had to be clues that eluded us. What were they? Why didn't we see them?*

Slouch was there when Worthy was killed, Angelo thought. *He was there until the morning, when Kate left with him. Kate said he was barking frantically when she arrived. Eliza heard him too. Why didn't he bark when Worthy was being killed? Why didn't he protect his master? Maybe he knew the killer. Maybe, but a dog still wouldn't sit silent while his master was being carved up with a box cutter and cut up with a chain saw. He had to have been incapacitated. He had to have been out when the carving and cutting started. Maybe he was given a shot of propofol too.* There had to be an explanation, and that was as reasonable as any.

Angelo pulled into the driveway between the carved wooden eagles. Eliza Dawkins greeted him at the front door. "Would you like some coffee?" she asked. "I just made a fresh pot."

"That's very nice of you," Angelo said. "Yes, with just a little cream, please."

Angelo waited in the living room while Eliza went to the kitchen to get the coffee. There was a small wet bar in one corner. On the counter, next to the sink, was a bottle of Laphroaig. It brought Angelo up short, but he reminded himself there must be a million Laphroaig drinkers in the world. Besides, Eliza Dawkins didn't look like someone who would have cut off Worthy's leg with a chain saw. Still, you couldn't be too careful. He'd better run it down.

Eliza returned with two coffees. She gave the one with cream to Angelo and eased into her favorite chair. He sat opposite her and sipped his coffee. "This is good," he said. "You're nice to see me. I wanted to thank you for your help and tell you about the trial."

"Yes," she said. "I've already heard. News travels fast in a small town. I never really knew Kate, but I feel badly for her. A lot of people out here knew her, and some think she was wrongly convicted. What do you think?"

Angelo wasn't about to say his office had charged the wrong person, so he parried the question. "There was a lot of evidence against her. Much of it was circumstantial, so I can understand how some people might wonder about the verdict. The jury found her guilty, and that's what matters. Did you follow the trial, Mrs. Dawkins?"

"Heavens, no. I have plenty to do without that. I just saw the result on television."

"Say," Angelo said in a none-too-smooth segue, "I noticed a bottle of Laphroaig on your bar. I didn't have you figured for a whiskey drinker."

"Oh, I'm not," said Eliza. "Trust me on that. My drinking days ended a long time ago. That bottle belongs to my daughter. She likes that brand, and she brought a bottle with her when she came over to make me dinner Saturday night."

Angelo perked up. "I didn't know you had a daughter, Mrs. Dawkins."

"Yes, she's grown up and has been on her own for a long time. I guess it didn't come up when you were here before."

"I'd like to hear about her," Angelo fished. He was alert.

"Her name is Elise. It's like mine, but different. She's a good girl, always got good grades. She and her husband lived in Charleston, but he was killed in Iraq, and she moved back to Hot Springs after my husband died."

"I'm sorry to hear about her husband. You seem very proud of her." The nibbles on Angelo's line were distinct.

"I am," Eliza said. "Did you happen to notice the carved eagles by the driveway?"

"Yes, I admired them. They're very beautiful."

"Elise made them for her father and me when she was in high school. That was the year she won the chain saw carving contest at the county fair. Funny, you don't usually think about girls using chain saws."

Angelo had actually been thinking about it a lot lately. The hook was in deep.

"Did Elise remarry after her husband died?"

"No. She really loved Joey. Her husband, that is. His name was Joey DiFranco. She had a hard time after he died. I think she may be starting to date again now. Finally. She doesn't talk to me about it though."

"What does she do for a living?"

"She has her own business, and she's very proud of it. She's a veterinarian. In fact, she took care of Slouch a couple of times when he and Mr. Worthy were staying at Justice Hill."

That's game, set, and match, Angelo thought, wincing at his mix of metaphors. "Well, I'd better go, Mrs. Dawkins. Thanks for the visit and the coffee."

He backed out of the driveway, glancing at the eagles. He drove until he could not be seen from Eliza's living room. Then he pulled over. There was a loose end he wanted to tie down.

"Ollie," Angelo said into the phone. "This is important. The woman you told me Worthy was having drinks with at Snead's a few months back. Did you know her?"

"Sure. She's the town veterinarian. Doc DiFranco."

Angelo called Scott O'Hanlon.

CHAPTER SIXTY-TWO

Ellie was brought in for questioning. Her computer and cell phone were seized and examined. The evidence against her was overwhelming. She engaged Kevin Donovan, a fine criminal lawyer in Harrisonburg, to represent her. She had no plausible defense, and, with her acquiescence, Kevin entered into plea negotiations with Commonwealth's Attorney Lily Cohen.

Deputy Tom Mahaffey found Ellie's April 6, 2016 email to Chris on her computer. He asked Ellie who Chris was and how deeply he was involved. She recognized that the question gave her an out, or at least leverage, but she didn't take it. She couldn't do that to someone she loved. She said Chris had never responded to her email. That squared with what Chris said when Deputy Mahaffey called and put the question to him. Chris was home free when his college friend, Dan Albanese, confirmed their dinner in Lexington on April 8 and beers into the early morning hours on April 9. Of course, Chris didn't tell Sam any of this. But then, he didn't know she had seen Ellie's email.

Kate's conviction was set aside based on new evidence. With the apologies of the court and the Commonwealth, she was released from prison. Angelo drove her home to Arlington. Slouch had been staying with a friend but was there to greet her, tail wagging enthusiastically, when she arrived.

Amos Neale and Lily Cohen filed a joint motion to dismiss Kate's appeal as moot. Lily apologized to Amos for having worked so hard to put his client, an innocent woman, in prison. "You were doing your job, Lily," Amos said.

"You had it right, though, when you told the jury, 'Hell hath no fury like a woman scorned.' You just had the wrong woman."

"Thanks," said Lily. "Did you ever figure out what was eating Judge Macaulay?"

"No. I've been crawling through the record and can't find anything to explain it. I was thinking about asking for an inquiry into her behavior, but I guess I'll let it go now that Kate's free. Judge Macaulay has a stellar reputation. Her actions in this case were subtle, and it would be hard to prove she intentionally acted in a prejudicial manner. Anyway, what she did seems to have been an aberration. No point tarnishing her reputation and alienating the court."

Others in the judicial and legal communities were less forgiving. There was no fire, but the smoke and rumors persisted, and the General Assembly turned its back on Jessie when she came up for reelection. Her judging days were over. The price she paid was indeed high. With Nell Richmond's encouragement, she resumed her law professorship at the University of Virginia.

CHAPTER SIXTY-THREE

The world seemed to be moving in the direction of normal by the fall of 2017. George Rafferty and Jason Worthy were dead, so there was no one left to hate. With the release of Kate Strange, faith in justice had been restored. Football was in the air and there was every indication that Virginia Tech would have another strong season.

Sam and Chris hosted the gang for Thanksgiving. She produced another beautiful turkey, having told Chris to take his turducken suggestion and shove it. They couldn't top the 1989 Haut Brion they had served in 2012, but they came pretty close with a 1995 Chateau Margaux that was out of this world. Bill opined that the Schweppes was of unusually high quality.

Bill and Chris were spared now that Ellie DiFranco had pled guilty. Bill was in the clear with Jessie, and Chris was in the clear with Bill. Sam was the only one who still had doubts that all the shoes had dropped in the Worthy murder investigation, because she alone knew who Ellie was and had seen her email to Chris. She was destined to continue living with a man she loved but had come to believe was a murderer.

Although Jessie and Bill were relieved of their burdens, they gave no inkling of the suspicions they had held. How would it help Bill's relationships with Chris and Sam to say he had suspected Chris of murder? How would it help Jessie's relationships with Bill, her mother, and Sam to say she had suspected Bill of murder? The suspicions, no matter how well-founded or deeply believed, were too awful, too unforgivable, ever to be told. Bill and Jessie had not told them, even to their spouses, and never would. Sam would never tell her suspicion either, even to her husband.

Because if they did reveal their darkest thoughts, the relationships among their band, the ties that held them close, the bonds Jessie had protected at extraordinary personal cost, would be shattered. Keeping secret their suspicions was the only way to spare them and preserve their friendships. Except for Jessie and Sam. They were already lost. But they would fake it, for the sake of the others.

They couldn't talk about these things, but they could and did talk about Kate and Ellie.

"Let's drink a toast to justice," Bill said, raising his glass. "Justice for Jason Worthy and Kate Strange." All said hurrah and sipped their wine.

"Ooh, that's good," sighed Jessie One. "I'd better have another taste just to be sure."

"I'm with you on that," said Jimmy. "Both parts of it."

Bill, the clearheaded analyst, weighed in. "It's really odd how this got resolved. Ellie DiFranco surfaces out of the blue, and her mother turns out to live next door to Justice Hill."

"From the reports I've seen," said Jimmy, "the deputy, Angelo Jones, did some strong detective work and broke this thing wide open."

Sam and Jessie were silent as the others talked. Jessie was silent because she had been involved with the case and felt shame for having presided over the conviction of an innocent woman. Sam was silent because she knew too much and was still afraid for Chris.

"Ellie must have loved Worthy or hated him or both to have cut him up like that," observed Jessie One. "I wonder what made her tick."

There was a long silence. Then Chris spoke.

"Ellie was a friend of mine. I should say she is a friend of mine. More than a friend, really. Her husband, Joey, was in the jeep with me in Iraq when I got hurt. Joey was killed. Ellie came to me for legal work in Charleston. It was a fluke. We discovered we were connected by Joey, and our friendship began."

The room was deathly quiet as Chris spoke. No one ate. No one breathed. Everyone wondered where this would go.

Chris told the story of their friendship, how it had developed and evolved. He talked about lending her the chain saw, and her gift of Preston. He talked about their monthly phone calls, how they depended on each other and confided in each other. He had told Ellie about Sam, and Jessie, about Big Joe and how he had lost his leg. He had told her of his hatred for Worthy for what he did to Sam in the Rafferty trial. Ellie had told him about meeting Worthy a couple of years after she moved back to Hot Springs, about dating him and being dumped by him, about coming to hate him as Chris did.

Sam was in rapt attention, so glad Chris was opening up, finally. Looking at her, Chris said, "I'm really sorry I never told you this, Sam. It started off as part of the Iraq experience that I never wanted to talk about. And then it became a friend thing, a private thing like you and Jessie have. It just never came up between you and me."

"It's OK," Sam said, reaching under the table to touch his knee.

Chris continued with his story. "It was just so weird, first our mutual connection to Joey, and then our mutual connection to Worthy. Anyway, our friendship was real, and strong, and mutually supportive, kind of like you and me, Sam," he said, glancing at her, "except obviously different.

"Then a little over a year ago, I started getting concerned. Initially, we had used our ties to Joey to build our friendship. Now it seemed Ellie was trying to use our hatred of Worthy to build it further. I was uncomfortable as the hatred theme grew. I hated him, too, but she had a raging bonfire going, and I was afraid of it. I started finding excuses to duck our calls. I haven't talked to her in over a year." He didn't mention her email.

"Have you talked to her since Worthy was killed?" asked Jimmy.

"No."

"You must have suspected her when Worthy was killed," Bill offered.

"Yes, but not so much. We had gotten to be quite close, but I never dreamed she was capable of murder. It wasn't until the trial, when the testimony about the chain saw came out, that I knew it was Ellie who had killed Worthy. The manner of the killing confirmed it. I understood what she had done and why she had done it. The X cuts were her vengeance for what Worthy did to her. She cut the leg off for me."

No one moved. It was difficult to take in the enormity of what Chris was saying and imagine the hell he must have been living, even as Sam and Bill were suspecting him of the murder. For a guy who didn't say much, Chris was letting it all out. He was acknowledging his guilt to those he held most dear.

And he wasn't yet done. "I should have told the authorities. I should have told you, Jess. I knew what you must have been going through with that innocent woman's fate in your hands. I had the information to free you from that. And I didn't give it to you. I couldn't. Ellie was too important to me. I'm sorry."

Chris had now finished his confession. He was crying. They all were. Finally, it was Jessie who spoke, and gave him absolution.

"It's OK, Chris," she said, taking his hand and holding it gently. "The choice you faced was impossible and unfair. We can be forgiven for protecting those we love."

Sam was drained when she and Chris retired to their bedroom. But she wasn't done yet. For the first time in a long time, maybe the first time ever, she had to tell Chris she loved him.

She had to tell Jessie too. Her forgiveness of Chris was an extraordinary act of love. It tore down the barrier between them. They would talk tomorrow. They would share everything.

ACKNOWLEDGEMENTS

I have to give a quick but heartfelt shout-out to several folks who stepped in to mark the trail, and sometimes save me from myself, on this first journey into the world of fiction.

My thanks to Marcia Trahan, my talented, responsive, and thoughtful editor. Marcia helped me with my first book, *A Lawyer or a Priest*, and I wanted the benefit of her candor and care once again. She pushes and criticizes and encourages in all the right ways, always with a gentle firmness. Give her book, *Mercy: A Memoir of Medical Trauma and True Crime Obsession*, a read for an exquisitely choreographed and beautifully written voyage to a place most of us have never been.

Chuck Rosenberg is a former United States Attorney. In writing about two criminal trials in *Justice Hill*, I relied on my experience with civil litigation and my general sense of criminal proceedings. Chuck was kind enough to read a draft and patiently correct my missteps. The one or two that remain are entirely my doing—I disregarded Chuck's teachings for the sake of the story. Chuck is a legal contributor on NBC and MSNBC and hosts a wonderful podcast called *The Oath*.

Christopher Rosow had a stunningly successful two-book debut in May 2020 with terrorism thrillers *False Assurances* and *Threat Bias*. He was half a year ahead of me in figuring out how to publish a book, and I shamelessly rode his wake. With great characters and story lines, Christopher's books are true page-turners. His riveting tales will inevitably find their way to a movie theater near you.

Thanks, finally, to my former colleagues at Crowell & Moring, and before that Jones Day, for making my life in the law so interesting and enjoyable that it continues to engage me, even in retirement.

REQUEST FOR REVIEW

It was a joy putting this story together and telling it as best I could. Thanks for giving it a read. I hope it surprised and rewarded you.

We learn and grow when we get feedback. If you liked *Justice Hill*, or even if you didn't, I would be most grateful if you would take a few minutes to give it a review on Amazon.

ABOUT THE AUTHOR

John Macleod practiced law in Washington, D.C. for forty-seven years. He was a founding partner and chairman of Crowell & Moring, a major Washington-based firm. He and his wife, Ann Klee, live on a farm in the Shenandoah Valley with an assortment of dogs.

www.ingramcontent.com/pod-product-compliance
Lightning Source LLC
Chambersburg PA
CBHW031342260626
47153CB00022B/1992